THE SECOND MAN

by Edward Grierson

"A leisurely, firm and dramatic tale, turning fairly enough on a point of feminine understanding, and notably literate in style."—*San Francisco Chronicle*

"Grierson tells a good story well."—*Kirkus Reviews*

THE SECOND MAN

BY

EDWARD GRIERSON

PERENNIAL LIBRARY
Harper & Row, Publishers
New York, Cambridge, Hagerstown, Philadelphia, San Francisco
London, Mexico City, São Paulo, Sydney

This book was originally published by Alfred A. Knopf, Inc. It is here reprinted by arrangement.

 For information address Harper & Row, Publishers, Inc., 10 East 53rd Street, New York, N.Y. 10022. Published simultaneously in Canada by Fitzhenry & Whiteside Limited, Toronto.

First PERENNIAL LIBRARY edition published 1981.

ISBN: 0-06-080528-5

81 82 83 84 10 9 8 7 6 5 4 3 2 1

THE SECOND MAN

Chapter One

I WELL REMEMBER HEARING OF MARion for the first time. I had been called to the Bar two years and had been in Hesketh's chambers for nine months when one morning Ross, who was immediately senior to me, put his head round the door of the room we shared and said: "D'you know what? We've got a woman coming in with us, name of Kerrison. They'll move you into the Black Hole, I expect" —a cubicle off the clerk's room used for storage of the mustier law reports.

I remember I wasn't pleased. Being the latest recruit to the chambers, I was naturally the most reactionary; I accepted the truth of the Bar's dictum that women were ill-advised (a euphemism) so to deny their own inexact natures. Of course you couldn't stop them if they insisted. I wished Kerrison, like all my fellow creatures, well. But if she'd come to me and asked for my advice, I feel sure I should have mentioned nursing and a great number of other worthy occupations and been very convincing about it. I didn't like the waste of talents. I didn't like the idea of the Black Hole either.

Hesketh's were provincial chambers. Sir Evelyn Parks had once been the head of them, but he'd gone to London and waned thin on enormous fees. Hesketh wasn't of that fashionable sort. He'd never applied for silk; he wasn't one for exchanging money for honours, which always rankles a bit with your north-countryman.

But he was good. He was really good. He was no orator. You don't win cases that way, not even with juries nowadays. But he was a deadly cross-examiner: one of the quiet, relentless sort that gets a witness down and worries the doubts out of him. Everyone knew he was the best man on the Circuit, or so at least the clerk, Jaggers, said; and he said it often, in chambers and out, to pupils and clients and anyone who'd listen. "You're coming to the right place, Mr. Irvine," I remember him saying to me, waylaying me in his outer office after my first interview with Hesketh. Jaggers was enthusiastic about all his team. "There's Mr. Hesketh," he would say, playing his trump card almost without a flourish. "Then there's Mr. Fenney. He hasn't many inches, Mr. Fenney" (he was five feet four), "or the grand manner, perhaps" (and he certainly hadn't), "but there's none better in the north. None better," Jaggers would repeat, looking his man in the eye as though daring him to produce a better on the spot. "Mr. Serpell has a big practice"—this was perhaps the truest, or shall I say the least optimistic, of Jaggers's claims, but it was done with less enthusiasm, for Serpell, a hard man, was immune to the Jaggers's charm. "And Mr. Ross has style and the *manner's* there."

"What will he have to say about Kerrison?" I wondered as I went to the outer office to hear Ross try the oracle.

"Well, she's a woman," Jaggers began, as though that answered everything. After a moment, recovering from this discouraging start, he remembered that she was now one of the elect. "A very nice lady," he went on, his voice taking on a booming quality. "Mr. Hesketh was saying she has a first-class record. Read law at Oxford and got a First: brought off the double with the Bar Finals and was a pupil with Mr. Crane in London."

"Why didn't she go into his chambers?" Ross wanted to know.

"Because she could come into *these*, Mr. Ross," Jaggers replied with a reproachful look, for he liked a high standard of internal propaganda.

"And she's coming when?"

"Tomorrow."

"Shall I have to share? And will you put poor Mr. Irvine in the Black Hole?"

"I'll have to clear it out and make it shipshape. I'll give you Belle's" (the junior typist's) "desk," Jaggers said to me, and I could see that in recompense he would be particularly kind about me to the local solicitors for the next few weeks.

But, as it happened, it didn't come to that. Serpell was prevailed on to double-up with Ross, and next morning when I reached the chambers I saw that a brand new desk had been installed beside mine and a young woman was sitting at it, her face appearing rather disconsolately over the large tomes that Jaggers had provided.

"I'm Kerrison," she said to me, getting to her feet.

She was about thirty, dark and trim with a good figure. My first impression was that she was attractive and nice but rather careless of herself.

"Good morning. I'm Irvine," I replied.

"I've heard about you"—Jaggers, of course, who had probably thrown in an accolade or two.

At this moment Jaggers himself appeared and introduced us. He had with him some barristers' briefs tied with pink tape—old cases of Hesketh's, actually—and he laid some of these on her desk in such a way that visitors to the room would fail to see to whom they were addressed. "Tide you over for a few days till you get some of your own," he explained tactfully. He looked across at my desk and I thought for a moment he was going to give me the treatment too. However: "No need for that with Mr. Irvine," he said in his heartiest propaganda voice, and I really think that he believed it.

When he'd left the room I looked at my roommate and saw that she was smiling—she had a pleasant smile, friendly but quiet like her whole personality. I waited to see whether she'd say anything about Jaggers, who was something of a collector's piece on the Circuit. But she was far too polite and conscious of her place as the most junior of his string.

"You don't want to mind *him*," I said.

"Oh, I don't."

"He's a good chap. Helpful. He wants you to feel at home."

"I do feel at home," she said, looking round the bare room with its desks, its two easy chairs that seemed to wait with hungry urgency for clients, the law reports and the "Spy" cartoon of Haldane hunched up like a toad on the Woolsack.

"They're a good lot altogether," I continued, to cheer her up, and I began to describe them, for there was something horribly catching in Jaggers's method, and practically every one of us, including Hesketh, went in for this mutual cataloguing.

She listened attentively, which is a good point in a barrister, but there was more to it than that; there was the social grace some listeners have of joining in, of sharing what you have to say.

At eleven we had tea in Hesketh's room. No one had a conference or was in court, and so we were all there. It was amusing to watch the reactions. Hesketh of course had seen her before. He was a plain man of business. This woman was now a junior colleague, part of the team, the oddly individualistic team of barristers' chambers, that bears no resemblance that I know of to any other organism on earth. He tried his best to be kind in his blunt, honest way, but I don't for one moment suppose that he appreciated the ordeal she was going through or that he'd have had much sympathy for her if he had. After all, she'd chosen this life: he hadn't asked her to compete with men in their last-ditch profession. So he gave her a cup of tea, asked her if she was comfortable, and then lit his pipe and blew clouds of independence all over the room.

Serpell, the third man and potentially the best, was more hostile. He was tall and thin, lethally sharpened on a thousand nice points of law. "You were a pupil of Crane's in the Temple?" were his words of greeting to her in his dry, donnish voice.

"Yes."

"Very busy there, I suppose?"

"Oh, yes."

"General Common Law practice? Negligence? Defamation?"

"We rather specialized in that," she said.

Serpell looked at her carefully, his head held sideways in the way he always read his briefs.

"Much divorce?" he asked.

"Not really."

"Town and Country Planning?"

"Yes."

He continued to cross-examine her: he was interested in Crane. All successful men interested Serpell, who was getting the way of it himself. He did not actually ask her Crane's income, but by the time he finished he could have assessed his taxes for him. Once he had got this, he dismissed her with the same nod he gave to witnesses when he'd finished with them in the box, and with a sigh picked up his cup, selected the only chocolate biscuit from the plate that Belle had brought in, and went off to his own room to devour it.

"Serpell's a keen man," Fenney said into the silence that lingered after him.

She looked at him gratefully: I suppose like all women she had a good nose for alliances.

"But don't you mind him," Fenney went on, balancing his teacup on his knee in the precarious way that always distressed Belle when she saw it. "You should have heard the interrogatories poor Irvine got when *he* came. And Ross. Remember? They say women are inquisitive!"

"They are, very," she answered with another glance at him. I think she had already summed up her new friend and had observed that this defence of her—

for that was what it was—was taking place after the assault was over.

"Then what can we tell you?" he said, responding. "That you'll like it here. It's better than London. You won't have to wait around for briefs the way I did." Fenncy was London trained: it was believed that his experiences in the Temple had been discouraging. "You'll get work right from the start. Jaggers, an excellent fellow, will see to that."

I think Jaggers, who had an almost mystical sense of group kinship, must have been on this wave-length at the time, for he now entered, almost at the run, announcing: "Petitioner for conference, Mr. Fenney, in *Scott* v. *Scott*"—which was an undefended divorce action with the barest number of guineas marked on the brief.

"I certainly like these chambers," she said to me when we were back in our room. She was too much the barrister and had the woman under too tight control to say more than that, and I had to guess at hcr approval of Hesketh, her awe of Serpell, her delight in Jaggers and gratitude to Fenney, who so obviously wanted to support the weak, though he had a tendency to do it at a distance. I couldn't imagine what she thought of Ross, for he hadn't made much impression and had hardly spoken. There was a bit of Serpell in him, I knew, Serpell with a sense of humour, unthinkable in the original, and I wondered if she had sensed it.

But I knew she was sincere and pleased to be with us, and that in turn gave me a comfortable feeling, so that I forgot my resentment at losing Ross as a room-mate and having another rival for the pickings of the smaller briefs; I even forgot that she was dowdily dressed; and later that evening, in session with Jaggers, I was enthusiastic about her. "A very nice lady," was his opinion. "Clever. She has the *manner*. We'll make something of her"—meaning that he would.

I have gone in some detail into Marion Kerrison's first day with us because it set the key to the relationships that followed and the feelings that ruled our business lives. I have found by experience that first impressions are normally a good guide: at every meeting we prepare the mask of personality that we feel to be the most becoming, but in the moment of adjustment the truth is apt to show through. We are deeply faithful to our prejudices too. Most of us cannot help liking or disliking others on sight; next day we may doubt our judgement, but something in us keeps harking back, and though we may have been wrong, we shall be sure one day to find some excuse, however trivial, for believing in our own clairvoyance.

For this reason, whenever I see Marion now in the setting of her maturity, I think back to that first morning and sense again the vague unease we all shared, the fear that animals show when some unfamiliar creature is put among them. I suppose we imagined ourselves to be men of the world. Hesketh and Jaggers were married, Ross was engaged—to a young woman as glossy as a model in a fashion magazine and with the same expression of camel-like contempt. But the truth was that no one, not even Jaggers, was really at ease with her. It was all right having Belle and Miss Egerton in the office, though they did get embarrassed sometimes over the outspokenness of witnesses' depositions. "You leave that bit to me, Miss Egerton," Jaggers would be heard gallantly booming. "Skip it, Belle," was the equivalent of this in another key. "It's these Harfield cases," he would complain to us, naming the local Gomorrah. "Beats me how they find the time for family life."

Miss Egerton and Belle were familiars, our executants. But Marion was part of ourselves. Of course there were a number of women at the Bar, and even on our Circuit, where some were quite old friends. But it was a very different matter to have one in our midst, sharing our problems, part of our small talk and our tea-drinking.

I shall never forget Jaggers bringing her her first Harfield brief—not a full-blooded one, but only tainted at the edges. "Well, these things happen," he said defensively. "Beats me why, but there it is. Of course Mr. Irvine could do it," he added, cheering up a little.

"Mr. Irvine has his own briefs," Marion said, "and a very sensitive nature."

Jaggers looked disbelieving.

"Well, do I accept this sort of thing for you or not? I was doubtful. I told the client so."

"Of course you accept it. I'm no different from the rest of them.'

Even in those days there was a firmness about Marion that impressed you. "There's talent," Hesketh had declared in one of his rare confidences. I think everyone realized that she had power and courage. Perhaps she had too much courage or displayed it too openly. "The Galloping Majoress" Ross called her after one of her early cases, in which she had hurled herself in a spate of indignant questions against a witness of iron integrity and the halo of a verger.

Very early on I found out for myself how good she was, for I came against her in court—it often happened that members of a set of chambers were pitted against one another—and with what appeared to be the losing case she won easily. She was a good lawyer but that was only part of the battle. She knew her practice, the ins and outs of paper-work, which is the basis on which careers are built, and in court she was in her element, though she never overcame the recklessness that went so oddly with her calm appearance. "You must go easy, Miss Kerrison," Jaggers reproved her after her first brush with the bench. "A proper little bitch, God bless her!" he was said to have confided afterwards to his cronies in the clerks' room, but she was making money for him by this time, and that always mellows judgement.

At first, I think, solicitors came to her for novelty, or just for the devil of it. "Who's this little fire-eater you've got, Mr. Jaggers?" I heard a professional client say.

"A very nice young lady," Jaggers replied, probably smiling like the Cheshire Cat at him.

"Um, that's not what they're saying. Well, we'll try her."

"You won't be disappointed, Mr. Summers."

Nor was he. She won that case against all the odds and a real "Tipperary alibi" of witnesses.

Soon the word was going round that there was an exceptional young woman on the Circuit. Of course the rush wasn't killing at first, for your average client is nervous about being represented by a woman and would as soon have the devil speak up for him. Most of the business and professional barriers had gone down, but in the law the ghost of the belief still survived that women barristers were temperamentally unsuited to the work; it was even darkly rumoured that women jurors didn't like them. So, to begin with, only the cranks and the impecunious and the downright curious came: nor would I say that at the start Marion was as good as her reputation.

How well I remember my own first case: the appalling moment when one first has to rise and hear one's voice presume on the stillness of a court. Worst of all, I think, is the sight of one's own client. I remember the thought flashing through my mind that he might know that this was the beginning for me, that he was the guinea-pig of my career. Poor fellow, I was truly sorry for him, and perhaps he was for me.

If Marion was nervous in that way she never showed it. Right from the start her manner was assured. Everyone in court was staring at her when she got to her feet that day. "Another of them!" the reporters in the little penitentiary provided for their discomfort seemed to be saying. There were some who were looking at her as a woman, and she always appeared her best in wig and gown, with her hair hidden and the Gothic cut of her face against the white curls. She had beautiful hands too, and they showed up well with the black of the gown. Even the policemen seemed to have stopped chewing the cud of their evidence and watched her closely; indeed the only person who seemed to be unaffected was the judge, and he no doubt was only impassive out of kindness.

There was much praise of her afterwards, though

she had lost her case, and Jaggers went round smiling and taking bows by proxy. She had the manner. Nevertheless, in my short spell at the Bar I had seen better maiden efforts. Marion herself was conscious of this. "I wasn't very good," she said to me when we were back in our room, hearing in the distance the rumble of Jaggers who was giving Miss Egerton and Belle a résumé of the glories of the day. "I was nervous."

"You didn't look nervous," I replied.

"No? Well, I was. I just picked someone out on the jury and focused so hard on him that it hurt. It made me feel better."

I knew that feeling well. You make a friend of a face, or bludgeon it into friendship, or go down metaphorically on your knees to it.

"But I wasn't good," she said again. "I should have got an acquittal."

"Nonsense."

"I should. That's the way Crane approached things. He never had any successes in his own opinion: only failures sometimes. Of course Crane was good," she added, as though forestalling my own thought. "I don't know where I failed. Lack of touch, I think. I didn't get close enough to the witnesses. So I lost for my poor man."

"You did a good best for him," was all I could find to say.

"No. He was innocent. I *knew* that."

I think looking back on it that Marion was right. In those early days she lacked what she'd called "touch," the understanding of witnesses' minds which is part of the equipment of all successful advocates. She was too impulsive, too much engaged with her own sensations—generous ones at all times—to enter into the sensations of others. As a result she antagonized witnesses she might have won over, and she gave juries the impression that she was being unfair. Even judges seemed to feel this on occasions, and she had one or two encounters of a lively kind—not altogether harmful events, for they helped her reputation as a fighter.

But in that conversation she had held with me after her first case she had also touched on one of the fundamental things about her advocacy, something that was at once a strength and a weakness. "He was innocent," she had said. "I *knew*." Of course I had heard other barristers say similar things and I'd always discounted them. But in Marion it didn't only amount to a passionate belief in the virtue of her own case; it reflected what I think amounted at times to a real flair and insight into the truth.

Women are perceptive, they say. I know Marion was. She may not have been perceptive about the feelings and characters of witnesses, but I am sure she often sensed in some extraordinary way the truth or untruth of what they *said*, in the box, or in conference, or even in the written "proofs" of their evidence which were supplied in advance with the briefs.

"All lies!" she scribbled across the deposition of a witness in one of her earliest cases. The witness had seemed reliable to me. But it turned out she was right. I often saw evidence of what Jaggers called her "second sight." Of course he built it up. "You can't fool *her*: she knows *everything*," I heard him announcing to one doubting soul.

There was no universal acceptance of these powers. "I hear our Kerrison does a little crystal-gazing," Ross said—he was tending towards the Serpell school. Serpell himself was too correct to say anything: he merely hoisted his eyebrows when Jaggers was under way till his whole face seemed in danger of taking off.

"But it's true, Mr. Serpell."

"Yes?" Serpell said, looking at him; he had a great range of expression, and there was a very distinctive one for Jaggers that would have disconcerted most souls.

"Well, you ask Mr. Irvine."

"And Belle, perhaps?"

"Serpell's jealous, that's the truth of it," Jaggers confided to Miss Egerton when they were alone together, for there were times when he promoted her and climbed down into the ring himself. "She'll make a career, that girl will."

Marion's practice soon began to confirm this unmistakably. Solicitors who had come once for curiosity came again. The local papers, starved for colour at this time, began to take her up. Court reporting, once so stimulating, has now been whittled down by law till it must be a most frustrating career. But our local reporters did their best. WITNESS COLLAPSES IN BOX, one particularly good headline ran. Barristers are not allowed to advertise or court publicity, and Marion was absolutely scrupulous in this, but publicity has a habit sometimes of holding on behind.

Occasional rumblings and murmurings against this could be heard from the other chambers on the Circuit and particularly from those in our town, where the pure spirit of professional rectitude was seen to have alighted; and one day Hesketh sent for Marion.

She was very subdued when she came back. I said

nothing. I guessed that Hesketh had reproved her and I felt embarrassed: I even imagined that she might break down and weep—so greatly had I misjudged her.

After a while I felt that she was looking at me, and glancing up I caught her eye. There seemed to be the glint of a smile.

"Well, what's the verdict?" I asked, for there are moments when it is best to show oneself over-curious.

"No photographs," Marion replied in a solemn voice and began to laugh. "There are to be no photographs of me; or portraits, rather, within the meaning of the Act."

"Did Hesketh say that?"

"Yes, and of course he's right. He was sweet about it, really."

"Someone's complained?"

"Yes. Hesketh said he'd no rights in the matter. He wasn't making a diktat. He just 'reminded' me of Bar etiquette, that was the word. He was so tactful, he tried so hard. But won't Jaggers be mad about it!" she ended up, turning back to her desk.

Shortly a case came her way that frustrated all these well-meant intentions. It started, as important cases sometimes do, with a small action—in the County Court in this instance, for payment for goods supplied by a tradesman to a wife. Out of this a divorce action began, which also in its essence seemed of a comparatively trivial kind—if you can use the word in such a context of disillusion. But as the case drew near to trial an astonishing background of misconduct of both parties came to light; names of quite prominent people crept into the briefs; and though the national Sunday papers would not be expected to promote the matter beyond page 3, the local furore showed signs of being tremendous.

Hesketh was brought into the case. Kenyon, who headed the other chambers in our town, was on the other side, his junior being one Gilroy Ashington-Duclair, who sometimes came down from London to lend us the light of his personality and to make the local compositors very angry and sarcastic.

In the event, when the case came to the first of its three hearings, before Mr. Justice Cray, Hesketh was far from well. For two days he fought on, enduring his recurrent ulcer pain with what I can only describe as irritable stoicism: on the third day, when the husband, the Respondent, was to give evidence, he was no longer able to take his place, and Marion's great chance had come.

That morning early, before she had left chambers, Hesketh telephoned her from his bed. I don't know what he told her, but I know from my own experience that this blunt man had in him a vein of true feeling for others and was capable of tenderness. Respect for talent or achievement could always move him. I feel sure that in the months he had known Marion he had formed a high opinion of her, and I think that he believed that she would seize her opportunity and that he conveyed that belief to her—probably in rather ribald form, for that was the way sentiment took him.

Certainly there was a flush in her cheeks as we walked over to the Assize Court, and when she spoke of Hesketh there was sincerity in her words of regret, though at the same time she must have known that her chance had come of rising far above the ruck, the phalanxes of the white-wigged who sit so hopefully in court with their few precious briefs under their arms and their faces set in alert yet magisterial expressions.

She may have been nervous, sensing the weight of a publicity around her such as she had never experienced before, but I don't think she was. As we went into court I could see that the news of Hesketh's illness was known, and she might have read a certain pity for her, and perhaps for her client, in the expressions turned towards her. She showed no sign of noticing. Gilroy Ashington-Duclair came in and gave her a smile of exquisite sensibility; Kenyon followed him with a nod, a rustle of silk and his now-let's-get-down-to-it air, and was handed a whole arsenal of law reports by his clerk, while Fenney, who was half-expecting a brief in the Criminal Court next door, came in and gave her an encouraging wave.

Through all of this she talked to me in a calm undertone of the cross-examination that she and Hesketh had prepared. "He would have been good with this witness," was all she said of him, but I remember it as one of the best tributes to a man of whom I have only pleasant thoughts.

The judge came in and settled down on the bench. Of course he had been told about Hesketh, but he looked at the empty place at counsel's table and then at Marion in an inquiring way, as though he half-expected that she would ask for an adjournment. She made no move and he gave her a little nod—there was something extraordinarily encouraging about it—and next moment the Respondent was being called, and Kenyon was on his feet with professional confidence and belief in the witness writ large all over him.

I forget most of the evidence given by the husband that day. I recall that the effect was damaging, and as I sat beside Marion I watched the judge to see how he was taking it.

A great deal more coolly than the Plaintiff, I could see. The poor woman—she was quite young—was in a fever of emotion throughout. She kept leaning over to her solicitor with some impassioned comment or denial, and every few moments Marion would feel a tug at her gown and hear whispered words of counsel. I admired her calm. Not by a word or a gesture did she disclose to them her dismay at this interruption of what should be an advocate's task during the evidence of a hostile witness—the study of that witness's demeanour and the nuances of his speech.

"Shall I tell them?" I whispered to her, seeing a slight movement in the muscles of her cheek, a sign I had noticed in her before when she was distressed.

But she shook her head. Even at this moment she was thinking of her client and making allowances for her. Perhaps, too, she had summed the witness up, for at one reply she had drawn a pencil-mark on the brief; it was her way of indicating the crucial answer, "Kerrison's Moment of Truth," Ross called it in derision.

The evidence of the husband came to an end. There was a rustle among the crowd. The witness glanced around, somewhat puzzled, and he made a move, as though he imagined that his ordeal was over and he might leave the box.

"No, but *I* have some questions too," Marion said, and immediately there was a great gust of laughter in court, one of those releases of tension that can be touched off by the most obvious remarks.

The judge made no immediate attempt to quell it. He knew that it would give the young woman the confidence she needed, and he too smiled a little. Most of us understood and recovered quickly, but when a few persons at the back persisted he held up his hand, a slight gesture, though it had its effect at once.

In a silent court Marion began her cross-examination.

I have heard most of her big cases, one in particular, the most famous, of which I shall tell in good time. But of all her efforts I think that this was the finest, the most fair and powerful and overwhelmingly persuasive. "You were on your best behaviour,' I said to her afterwards. I think that she may have felt the influence of Hesketh beside her, counselling and restraining; he had planned this approach with her in hours of conference; it was his work at heart, though she embellished it with a thousand touches and crowned it with that flair for the truth that I have already mentioned as her outstanding gift. This time, for once, she was never rash. She was courteous; she seldom raised her voice, yet the beautifully phrased tones could have been heard in every corner of the gallery.

Slowly, with a perfect economy, she drove the witness to the wall. At first he was unwisely contemptuous of her and showed it. It did him no good. He was sarcastic; he scored; and his scores rebounded. She turned his words. She held them up; comparing them, and presented them to him again; and got fresh answers, and played with these. I have never heard a witness so condemned out of his own mouth. Yet at the end she was still treating him in the same way; as though she trusted him and *expected* the truth and found herself bewildered by the lies that came up like changelings.

It was a marvellous performance for so young a woman. You could feel the atmosphere of astonishment in the court. There would be a gasp sometimes at the witness's answers. You would have believed him a blundering fool if you hadn't heard his earlier evidence, so clever and tendentious. And when she had finished, without a glance at him, she sat down, apparently as unmoved as when she had risen. Only those close to her could see that she was trembling and on the verge of tears.

That evening when the court rose the judge sent her a note. I saw it at the time: an immensely judicial note that gave nothing away and yet made clear his appreciation of her talents and courage. For once, even Jaggers could find nothing to add; indeed he was strangely subdued, like a mother whose daughter has turned out a more indisputable swan than she had prophesied. I saw him at the centre of an admiring ring of clients and clerks, looking embarrassed about it all. But I knew how proud he was.

As soon as I got back to chambers I telephoned Hesketh and told him what had happened. He did not sound surprised. Hadn't he said the girl had talent? His ulcer, he declared, was particularly bad, and he rang off, but not for a moment did I make the mistake of assuming that he was displeased. "A fine cross-examination," was Serpell's tribute, which was generous, for he disliked her; and I think she thought more of it than anything Fenney or I could say. As for the papers, I am afraid they behaved alarmingly, writing her up for all they were worth, and there were pictures of her leaving the court with the hind end of Gilroy Ashington-Duclair. "I'm afraid Hesketh won't like *that*," she said next morning when we showed her them.

"Nor will Gilroy," Ross put in, laughing like a hyena over so much displaced elegance.

When we went over to court that morning the atmosphere was transformed; you could have guessed from the feel of it that Marion had arrived. It was a more normal atmosphere, no longer sharpened by doubt. The policemen at the doors were as friendly as ever, but the journalists were no longer attending; they were slumped down in their box with the air of having gorged on her. A rather wan smile from Gilroy, a brusque nod of rivalry from Kenyon, no sign from the judge who had retreated into the rarefied regions. The aftermath of triumph is like that. I remember I felt resentful on Marion's behalf. It seemed wrong that they shouldn't all be cheering and that Hesketh should have kept silent that morning at the end of his telephone. I took it as a personal affront that Jaggers should be with Fenney in the Criminal Court on some pettifogging case. But I noticed with pleasure that our solicitor was much more respectful than he had been in the early stages of the day before. "You did a great job, Miss Kerrison, I thought the case was lost," he had said to her outside in the Plaintiff's presence, surrendering every credit except of having found her.

The Plaintiff herself had joined in, a much gayer figure now, with a mauve straw hat that looked like a kind of bet on the result. "You were so good, so wonderfully good. All those lies!" she ventured.

Marion was cool with her. She had not found that

her client matched up to her own standards of truth and she could not like her, though I am sure she was sorry for her and thought of her as a victim of life.

"It's all right now, isn't it?" the woman asked. "I mean those lies came out. The judge sees the rights of it."

"I don't know," Marion said, and turned away.

Once on her feet, however, with her speech to be made, her sense of the justice of her case overcame her. Here she was in a new role. As I have said, Hesketh was no orator, Serpell's voice was displeasing. I had not heard from anyone in our chambers the kind of speech she made that day. She was so eloquent that the court stenographer had difficulty in keeping up with her. But she was reasoned also. She never made the mistake some do of talking to the judge as though he were a jury—which is only less heinous than talking to a jury as though it were a judge. She spoke calmly, never getting indignant over the things the other side had done and said, though she sounded disappointed in them sometimes. She made no attempt at irony, though she was capable of that also.

While she spoke I watched the judge. He seemed most of the time to be staring out of the window at some starlings nesting outside. Occasionally he looked at her, and these were at the vital points, so I knew he was listening. Once he interrupted her with a question. She replied in the same measured voice he had used, not excitedly as beginners do. I was astonished, for I sensed how she must be feeling, and I knew that her temperament did not easily brook opposition and that she was always in danger of breaking out. The shade of Hesketh, it appeared, was still beside her.

"Yes, my lord, but may it not be . . . ? Your lordship will no doubt consider . . . I would respectfully submit to your lordship . . ."—soothing words: if only she had always followed that precept all her life!

After hearing her, Kenyon's speech sounded very bumpy and uncouth. The judge could not help noticing it; he became so sharp with the advocate that when the latter persisted I saw Gilroy plucking gently at his elbow—an exquisite conscience to have beside you! Kenyon shook him off angrily. He saw that only combative measures would do: he could not hope to echo the still voice of reason that Marion had used.

But even combativeness didn't pay. By tea-time it was all over and she had won. Applause broke out, instantly suppressed. The Plaintiff was in tears, wiping her eyes with a lilac handkerchief and blessing Marion and justice indiscriminately—it was perhaps as well that the judge didn't hear her.

I was delayed in court by a solicitor client and I got back to chambers some half-hour after Marion, at a time when Miss Egerton was putting on her hat and Jaggers seemed to be trying to will Belle into finishing the last of the day's letters.

When I went into my room I saw Marion sitting at her desk, working at a brief—I recognized it as a small five-guinea County Court action set down for the next day but one.

"You're staging it on purpose," I said to her.

"What do you mean?"

She was genuinely surprised: she didn't follow me.

"But I've got this case coming on, don't you understand?" she said, when I tried to explain what I myself would have been doing in her shoes. "And I don't like celebrations," she went on—I think she rather feared that Jaggers would somehow contrive to make a public toast of her.

"I could take you out to dinner," I suggested.

"I told you, I have this case. I've hardly started on it."

"Well, a drink, then?"

She hesitated. "If it's just one," she said.

"One: and cross my heart."

We went out together and began to walk to the wine bar near the station. It was a spring evening and everywhere people were strolling more slowly than usual, and there was the glint of a bank of tulips at the end of the street.

"I like this town," she volunteered suddenly.

I knew she came from the south, a country-bred girl, and I was startled by these words. That she should like the chambers and the practice was understandable, but our city was another matter—no beauty spot, though it had a certain pawky charm.

"You can't: you weren't born in it," I protested, as most of my fellow citizens would have done, for local patriotism in the north is jealous and always a little in fear of being patronized or laughed at.

"I still like it," Marion said, looking around at the soot-blackened buildings in the Mammon-Gothic of an age of faith.

"I don't know why you ever came to us," I grumbled as I led her down into the snuggery of casks and plush seats. Several people were there and I recognized some of them: the new aristocracy of money made in the mills and warehouses. "Well, all right, you're here. I was here first. I'm as good as you and better, remember that," they seemed to be saying to every new arrival. I gave them the same look back; they expected it; they were the best hearted of men so long as you didn't try to jostle them in a queue. I had been brought up with them and knew their shrewd and excellent qualities, but I sometimes wondered what Marion from her more sheltered world thought.

"You see?" I said to her, as though she really *would* see what I meant. One or two of the "regulars" were staring at her; perhaps the word of her success had gone round. If it had they certainly would have respected her, for they admired achievement. She had asked for a madeira, which was a speciality of the house, and I brought it back to her in one of the plain glasses in which wine is served in my town, and rightly.

"What is it I should see?" she said to me.

It suddenly occurred to me that she was looking her best. The light spring coat she wore was admirably cut; there was a froth of lace at her wrists and throat, which may have been years in or out of fashion for all I knew, but looked nice.

"That you're a rare bird," I said to her, "and in a quaint nest. Now I'm going to drink to you."

We touched glasses.

"It was a milestone for you today," I said.

She smiled. "No, go on as you were doing: Delphic talk. I liked that better, though I didn't understand a word."

"Don't you want to remember today?"

"No."

"And *I* don't understand that."

But I did. She had arrived. And I hadn't. She had great sensibility.

"We'll have it your way," I said, accepting her mood, which perhaps suited mine also. "Forget to-day and tell me about yourself and why you came here."

"You're trained under Jaggers and you ask that!"

"Why did you come?"

"I heard of Hesketh. I thought there would be better chances for beginners away from London. And Crane wouldn't have me."

"Well, you can laugh at that," I said warmly, feeling a sudden anger against Crane. "You'll go back one day."

"I don't want to go back. I told you I like it here. This suits me." She leaned back against the plush seat. When she tilted her head you saw how finely shaped her throat was. I suppose she wasn't a beautiful woman according to the fashion of her time: her face was too thin, her nose too large. But she had great distinction. She was that kind of person who in old age gives the impression of a past beauty. I confess I smiled a little at her words, for the last thing I would have said suited her looks was this Edwardian bar, so masculine, smelling of must and the good cigars that had been smoked in it.

"You don't believe me," she said, seeing my amusement.

I shook my head. "No, I should have said you were from another world—green lawns and lily ponds and one of those old houses with gables. . . ."

"And jackdaws in the chimneys. I suppose I was."

"Don't you miss it?"

She sipped her drink. It was a very good wine indeed and I was glad to see the solid respect with which she treated it—I had a vision of Gilroy at the port on a bar mess night, fiddling and scraping like a high-church curate.

"I don't miss it at all," she said. "I always wanted this life. I think you have it best in a town like this: you're not cut off from people as you are in the Temple. There you have the Strand on one side and the Inns of Court on the other and a line down the middle. There are the Law Courts, the holy of holies. But here you have your Assizes and Sessions in a town hall, with the town clerk upstairs bothering about the rates, and a choir rehearsing 'Messiah' in the room next door. That's the way I like it."

It was the longest speech I had ever heard her make outside court and I could see that she meant every word of it.

"Look here," I decided suddenly. "Let me take you out to dinner. We could go to 'The Five Hills,' there's a band there. It's very typical of up here, full of the right colour," I added in a cunning voice.

"But there's my case."

"You can do it tomorrow."

"I suppose I could."

We went out in my car, my extravagance in those days. "The Five Hills" was just inside the city boundary in the almost-country, with only the distant view of a housing estate and the pall of commercial haze to the south to remind you of where you were. It was really untrue to say, as I had done, that it was typical of my town; it was a road house of a kind you can find on any main artery out of London. There was an open-air swimming pool, a kind of gesture of defiance at the northern weather, and pleasant lawns and flower-beds. Inside were bars, a billiardroom, and a restaurant where the food was good, its tables enclosing a small dance floor of the usual pattern.

Here the young men in their sports cars brought their girls, and a few wealthier-looking clients might be seen with ladies whom one hoped were their wives. Ross and I had often gone there in the old days of his freedom on Saturday nights, and on one disastrous occasion had taken his fiancée. It had been a crowded evening and she had not been pleased. "Fact is Vivienne was a bit *allergic*," he had confessed to me next day with what I thought was a rather hunted expression. Not even the ride home, it appeared, had retrieved things. "He's got a handful with that tart, has Mr. Ross," Jaggers said, though I must say he was always at his most sycophantic on the occasions when she called at our chambers. "Be a client of ours one day," I heard him prophesy with relish to Miss Egerton, for he had a hankering for divorce practice and was always hoping for something really scandalous to turn up.

I could see at once that Marion, by contrast, recognized the good qualities of "The Five Hills." She looked more animated than I had ever seen her as she sat down at table—not a very good one and a long way from the floor, but she wasn't the sort that minded.

"See what I mean?" I asked, displaying the amenities of the place.

"Yes, I like it."

We had a bottle of wine, being fully launched now on a celebration, though of an unexpected kind. Also we danced. I was a modest performer myself, but I could see that she was good. I didn't dare say anything, for I was afraid that if I complimented her she might recognize my surprise. Somehow I hadn't associated her with such talents. I had seen only Kerrison, I suppose, the professional colleague, and it was something of a shock to discover the woman underneath—not that it happened all at once, in any sudden revelation, but rather by degrees.

Perhaps the first effect was more of embarrassment than anything else.

"The band's not bad," I found myself saying, as I had said to a multitude of Paul Jones partners. It was odd, for we had been conversing very easily before. I have noticed this about dancing: there is nothing half-and-half about it; it puts the barriers up or it takes them down. It can make husbands and wives seem strangers to one another, and it can make strangers feel the most delightful affinities, so that it may be said to be a very bad introduction to anything except a love affair.

Of course no such thoughts were consciously in my mind. I just didn't enjoy myself. It was too early in the evening for sentiment; I suppose the man with the amber and mauve spotlights was still enjoying his supper, and all around us people were being brisk, whirling and dodging about. It wasn't my mood and it was a relief to get her back to the table.

"Better go on from where we left off," I said, pouring some wine into her glass.

But it wasn't easy. I imagine that in the course of

that dance something, some intimation, had passed between us; the ground had shifted a little and we were both uncertain where we stood.

"We mustn't be too late back," she answered, glancing at her watch.

I believe if I'd said: "The night's young," as I nearly did (for at moments of embarrassment one is capable of any banality), our evening might have ended there, for her County Court brief was waiting for her and the calls of duty are unanswerable at certain times.

But I was quick enough to agree with her. The danger soon receded. I think she had enjoyed the evening, and that she liked me and was grateful and a bit curious, which is the best social oil. She began asking me about my life. Why had I chosen Hesketh? What did I think of our town? She knew already that I wasn't married, but Hesketh's and Serpell's wives were ready-made topics and she was interested in Ross's Vivienne, whom she had seen decked out in furs so expensive that one kept looking behind her for the elderly admirer—a mill-owner, no less.

"She's beautiful," she said.

"Ah, yes."

"Will they get married soon?"

"When Ross gets himself a fat enough brief," I nearly answered, for I shared Jaggers's cynical views of the relationship. "They keep talking of it," I substituted, which was nearly true, for Ross himself had done little else in the time I had known him.

"Yes," she said musingly, "I think he's the marrying kind."

Just for an instant the uncharitable thought flashed through my mind that she might be making similar calculations about me. Young men are prone to such delusions. But at the same time I had enough detachment to admire her sharpness. Ross, in spite of his Byronic looks, undoubtedly was the marrying kind, though it took a girl of Vivienne's stamina to prove it. Fenney, on the other hand, who seemed to be waiting as humbly for matrimony as he did for briefs (and without Jaggers to help him), was in reality much the more unlikely proposition—or so I had always believed until this moment when another idea occurred to me.

I don't know what I expected: hardly that she would ask directly about him. But that is what she did. There was a simplicity about her that sometimes disconcerted people: they forgot her training, her determination to be a barrister, a member of a team without distinction of sex. It was one of the problems she had had to face, and she did it without shyness or false heartiness.

I must have shown by my answers that I was surprised by this approach, for she sighed. Were men not curious about one another? she asked. Hadn't I been curious when I joined Hesketh's chambers? About Jaggers, surely?

I admitted to Jaggers.

"And not about the others? I suppose being a woman I'm different from all of you. In everything."

I did not know what to say, for I was struck by the poignancy of her words. I saw that they were true and that she was the outsider, she wasn't really wanted. Even Jaggers would rather that Fenney had her briefs. No one wanted her in court, taking the clients away, or in chambers where one had to mind one's words now. I felt suddenly very sorry for her.

But I didn't see how I could show it: certainly not in the way Ross in his pre-Vivienne days would have attempted it, in the car going home or even here, perhaps, at the secluded corner table with the shaded lights. She would certainly have surprised him if he had. Yet, though nothing had been said directly, I felt sure that she needed help. Of course she would have denied it, being self-reliant as a point of honour, but it occurred to me that her last words were an invitation and that secretly she wanted me to pry into her life, to see its daily frustrations and to exorcise them.

"I don't think you're so different," I told her, and as I spoke I was seeing the watchful eyes of the reporters on her, and the public making due allowances for her sex, and even poor Jaggers censoring himself like mad. "I don't think as a barrister you're different in any way."

"Not more inquisitive?"

"No."

"Or more illogical? Or fey, or whatever it is men think women are?"

"You're new on this Circuit: You must give them time," I said. "And a few more beatings. Nothing makes people feel more equal to others than being soundly beaten by them, it's human nature. It only needs another case like you had today."

In the midst of this eloquence I saw that she was smiling—a very feminine smile that contradicted the whole tenor of what I'd said. "Well, what is it now?" I asked her, not altogether pleased, for I sensed an unaccountable irony somewhere.

She glanced across at me and raised her glass.

"Nothing, except that it's come."

I must have looked absolutely bewildered, for she went on in her quiet voice, as though I were some client: "The case has come, I mean, the one you're speaking of. Tonight in chambers, just before you got back from court."

She paused and added: "They've given me the defence in the Maudsley murder case."

Chapter Two

EVERYONE ON THE CIRCUIT AND indeed in our town must have heard of the murder of Miss Maudsley: it had been in the headlines for weeks, rising to a shrill crescendo with news of an arrest.

Miss Maudsley had been an old lady of over seventy, a relic of one of those manufacturing families that established themselves in our town in the middle of the last century, building rows of hutches for their workpeople in the industrial quarter and a mausoleum of decent size—for they were never ostentatious—on the residential side in the midst of a garden depressingly stocked with evergreens.

The family had made money: that was common form in those times. But they showed their individuality in the fact that they did not continue to make it. In the 1920's, that era of doubt and conscience, Miss Maudsley's three brothers had sold the mills and had moved away—one to philanthropy (in another town), one into the wealthy fringe of outer London, the third overseas, where he had invested his money in sheep-farming and with an extraordinary expertise had contrived to lose it.

Miss Maudsley stayed on in the old house. She was well provided for. But in spite of that, the air of melancholy which had attached to "The Towers" from the beginning deepened with the years: the house was well kept, but the garden, for which she could not get help, decayed; the drive (for of course there was a drive, a tortuous affair that wound eternally between the laurels) became starred with weeds, the wind rustled in the dark overgrowing thickets and trees.

Miss Maudsley was a lonely person. Her brothers died. They had not been a very fruitful family. The philanthropist went to a lonely grave. The squire had two children, a boy who was killed on the Normandy beaches and a girl who inherited the trim estate in the stockbroker country. One son was born of the Australian branch, penniless like his father. He would have heard tales of the old prosperity, those sagas of the modern age, and one day he packed his bags and was next heard of in England, writing plaintively to his aunt for his fare north from London, which, after so great enterprise on an empty pocket, has always seemed to me one of the quaintest mysteries in the case.

Miss Maudsley, I have no doubt, was glad to help him. From the contents of her house, the albums and trinkets, I judge her to have been a shy but warm-hearted lady devoted to her past. I think she loved her house and her family, though she may have loved them with that careful, miserly sentiment of old people who have seen better days.

The photographs show her to have been a small,

delicate person, pretty in youth—there was the hint among the papers of some disastrous love affair—but in old age a trifle prim. I think she was afraid of the world. It must have seemed to her that it had treated her family unkindly. She will have remembered the great days of balls and carriages, and the thronging mills, and her father in his mayoral chain of office—there was a portrait of him in the drawing-room of "The Towers" by some artist, long forgotten, who must have made a fortune for himself by limning prosperity so faithfully.

She will have felt the fall from those golden times when she thought of her dead brothers and looked around her at the velvet curtains, faded now, and the enormous table at which no one ever sat. She became withdrawn from the world, as disappointed people do, and on her guard. More might be taken from her, perhaps the house itself sold, as the mills had been, and there would be nothing left.

On such a person, John Maudsley in the flesh must have come as an unwelcome surprise. He was large, and most of her family had been small, distinguished people. He was not very clean. He not only had no money but constantly told everyone so, which to a woman who had been engaged in keeping up appearances for thirty years was a kind of treason to the past.

In spite of this she made him her heir; in spite of their quarrels—for they quarrelled bitterly—he remained so to the end.

But she was cautious with her money while she was there to guard it. For a short while he lived with her, but the allowance she made him was wholly inadequate; it wouldn't pay for his cigarettes and beer, and he liked beer. He liked all forms of good living. He liked them so much, and was so short of cash to pay for them, that he became involved in certain transactions in our town which, not to put too fine a point on it, were shady. He suffered one prosecution that he managed to keep from her. But there was also an affair with a woman where he was not so fortunate, and a scene occurred between aunt and nephew in the course of which he was told to go.

Miss Maudsley was left alone. She had only one real friend, a neighbour, a Mrs. Pye. She seems to have felt her loneliness more acutely after the departure of John (which to me argues something in his favour); at all events she, who had lived so many years by herself with only the old family cook, now took a companion, one Jane Birman, who had done this sort of work before.

This Jane was the impecunious daughter of an army officer, a woman of about forty, by no means ill-favoured in a faintly hungry, feline way, though her looks had hardened. Five years earlier she might have endured the unholy régime of John with something more than resignation and would have been martyred—as must inevitably have happened—in the nicest manner. As it happens, she never met him socially. He called once when she was on her day out, and on her return she found her employer much distressed by his demands for money. Apparently he had been disappointed and told to leave.

He was living at this time in another town ten miles off, selling vacuum cleaners from door to door. It would have distressed poor Miss Maudsley even more. He was also again in trouble with the police: a little receiving of stolen goods, though in fairness it must be said that he was acquitted—Gilroy defended him on a dock brief, and the contrast between the two of them has always amused me in retrospect.

Forbidden to call, he wrote. He wrote often. He seems to have believed that he had a good case and he did not want to spoil it by too much variation. He was Miss Maudsley's nephew, her flesh and blood; he was in need; he had the chance of a good job (kind not specified) if he had a little capital to start with. Five hundred pounds was mentioned.

I saw those letters. There was something strangely artless and touching about them. I don't think he can have been a very good receiver or operator in the other small rackets of which he was suspected.

And Miss Maudsley saved all his letters. She kept them, along with her niece's polite rebuffs, in a folder of her father's in a drawer of which she kept the key—it was found hanging round her neck as she lay dead in the bathroom at "The Towers." Poor lady, how horrified she would have been to find herself at the centre of such a story, how she would have hated the headlines, the photographers trampling the lawns!

Just before six, at dusk on the evening of March 10th, about two weeks after John's last visit, Jane Birman, who had been on a social call at Mrs. Pye's, returned to "The Towers." According to her testimony, as she came up the drive she saw that the lights were on in the window of the living-room downstairs. She assumed that her employer was there, where she had left her and where she was usually to be found at this hour. On entering the hall, however, she noticed that the door of the living-room was ajar.

The main staircase at "The Towers" faces the doorway as you come in; it is a mean, narrow stair for so large a house, rising with one sharply angled bend onto the first landing, off which four rooms open; a bathroom immediately on the right, then Miss Maudsley's bedroom, Jane Birman's bedroom, and a room used for storage—the cook lived on the second floor.

From the hall Jane could see that the stair light was on. She seems to have decided to go up to her room to take off her hat and coat and deposit the magazines Mrs. Pye had lent her, for she was a great reader. At the top of the stairs she switched off the stair light, wondering a little to have found it on, for since John's appearance Miss Maudsley had become miserly about such things. She noticed no lights from under any of the doors. There was a window above the stairs, and in the half-light of the dying afternoon Jane went to her room.

A moment later she heard the sound of a door opening—it seemed like the bathroom door—and footsteps on the landing.

She was not exactly startled, for, after all, two other people lived in the house, also the living-room door had been open and the stair light on, which pointed to Miss Maudsley having come up. But Jane had been sure that there had been no light from under the door upstairs; and then the footsteps, even on the thick carpet of the landing, sounded different in some way from her employer's step. That is what Jane said in evidence.

She opened the door, leaving her light on, and looked out. Just below her, his head half-averted, a man was going down the stairs. He was moving rapidly. She could not say whether he had heard the door open or seen her light.

Jane Birman's next actions have formed the subject of much controversy. If she did not know the man, some people wondered, why did she not cry out? If she did know him, why did she not speak to him?

But, assuming for a moment the truth of her story, why should she cry out or be alarmed? Miss Maudsley was solitary but not entirely a recluse; people came to her house at times. Such questions also ignore the whole point of Jane's position in the house. She was on excellent terms with Miss Maudsley but she was still her companion, a subordinate in spite of everything.

But did she have no inkling, people asked, of what had been done? To me at the time it argued a great deal of superstition to think that. And those who thought it expected her to cry out! Did it not occur to them that it could have meant her death, as may often have happened in the double murders of the past?—witness poor Mary Rogerson who must have seen Dr. Ruxton kill his wife.

Whatever the truth of her motive, it is certain that she went to the head of the stairs, as she said, and from there watched the man go down. She expected him, she told the court later, to turn in at the door of the living-room. But he went on. He opened the front door and walked out.

It was at that moment, Jane has testified, that she became frightened. She ran down the stairs. The living-room was empty. She switched on the stair light and ran up again. She knocked at the door of her employer's room—a revealing touch that lights up for me the deference with which the old lady was still served—and receiving no answer she went in. That room was empty but in disorder.

She pushed open the bathroom door. It would not swing wide: there was some pressure against it. She cried out now, though no one heard. She switched on the light and stepped through the half-open door.

Miss Maudsley lay crumpled up between the door and the bath, one of those old-fashioned baths on legs. Her feet were under the bath, She was dead. Her face was blue and "horrible," in Jane's words. She was right: I have seen the police photographs. "There was a scarf round her neck"—I am using Jane's evidence as given in the shorthand note at the trial—"and it was twisted and knotted. It was horrible. She had raised her hands to her neck; there were scratches she must have made."

"How was she dressed?" Kenyon, for the Crown, asked her.

"In her day clothes, a lilac dress she wore. It was an old-fashioned dress, with lace, you know."

"Was her clothing disarranged?"

"Oh, no, *nothing* like that. Of course there was dust on her, she was all dusty."

"Did your employer wear glasses?"

"Yes. They were beside her. Broken. They were pince-nez, gold ones. I think she could see quite well really."

"Was there anything else about her clothes?"

"She was wearing felt slippers. She always wore them in the evening."

"Having discovered the body, what did you do?"

"I called the cook."

I have always found this particular answer to have

a flavour of true poignancy. The cook was over seventy, like her mistress. She wore very much the same sort of clothes; she had begun as a parlourmaid in happier days and had that extraordinary and fascinating primness that seems to have deserted the modern world. In fact, her reactions to the cruel sight that greeted her were as might have been expected. She broke down. She had the vapours—more realistically than her mistresses had ever had them in the past. Recovering, for she was a staunch soul, she wept. "Poor lady," she kept saying. And in the midst of these tears she did what Jane might have done: she said that the police must be phoned for.

They arrived in several cars, sweeping up the drive in a blaze of light. Detective Inspector Kent was the officer in charge, a very sound man whom we all got to know well on the Circuit; he kept racing-pigeons in his spare time.

They inspected the body. It seemed clear enough that Miss Maudsley had been killed at about the time of Jane's arrival in the house. I have often thought of the murderer up there in the small bathroom, with the body at his feet and the sound of steps mounting.

Miss Maudsley's room was a shambles—the word "untidy" that Jane gave it in evidence was a classic of understatement. The drawers were pulled out; the jewel case was open, its hinges bent back; only a few semi-precious stones remained, and a miniature of Miss Maudsley's mother, the mayoress, its glass smashed to fragments.

The detective inspector, having noted these things and left his subordinate to make an inventory, went downstairs to the living-room with Jane. He will have offered her a cigarette. I have no doubt he was kind to her; he was naturally kind, even to his pigeons when they returned, shamefully late, from some race. She will have told her story: they will have come to the man on the stairs.

How much has been written about him! Of course when it came to trial the conversation between Jane and Kent was not disclosed: it was not evidence. In court he told his story of what he did and saw in that house, and she told hers. The questions he asked and her answers were not relevant. It is no more than deduction when I say that I believe she was hesitant to identify that man.

"It was rather dark on the stairs"—so runs her evidence.

"What lights were on?" Kenyon, for the Crown, asked.

"There was a light from my room."

"Was your door fully open?"

"It was half-open. It gave some light."

"Was there any other light?"

"There was the window."

"What time would it be?"

"About six."

"Was there still daylight?"

"It was dusk. There was a greyish light."

Those were careful answers. I think we can assume from them that she was hesitant at first.

But she identified John Maudsley in the end.

Naturally the police didn't arrest him straight away. If he'd disappeared I suppose they would have issued a statement to the press saying that they wished to interview a certain person "who it is believed may be of assistance to the police," one of those delightful euphemisms for "murderer" which so bewilder the public. There are good reasons for such caution, though I think only policemen and lawyers understand them. In this case, however, there was no need, for the suspect was at home.

The inspector found him soon after nine o'clock that same night. Maudsley was in bed in the room he rented—I say rented, though naturally he was a month in arrears. He had charm, however, as I had diagnosed from certain aspects of his relationship with his aunt, and the landlady, far from being restive, seemed to be very much on his side—she was a personable widowed body who may have had hopes, some of which I think it possible had already been realized.

Interviewed in his bedroom among the cigarette stubs and the disordered sheets, Maudsley professed himself astonished at this visitation. "My God, no!" he exclaimed, on being told what had happened, or as much of it as Kent thought good for him. "The poor old sheila!" he followed up, shaking his head, for like most second-generation migrants he was rather more Australian than the "Diggers" themselves—I have always liked it as an epitaph.

The prologue over, the inspector began to ask questions, cautiously, for there are formidable legal pitfalls dug for investigators at this stage of a case. Maudsley was cautioned in due form. "Break it down! My oath, you can cut that out!" the suspect replied, and that went down along with the rest. We are fortunate here. What Kent asked and what Maudsley answered, unlike details of the interview with Jane, are known to us, for the inspector gave evidence of it in court; also we have Maudsley's own word, and I should say at once that the two stories tally.

Fortunately for the inspector his suspect was willing to talk; in fact, he volunteered everything. I can well imagine the scene: the watchful Kent; the subordinate writing it all down, not a bit the way police officers do it in folk story with blunt pencils and little notebooks with ruled lines on them; the expansive Maudsley, for I am sure he would have been expansive, it was his way. At one stage he appears to have offered his interrogators a drink ("grog," he would have called it); there was a half-empty bottle of gin on the washstand. The landlady had also weighed in hereabouts, knocking at the door and calling an invitation to tea through it. It was courteously refused.

The interview continued and a prompting question came up. Where had he been that day?

Where had he been? He had been at work of course. At work with his vacuum cleaners that morning. He'd sold one. Did the inspector want the address? The inspector did, and he supplied it. Dinner at home (he meant his midday meal). He'd gone to the pictures afterwards—apparently the sale had made it a red-letter day. He'd been to the "Royal" cinema, where the girl at the box-office might remember him. She didn't, actually. He'd walked back from there, dawdling a bit.

"Did you call in anywhere?"

"No."

"Did you meet or talk to anyone?"

"Yes, a chap called Mathers—or it may have been yesterday."

It turned out to have been yesterday.

He had come back home for tea after that, about

five-thirty. What time had the old lady been killed, by the way? I don't suppose he got *that* out of the inspector, but it was a gallant try. Since tea he had stayed in.

"Doing what?"

I think it more than probable that at this stage Maudsley may have given the inspector a wink, but nothing as unchaste was echoed in the immaculate police evidence. "He said he just stayed in, reading and suchlike," the inspector told the court without batting an eyelid.

The landlady, Mrs. James, supported this alibi in part. She was tentative about it. "I can't be certain with our clocks," she said, laying what blame was likedly to accrue squarely elsewhere. It was six or thereabouts, in her opinion, when the lodger came in for his tea. It was a proper tea, she added, no doubt feeling the honour of the house to be involved. "There was an egg, and apple pie—my own bottling," she later assured the court. "And some tea-cake and drop scones, and jam with it."

"Could it have been after six when he arrived?" the inspector had asked her.

"I don't think so. No. I'd have heard that clock strike"—pointing to the somnolent looking coffin with suns and moons on it that stood in the hall. "But you can't tell with them."

"Could it have been half-past six?"

"Oh, no.'

The inspector seems to have been disconcerted by these answers. Some policeman's instinct must have warned him that this shaky testimony might carry more defence weight with a jury than the stop-watch alibis some witnesses produce. Everyone was bound to sympathize with Mrs. James and her efforts, sorely hampered by her clocks, to tell the truth. Six o'clock, perhaps. But not half-past. They couldn't be *that* wrong.

In fact, when the inspector checked them he found that they were only wandering five and seven minutes respectively on the slow side of true. Mrs. James suddenly assumed the proportions of a formidable witness for the defence.

He went back to Maudsley, who was lying on the bed watching the young police officer with friendly interest. He cautioned him again.

"That's all right," Maudsley replied. He was as ready as ever to talk—about his aunt or anyone else. He provided details of the family. "There's just one other sheila, her niece, a sour little piece, my oath! The others have all passed on—to Paradise, one of 'em" (the philanthropist). "He worked his passage hard enough."

That was Maudsley. He was not in the least distressed by his own position, though his aunt's death drew from him certain words which, though flippant, were capable of a tenderer meaning. He had courage, no doubt of that. The inspector, for all his experience, didn't know what to make of him: whether this was absolute innocence or absolute callousness. They are strangely akin.

But he now had his case. The statement was read over and Maudsley signed it. I have no doubt that when that was done he offered his visitors more "grog," and saw them to the door, being cheerfully macabre and helpful to the last.

The inspector went back to the station, leaving a discreet watch. He examined the dead woman's jewel case again, and her will; he read the letters the nephew had sent her. He consulted with his superiors, and next morning he took out a warrant and went down and arrested his man.

"You've got it wrong, fair dinkum," Maudsley said.

That was the brief they gave to Marion for the defence.

Chapter Three

AS MIGHT HAVE BEEN EXPECTED, the reaction in our chambers to this news was mixed. Hesketh can hardly be said to have reacted at all. He knew that if barristers sometimes behaved like prima donnas they had a less sympathetic audience in the stalls; he had congratulated Marion once, as was proper, at the end of her first case, and as far as he was concerned it would have to last a lifetime. Nevertheless I am sure that he was pleased. Fenney, running true to form, was as excited as Serpell and Ross were indifferent. There was always something irritating about Fenney's enthusiasm and I found his fuss over Marion hard to bear, as I suppose was natural, for praise is competitive. He was really fond of her and not in the least jealous of her success. It so happened that that week he himself had a brief, and it was touching—if you were given to sentiment at all—to see the way he neglected it and gave Marion the benefit of his experience.

As for Jaggers, he was transported, there is no other word. "This is big, now this is really big," he kept saying. "I didn't think we'd land this"—for there were things for which even he was chary of claiming the credit.

He was a little dashed to discover that the prosecution was going into the chambers of our rivals in the town—Kenyon leading, with Ralph Loader and Marcus Stein. "They're only for the Crown," he said, recovering.

Mention of Kenyon, however, had given him an idea.

"Of course there should be a Queen's Counsel in this case," I heard him assure Maudsley's solicitor, Mr. Clive.

No answer.

"You know Kenyon's on the other side?" which was as good as saying, "So you'd better get Hesketh quick."

"I've got a very queer client," was all that the solicitor replied to that.

"My God, he must have!" Jaggers reported to me, wide-eyed. "What does he think this is? Income-tax dodging or something?"

"Perhaps Maudsley doesn't want a leader."

"Not want Mr. Hesketh?"

"Any leader," I said diplomatically, for I could see I was spoiling his day. "Perhaps he's allergic to them."

"Miss Kerrison will see it, if you can't," Jaggers retorted quite sharply.

He certainly handled her with tact. "It's not that you *can't* do it, Miss Kerrison. I know you can. But you've never been in a murder case."

"No."

"The atmosphere's different. I admire the way you take on the same cases the men do. It's all right in chambers. But in court things have to be *said* and you have to be heard saying them."

"You mean the jury mightn't like it?"

Jaggers clearly did mean that but he couldn't say so. He was already a bit afraid of her. I wouldn't have cared to say it to her myself, though I confess that I felt very much as Jaggers did, for I had seen the faces of jurymen (particularly the men) when some lady barrister was telling them of facts they had never hinted to their wives, even at the end of the honeymoon.

"I think we should have Mr. Hesketh too," was all he said.

For the next few days the conferences in our room were continuous. I was banished to the outer office, where I sat with my briefs between Miss Egerton's typewriter and Belle's teapot. Miss Egerton was an experienced business woman. Belle was young. She had always worked in blinkers, as it were. Each day she saw the finished product of our labour come out of our rooms in long-hand scrawls which she did her best to decipher, but never before had she been privileged to see a barrister actually in the throes, and she watched me breathlessly, waiting for the light of inspiration to dawn. I must have been a great disappointment to her. Fortunately she had other outlets for her romantic mind. "I wonder what they're doing now," she would whisper to Miss Egerton, with one eye on the door of the room from which a murmur of voices came. The wheels of fate turned visibly for her: justice had a face, and a mind like her own, inquiring and compassionate, but somehow infallible. "Miss Egerton."

"Yes."

"Did you see the brief?"

Miss Egerton righteously shook her head, though I am sure that Jaggers would have shown her the more horrific passages.

"I expect it's *awful*, just awful."

"Belle, there's someone here trying to work," Jaggers reproved her from his desk, with an encouraging look at me.

She relapsed into silence. But it was soon sure to be time for tea; it seemed to come up endlessly; the soundless typewriter also in the course of years had degenerated somewhat. I got very little work done but I have never regretted those wasted hours, for there was a pleasant old-world flavour about Jaggers's kingdom.

In the course of time Marion became concerned about my exile and looked around for expedients. Could I not be in the room during the conferences? she asked Mr. Clive. "Why not in the case?" the solicitor said at last, diagnosing the way her mind was working and perhaps imagining other things also, for he was of the kind who believed in keeping happy those who worked for him.

Jaggers, approached about the possibility of a junior brief for me, was enthusiastic. "Mr. Irvine is the *very man*," he assured Clive; though, of course, he added, there would come a stage when a leader was required, in which case . . . Naturally I was delighted to have this chance. "It will be the making of you," Jaggers told me, and he must have been so eloquent about it that the next time I passed through the outer office I saw Belle looking at me with quite an awed expression.

So I came into the Maudsley case. I have never thought of it as my case, though. It was always Marion's. She would want to take the blame for the mistakes, just as I know where the praise should be.

For the next two months we lived with it. We became familiar with every word the witnesses used. We knew by heart the letters Maudsley wrote and the quirks of the old lady's will; we knew every stone that had been in her jewel box. Twice we went to the house. We came up the drive as Jane had come that night, seeing the lights in the living-room, and went up the stairs as she had done, and came to the landing in the grey murk of dusk.

I have always been susceptible to the feel of past events. It gives me a never-failing emotion to stand in the castle of Blois imagining that winter's morning in 1588, the Duke of Guise by the fireside, the king watching him through the curtain, the assassins at the door. "My God, he looks even bigger dead!" the unhappy king cried, and he touched the body nervously with his foot. It is one of those phrases that reveal the characters of men. Of course this is emotionalism in me, the mind of Belle. No intellectual person would have been moved as I was once in Canterbury. I had arrived late at the cathedral when the sightseers had gone and only a verger was walking in the gloom. He took me round and showed me the spot where St. Thomas stood—there was a stain, he said, and I peered dutifully down, irritated as we always are when people take us to be gullible. But then he pointed. "It was through that little door at about this time that the archbishop came to the high altar. And then the knights . . ." I did not see them then as Eliot has seen them in his great play, figures of the theatre, suave or foolish, arguing their case, and the audience laughing, surprised and delighted as a congregation at a witty sermon. For a moment I heard the loud voices and the mailed steps in the nave.

The mind of Belle. Of course Marion didn't have it. On our first visit to "The Towers"—"It was here," she told me, and she pushed open the bathroom door and walked in. It wasn't that she was callous. But she had a job to do. Pity for the dead woman was a thing apart. "The head lay this way," she said, "and the feet were stretched out here. He killed her outside and dragged the body in, perhaps when he heard Birman on the stairs." But even these words were spoken in such a way that they had a strangely unpictorial quality. She was "reconstructing" the murder, as the police say: she wasn't living it. I am sure she had no unease in that house in the half-light, no sense of the so-lately dead whose possessions were all around us—the soap in its dish, the toothbrush in the rack.

For all that, she was seeing the *events* more clearly than I had done. "The murderer came into the house when Birman was out. He'd planned a robbery. He entered at the back and went upstairs. Somehow the old woman heard him. She followed him up in her carpet slippers. Perhaps he heard a noise. He came out—and there she was on the landing."

"Poor lady," I said, unconsciously using the cook's words.

"Yes, poor lady. But that was the way of it."

Day after day we worked through the brief. It was not pleasant. The photographs were horrible and even Jaggers after one glance put them aside. Maudsley's letters to his aunt were a great relief from them, the expressions of a financially injured soul, never precisely threatening, though there were one or two phrases that must have been pleasing Kenyon very much: "It is unwise to treat me like this. . . . When other people have made promises I have seen that they kept them. . . . I *must* have money"—this was repeated several times with varying degrees of forcefulness.

"How much did he have when he was arrested?" Marion inquired, marking these passages in pencil.

"Fifty pounds in notes," Mr. Clive replied: he was our constant familiar in these discussions, though he seldom spoke.

"Had he anything more? A bank account?"

"Yes."

"Anything in it?"

"A few pounds."

"So he had motive?"

"Yes."

"He needed money for this business he wanted to buy, that's one side of it. He was her heir and they'd quarrelled, and that's another. He was afraid she might disinherit—his words can be read like that."

"Certainly."

"Well?" Marion said, looking at the little solicitor whom she had come to like and trust. "Is he the sort of man who could have done it?"

"He could have."

But they went on further. It is not wise for counsel to speculate about the guilt of clients, particularly when they are in doubt themselves. You could see the doubt in Clive's face also. It is true of most murders that the obvious person is guilty. You could say also that murderers generally are of two kinds. There are the unpredictables, the hitherto honourable, the Crippens of the world. One can imagine the consternation of his friends in Hilldrop Crescent. Yet, on the other hand, there are men who seem to be predisposed to it, the Heaths, whose history is a rising tide of small dishonesties shading into violence towards the end. Of course only a minute percentage of such men kill. But I have had an eerie feeling sometimes, watching some prisoner in the dock, that here was a murderer met on the way—the mind of Belle again, but some men by their face or manner induce such thoughts.

Maudsley did.

I shan't forget our first meeting with him. We had driven out by taxi, Mr. Clive sitting between us hugging his bowler hat, a rarity in our town. I had never been inside a gaol before and I found its atmosphere peculiar, a compound of school and hospital and fortress turned outside-in. Years before, when I was a small boy, my father had taken me into the public gallery of the Law Courts, and I remember distinctly the impression I received that the judge and the jury were really there to deal with me. "Can we go now? I mean, will they let us?" I kept whispering, and it became a joke in the family. The gaol gave me just that feeling. Everyone was kind, with the brusque kindness of officials who know the ropes, but the small boy within me was still whispering.

Then Maudsley came in. I had seen photographs of him, but even so I was unprepared for what I saw. He was much bigger than I had imagined. Miss Maudsley had been a frail person, as her mother had been also, and the neat mayor of the portrait. This man seemed to come of a coarser stock. He had the small grey Maudsley eyes but they were set in such a large frame that the effect was strange and somehow repellent; they gave a mean look to what was otherwise a cheerful and open face, with a big mouth and a nose with a slight humorous twist to it. "The *faux bonhomme*," I said to myself. I can't say that I liked him. My first impression unmistakably was that he fitted the murder, the forced jewel box, the broken miniature, the scarf drawn savagely tight.

But Mr. Clive was introducing us, it might have been any business conference anywhere, and Maudsley was looking at us in turn and forming his own conclusions. I don't think they were much more favourable than mine.

"So you're Miss Kerrison," he said at last in his exaggerated Australian voice.

I imagine he'd seen pictures of her leaving court after her big case, and they had been flattering ones. Perhaps he wasn't prepared for the day-to-day Marion in her sombre clothes, for I have noticed that clients are almost invariably disappointed to meet barristers out of wigs and gowns; they feel cheated somehow.

"This is your counsel," Mr. Clive translated coldly.

Maudsley gave her a nod as though to say: "Well, it's done now, and anyway you're not so bad." You could see at once that he had a familiar way with women which worked or didn't work according to the subject. Marion appeared unmoved. They stared at one another, but it was he who glanced away.

"We'll get down to the case," she said.

For the next half-hour she cross-examined him. It was a stern performance. He must have assumed that she had taken a dislike to him, for once or twice he broke out in protest and had to be soothed by Mr. Clive. Marion herself made no attempt to calm him. She was testing his evidence by prosecution standards. "Answer, you must answer," was all she said.

He did his best, but for myself I can't say that I believed him. I had the impression all the time that he was evading something. His story of his movements on the night of the murder was particularly scant and unconvincing.

"You say you went to the pictures after lunch?"

"After my dinner, yes."

"You know the girl in the box-office doesn't remember you?"

"So I've been told."

"What was the film?"

"Some bush film it was."

"Who were the stars?"

"I can't remember."

"Describe it."

"There was a man in the bush and some lions and buffalo. He was a hunter. And there was a girl with him. He was some hunter all right."

"You could have known that from the posters. Isn't that vague?"

"It was a pretty vague film, fair dinkum," Maudsley said.

"Very well. And after the picture you walked home."

"Yes."

"And you thought you'd met someone, only you hadn't."

"That's right."

"At half-past five you were back?"

"Not later than six, anyway."

"Did you go out again?"

"I did not," Maudsley said with the ghost of a smile.

"So you weren't near 'The Towers' that night?"

"I was in bed."

Marion looked from her brief to Mr. Clive, to Maudsley, who had quite recovered from his anxiety and had relapsed into the easy flippancy that was either his character or his stock-in-trade.

"Has it occurred to you that this case is menacing?" she asked suddenly.

He stared at her. "Of course."

"I don't think it has. And yet there's motive, identification at the scene of the crime, misleading statements you've made—lies, they'll call them. It may not be enough. You've your alibi and it could save you." She paused, and when she went on her voice was grave. "But if it's untrue *in any particular, however small,* it can hang you. Do you understand that?"

"Oh, yes," he said easily.

"It can hang you as certainly as if the jury had seen you in the house that night."

He smiled, as though inviting her to go on and imagine some more.

"I'll ask you again. Were you near 'The Towers'?"

"No."

"You had motive, do you agree?"

"I suppose so."

"You were in need of money. Did you know about her jewels?"

"Yes."

"Did you ever see them?"

"She showed me the box once."

"Did you ever take any?"

Maudsley stared at her indignantly. "Take any!" he exclaimed. "What do you think I am?"

From a charged and suspected murderer it was in its way a classic answer, and perhaps it was the ironical flavour surrounding it that made it sound so completely convincing. Marion nodded and began packing up her papers.

"Doesn't anyone else want to ask me anything?" Maudsley demanded with a glance at the supernumeraries.

It was said very impertinently, and I could see Mr. Clive flush and prepare to get on our dignities for us.

"*I've* one thing more," Marion said. "I think there should be a leader in this case."

"A leader?"

"A Queen's Counsel," Mr. Clive explained.

"Who'll pay him?"

"The State will."

Maudsley thought for a moment. He stared at Marion, weighing her up. "Oh, I don't know, I'll think of it. But I should say this lady here will do me fine, just bonzer," he said with the suggestive glance and voice that had probably slain poor Mrs. James. It was deliberate. He hadn't enjoyed the interview, the sharp questions; she had hurt his pride, that assertive cockerel pride some men have. I think he was in the mood for taking any risk so long as he could score off her, and his humour took this way of doing it, accepting her as a *woman*, with just enough reservations and condescension to hurt.

He must have been disappointed by the way she took it. "Think it over carefully and let Mr. Clive know," she told him, putting the papers in her brief case, and with a nod to him she led the way out.

No one spoke much in the taxi going back to town. "I told you he was a queer customer," the solicitor said as we got out at Hesketh's chambers, and you could see that he felt himself personally responsible for the client.

"Oh, he's all right."

"He's a surly type,"—Mr. Clive had too much tact to refer directly to his rudeness to Marion.

"Yes."

"What sort of witness do you think he'll make?"

"A very bad one."

Mr. Clive gave a sigh. He knew that it is in the witness-box that most murderers are hanged. Conceit kills most of them. I would hazard that nearly all murderers are abnormally conceited men—Rouse, Sedden, Fox, Vaquier, Landru, Haigh, Heath, and even Christie—that sin is inherent in the crime itself and is disclosed with terrible clarity under cross-examination in the box.

"Clive thinks he's a dead duck," I said to Marion when we were alone in our room again.

"Yes."

"Is he right?"

"Perhaps."

"That alibi now." We exchanged glances. We were both seeing Mrs. James. Her testimony seemed strong and fair, but mistresses make bad witnesses as a rule: they either abandon their lovers or compromise themselves. I think we both hoped very much that the poor lady would not be presented in these clothes, but there seemed little hope of it with a man who could give a touch of the seraglio to a conference in prison. "I'd watch that alibi," I said.

"I shall."

"I suppose we've got to use it?"

"Yes."

"Though he's the sort of man," I said, "who doesn't understand truth. I don't think he understands what's happened to him. Conceit again. He's quite good-humoured about it, just the way he was, I suppose, when he was swindling people. He's above us. He's as unreliable as Jupiter. You can't trust a word."

"I do," Marion said.

I looked at her in astonishment. "You can't mean that."

"Oh, but I do. He's innocent. He never killed Miss Maudsley."

It was that same evening we learnt from Kenyon that one of the dead woman's jewels had been found in a cistern at Mrs. James's house.

Chapter Four

THE CASE OF THE QUEEN AGAINST Maudsley was a focal point with me. Till then, I had spent my time watching from the inside the public activities of others; there are few occupations to disenchant you so quickly or completely. A little later in life the "gravitas" that surrounds barristers like an aura sat more naturally on me and I was able to take my place on the stage without excitement or envy. But it is not easy to keep one's balance in the midst of one's first murder case.

How can I describe it? I have heard pundits say that a murder trial is like any other; more straightforward, if anything, for there is seldom much law involved and witnesses are more likely to tell the truth. I suppose there is force of a kind in this, though I know that these pundits are wrong. The sense of life and death is never absent from such a trial. Of course the judge and counsel are trained to subdue the personal in themselves, but I have never yet met one who succeeded completely. At the end of the story, beyond the droning voices and the court stenographer in his black suit writing it all down, is the cell in the grey morning light and the sound of footsteps in the corridors. In France the executioners come creeping to the door, trying to make no sound, but I think our own way is macabre enough.

The jury and the witnesses have that same picture also. They know that their words may condemn a living soul. And then there is the wretched man in the dock, the knowledge that he may have killed, that the body shown in those glossy photographs on counsel's table may once have lain under his hands.

The hands of murderers. Some artist should draw them, as they drew Landru for the Paris papers: restless hands clasped on the ledge of the dock, twisting a handkerchief; busy hands that write endless notes; careless, doodling hands; the impassive hands of workmen. I see them as symbolic. Even reporters, the most disenchanted of men, have told me that the atmosphere of murder is never matched elsewhere, the mark of Cain on us, the old savagery that persists in the stockbroker reading his "thriller" in the train.

I know that during these weeks when I was working on the Maudsley brief the world outside had a very dim appearance. It seemed to me that the whole Circuit was watching and envying us. In fact, looking back on it, I can see that there was a measure of interest. "I hear you and Kerrison have got the Maudsley brief," people would say to me, and one evening my neighbour in the bar mess so far forgot the rule against talking "shop" as to draw down a rebuke from the "Junior," a sort of adjutant who mirrored the Circuit leader's urbane conversation from the lower end of the table.

Marion was not allowed at these mess evenings where she would certainly have felt herself out of place. They were relics of the old convivial days when the Circuits were real clubs for a travelling band of brothers and not mere satellites of London. Like so many ancient things they have a use in our times, but rather a strangulated one: people tend to come out of duty rather than nature, and suffer the indifferent meal and remember to pass the port the correct way round. Afterwards it was the custom with some of us to go across the way to a hotel and have a game of snooker; it made a pleasant end to the evening, though no one —Ross excepted—was any good.

On this occasion, about a fortnight before the trial, I found myself with Ross and Loader, Kenyon's junior, and Gilroy Ashington-Duclair who had come down from London on one of the naughty and fashionable divorce cases in which he specialized.

We spun for partners and I drew Ross. "Oh, God! Well, never mind," he said, setting the red balls in their frame.

Games are great indicators of character. Ross's was the misspent youth, all right; Loader played with solid care, you felt he hardly found the game respectable; Gilroy put an exquisite edge on every shot.

"How's Portia?" he said to me while we were watching Ross perform—he still bore her a grudge for those photographs, I think.

I replied: "She's all right."

"Any news?"

I looked across at our opponent, Loader, who in his expressionless way was chalking his cue. "Shop again," I said.

"Oh, come," Gilroy retorted, "we're not in the mess now. How's she bearing up?"

"Quite well."

"Do you like her as a leader?"

At this point it became his turn and he bent down behind the cue ball, showing an expanse of beautifully laundered cuff. The shot when it came was hardly up to it.

"No Hesketh, I hear," he resumed, straightening up.

"Not so far."

"Just the two of you. The innocents. I expect the press'll catch onto it."

"Very probably, and they might print some pictures too."

He gave his high cackling laugh. "Ah, my dear chap, we must *always* cede the limelight to the ladies. Perhaps you'll find that."

"Your turn," Ross said, nudging me. There was a choice of shots, but from experience he no longer suggested which of them I should take, since he confidently expected me to miss either. "You know we've half a dollar on this," he reminded me tartly as I obliged.

Loader went up to the table and potted the sitting red ball I had left him, and a green and another red.

"*All* the limelight," Gilroy said. "Never forget Portia's a star part."

Such, I think, was the general feeling on the Circuit at that time. There was resentment. Many were jealous, and even the older men, who truly believed in the fraternity of the gown, were shocked at what they thought her too-public method; they never made allowances for the way she had been forced into the headlines by circumstance and her own abilities.

Marion was perfectly aware of this. I don't think she cared much on her own account, for only the weak fear making enemies; it is the eternal schoolboy in them, and I have noticed that all the successful-to-be accept the envy and dislike of others as favourable weather signs. But I think she cared on Hesketh's account. She was afraid that he would be disappointed in her and hurt by the way the big brief was eluding him. She cared a lot for Hesketh's opinion. Yet characteristically she brought no strong pressure to bear on Maudsley and Clive to get her leader brought into the case. She did not mix sentiment with business, and in this she exactly matched Hesketh.

It took a man of Fenney's sensibility to misinterpret these two strong personalities. "I'm saying this as a friend," he began, coming into our room one day with that beneficent air of his that always riled me.

It is never a good beginning and Marion waited, probably guessing what he would say.

"I've been thinking. I mean, I don't want to interfere. I know you can do this case and do it well, get him off if anyone can. But is it wise? Hasn't Jaggers spoken to you?"

He must have known very well that Jaggers had done very little else.

"I mean, *Kenyon's* there," he went on. "It needs the old man to deal with Kenyon, he's used to him. I don't want to interfere. But there's been a sort of established pattern in these cases: Kenyon on one side and our lord and master on the other. Everyone half expects it."

"And does Hesketh wholly expect it?" Marion demanded sharply.

"Well, yes, I believe so, in a way. Of course it's not my business."

"Did he say so?"

"Oh, no." Fenney looked alarmed. You could see

that he was suddenly aware that he had fallen into an imprudence. "You mustn't breathe a word of it to Hesketh," he warned her.

"Why not? If that's what he thinks."

"Oh, no, you mustn't."

"But if that's what you say and . . ."

"My dear, I've said nothing, nothing at all, believe me." He was agitated, for he was greatly in awe of Hesketh. "I just thought you'd see."

After he had gone we smiled at one another. "That was naughty of you," I said to her. "Very naughty."

"I know and I'm sorry. I like Fenney."

"And he means well."

"Well, he does, and you needn't laugh about it," she rebuked me. "You're as bad as Serpell. Why are you so antagonistic to the poor man?"

I denied this strenuously.

"You are antagonistic," she said, looking at me thoughtfully. "Though how he's harmed you . . ."

"He hasn't harmed me, as you call it. He's just an ass."

She opened her mouth to pursue the matter but seemed to think better of it. "Well, do you think Hesketh really *is* hurt?" she asked me, changing course.

"In a way, yes. He's like all of us: he loves briefs."

"So what should I do?"

"Nothing. What can you do? Maudsley wants you." I may have said this a trifle tartly for I hadn't liked her defence of Fenney, which, if I'd only had the sense to see it, I had forced on her. "It's your case, whether you like it or not. My guess is that you do."

"Of course I do. It's a great opportunity."

But the more we studied the brief the more we saw

what its probable outcome must be. The Crown's case, which had seemed so tenuous, was beginning to take dangerous shape. Maudsley was the cause of this. From the outset I had suspected that he was a morally colour-blind man. Such men don't so much tell lies as fail to distinguish truth. I have heard the guiltiest criminals declaiming their innocence after sentence and obviously believing every word: indeed, the injured innocence of the guilty is worthy of the pen of Dostoevsky.

Marion would not agree with me. She admitted that Maudsley had lied—she could hardly do otherwise after the discovery of the ring. But she remained convinced that in essentials he had told the truth.

"Even about the alibi?" I asked her.

"I think so, yes."

"And the lies about the jewel? How do you account for that?"

"Of course he stole it some weeks before."

"A present for Mrs. James? Why was it hidden, then?"

She gave me a pitying look.

"People like Maudsley don't need to give presents to people like Mrs. James," she said. "The gratitude's all the other way. The ring was in cache."

It was certainly fortunate for her that she felt like this, since she had to defend the man. I confess that for myself I could see no hope in the case. A lying witness, identification, the discovery of the jewel. It is not the *duty* of counsel to be deceived and I pointed this out to Marion.

"Do you want to return your brief?" she demanded, rounding on me angrily.

"Of course not."

"It sounds like it. Are you saying that I'm deceiving myself?"

"No."

"Because I tell you again: he didn't do it. He's an innocent man."

Two days later we went to the prison and all my impressions were confirmed. Maudsley seemed delighted to see us. It was dull in the cell, he said; there didn't seem to be anything about him in the papers; he was greatly looking forward to getting out—what was the position about the old sheila's money, by the way?

Mr. Clive gave him a pained look and told him he understood there was forty thousand pounds in shares and the house.

Maudsley whistled. "She was a warm old girl. And I'm the heir?"

"Yes."

"When do I have it?

"It's a fair cow, that!" he exclaimed on being told that for the time being (one of Clive's better interpretations) he couldn't touch it. The sum of forty thousand pounds, to say nothing of the house, was a cheering thought, however, and I could see some ideas already forming as to how he'd spend it. Of doubt about the issue there wasn't a trace. He was innocent, so his mind was assuring him. He was astonished and grieved at the harsh way Marion handled him.

"The last time you were here you may remember telling us about Miss Maudsley's jewels."

"Oh, yes."

"You said you'd never seen them, though she'd shown you the box. You hadn't taken any."

"That's right."

"How do you account for the fact that the police found an emerald ring, the property of Miss Maudsley, in the cistern at your house?"

He stared at her. "Could they do that? High-handed bastards! Well, it's a fair cow," he said.

It was a long time before we even got an explanation out of him, and that quite clearly wasn't the true one. "She gave it me." When? he was asked. On his last visit. Why hadn't he told us that before? He hadn't liked to. Why had he hidden the ring? For safety. As a precaution against theft. Who was he afraid would steal it? Mrs. James?

At that question Maudsley's sense of humour, always his vulnerable point, overcame him and he burst out: "Look here, what's the good? I took that ring." Apparently he had been alone in the house with his aunt on his last visit, two weeks before the murder, and had nipped upstairs ostensibly to go to the lavatory and had stolen the emerald, which was a small stone and one she was most likely to overlook.

"Was the box open?" Marion at once wanted to know.

"Of course not."

"Then how did you get the key?"

His eyes flickered for an instant and he answered: "I knew where the old sheila kept it."

There was a pause before Marion said in a small voice: "She kept it round her neck."

"She had a duplicate, fair dinkum. Silly, wasn't it? Old women are like that. She had a duplicate in a little box. There were all sorts in it: clock keys, boxroom keys. Those boxrooms were always kept locked. There was damn all in 'em. I know, for I looked."

Thinking back on it I can see that we were naïve to

be as excited as we were by these words. I suppose we had really feared that he would introduce a fiction of duplicate keys made at his order by some friend of his (whose name he couldn't remember) whom he had met at some street corner (name supplied), keys that he'd disposed of down a drain; and the story he had in fact produced was so much more reasonable. Actually we were no further forward except in a negative way. When a man admits to stealing once it is not hard to assume that he has stolen again, and the jury might well believe that this admission of means and knowledge was just another link in the chain connecting him with murder. Nevertheless, the fact was that his credit in our eyes revived. He had been evasive and stupid rather than artful in his answers, and the bit about the boxrooms, pointless in its way, was strangely convincing.

"We must get that key," Marion said with a glance at Clive, whom she had a tendency to treat as a secretary of the more confidential kind. Mr. Clive said he would see to it.

"Well, that's all, then."

Maudsley seemed surprised. He could see that he'd pleased her but he didn't quite know why, for I'm afraid the nuances of truth were beyond him. No more questions? Hadn't we anything more? At our first meeting his sex antagonism had been too much for him, but now he seemed quite grieved that the interview was over. You could see that he would be the type of witness who relishes questions; that is the worst type of witness. Most people are like that, they enjoy being asked questions. Interrogation must be tremendously exciting after the dull routine of prison; it is on this that police states rely for the first steps in "brainwashing," and a trial in a court of law achieves something of the same result. I felt suddenly very sorry for him. "You'd better get that fellow gagged on the day," I said to Clive as we went out to our taxi.

He nodded gloomily. "He's too eager, Mr. Irvine."

"Too eager by half. Kenyon's going to have a field day."

I noticed that Marion was looking at us sourly. "You'll see," I couldn't help adding for her benefit, though I was sorry for her too.

I couldn't say more in front of Clive, since legal etiquette is rather Medean and for all his doubts of Maudsley he would have been as scandalized as Marion if I had expressed what we were feeling. But I knew it should be said.

"What about dinner tonight?" I suggested to her when we were back in chambers, seeking a more informal atmosphere.

She agreed with a surprising promtpness—in fact, for a moment it occurred to me to wonder whether she too wasn't looking for an informal setting to tell some home truths to *me*.

But she was all friendliness at the road house. I suppose we made a quaint pair in our sober clothes among all the *décolleté* and club ties. Jaggers always insisted on a strict adherence to rules: not for him the chalk stripes and soft hats that were invading the Circuit. "Mr. Hesketh thinks a barrister should look like a barrister," he would say to us, not without doubt, for Hesketh himself had the weakness and would sometimes arrive in a horrible grey trilby which his wife was goading him to wear.

Marion certainly looked the barrister, or at least the professional woman of some kind, in her severe costume and blouse. Nevertheless Ross had long since professed to have found a change in her. "Our Marion is becoming feminized," he had said to me with a glance of unmistakable significance. "Style, *the lot*, the treatment, my poor friend." I must say that I hadn't noticed it, perhaps because I had been quicker than he to discern the woman in her and the male eye is limited in the number of perceptions it can make.

Perceptions can be forced on one, however.

"You look pleased," I said to her as we sat down opposite one another.

That was the way it struck me. I think we only imagine that beauty is a reflection of something within. Perhaps the only difference between the Marion I had brought to this place before and the Marion I saw now lay in those subtleties of clothes and make-up that Ross had detected. I was never observant. I couldn't have told you that her stockings were finer and her costume better cut. But it did seem to me that she was happier, and beautiful as she had not been before. I felt in myself a surge of happiness: which may have been not so much the response as the instigator of it all.

"Pleased?" Marion was saying. "And shouldn't I be?"

"Yes, and I'm glad. Is it the breaking out tonight?"

"That, of course."

"And perhaps something Maudsley said this afternoon?"

She gave a shrug of the shoulders and it occurred to me that for once she had forgotten all about him. I was free to find this very flattering. No one, however, altogether likes being robbed of a duty and I had brought her there to discharge one, or so I told myself. "You shouldn't be too encouraged by anything he says," I went on, putting it very much lower than I had intended.

She smiled at me. "No? Well, you're a great corrective, Michael."

"Thank you."

"Ah, now I've said the wrong thing. Perhaps it's better than that *you* should."

I saw then that she had known perfectly well what was in my mind.

"Naturally, Ross would say that you're a witch," I said to her.

She was all innocence. "Oh! Why?"

"For reading me like that."

"Men aren't difficult."

"And Maudsley?"

"Is less difficult than most."

"Yet you believe in him?"

She thought for a moment. When she looked pensive she went some way to justify the unkind things Ross said of her: her brow furrowed, she looked as stern as a stipendiary.

"I believe in *him*, not in all his answers," she replied at last.

"The court will hear the answers. It may not have your instinct."

"Which you distrust?"

"In this case, yes."

"Well, that's very frank."

"I'm not claiming frankness as a virtue, Marri," I said.

"A duty, then?"

"Yes, if you like. I'm in this case, too, you know."

She didn't like that; but it was necessary reminder and I am sure very good for her.

"I'm not likely to forget you're in it," she answered huffily.

"Oh, come off it, Marri!"

After a moment she began to smile.

"Why! Am I such a dictator, Michael?" she asked in her wheedling voice.

"Don't you know you are?"

"Yes, I suppose so. You must correct me."

"Oh, I will."

"Hold me back."

"Yes."

"Particularly when I'm certain about things."

"Particularly when you're certain. And now go on and tell me he's innocent again."

Chapter Five

REGINA VERSUS MAUDSLEY WAS SET down for the next Assize before Mr. Justice Lorne, who had reached the bench in the previous year. He was a man who had shone at the Bar, and his promotion was said to have been the signal for great rejoicing in the Temple, where the blessed manna of his practice was released on the laps of the deserving.

Jaggers, who always kept abreast of developments, reported him to be a "strong" judge, somewhat conscious of his divinity, as is the way with new gods. "You want to watch him; he's difficult, he was very rude to Mr. Hesketh once," he told Marion in a voice which suggested that Mr. Justice Lorne would be likely to do at least as much for her. Jaggers already had doubts about her too independent spirit. "And you must watch *her*, Mr. Irvine," he instructed me. "You must hold her back." I said that I would try. "Ah, but can you do it?" he replied, shaking his head over me lugubriously. "She's difficult too. A pair of them. And Mr. Kenyon on the other side!"

In these last few weeks before the trial Jaggers had

become thoroughly pessimistic about his great case, which was an extraordinary departure for him. The loss of Hesketh's brief as leader rankled terribly: it was a denial of the natural order of things, and this affected him far more than the loss of his own cut of Hesketh's fees. There were times, I think, when this incorrigible propagandist would gladly have thrown the whole thing up and seen it go into other chambers. A failure —and for once he believed he foresaw failure—would have the worst results on Marion's practice, he told me —he didn't refer to mine.

I can't say that I was much more optimistic as I worked through the minutiæ of the case. It was often dull work. We had to become familiar with every detail, with times and lighting-charts and the inventory of Miss Maudsley's jewel box:

3 diamond rings (one solitaire)
1 diamond pendant and platinum chain
1 pair of diamond ear-rings
1 diamond bar brooch
1 rope of pearls
1 ruby necklace with gold chain
1 sapphire and diamond ring
1 sapphire and diamond brooch
1 emerald ring
1 gold chain bracelet set with diamond and turquoise
1 topaz and silver necklace with matching ear-rings and bracelet
1 cameo brooch
1 bracelet of cairngorms with brooch and ear-rings to match

1 miniature of Miss Maudsley's mother
1 heart-shaped gold locket

The emerald was the one found with Maudsley. The miniature, the semi-precious stones and the cameo brooch were still in the jewel box. All the rest were missing, ranging in value from the diamond solitaire ring at £2,500 to the heart-shaped locket which might have been worth ten pounds to anyone sentimentally inclined.

That was a small and unimportant aspect of the case, which resolved itself increasingly as time went on into the problem of the identification, the evidence of Jane. What sort of woman was she? That was the question we always kept before our minds, though we had nothing to go on beyond the rather indeterminate results of inquiries which Mr. Clive had caused to be made.

Jane Birman, it appeared from these, was the younger daughter of an army officer whose pension and private income had never been adequate to his tastes. She was part educated, you could say no more than that. At times, when certain speculations went well, she was sent to schools where the most exacting standards in the way of clothing lists were enforced; others were perhaps a little nearer to Llanabba; but one and all failed to make much of this quick but farouche and ignorant child. A career as a teacher in one of the less eminent of the establishments she had suffered in was accordingly decreed when the time came for her to go out into the world, but she and her embryo pupils were mercifully saved from this by the war.

She did well in uniform, and this was probably the

happiest time of her life, when she had a job that suited her and a reasonable amount of money. She rose to be a sergeant, was commissioned, and went overseas into the thronging garrison life of the Middle East, where engagement rings were to be found in the kitbags of most single ladies.

Yet she returned a spinster, which was strange, for by all accounts she was a good-looking young woman, amusing and high-spirited. Perhaps it is permissible to infer an emotional upset somewhere on the way, for after her demobilization it became clear that she had changed. Her father was dead, she had a small inheritance and her own savings and might well have found a niche for herself in some busy West Riding firm; instead, she chose to go of all things into a tea-shop business in a small country town, a venture that was not prosperous.

Her career as a lady's companion followed naturally from that: four employers, some testy, some benevolent, all in some degree infirm, ending with Miss Maudsley among the lace and *petit point* embroidery.

The new life seems to have set its mark on her: she became outwardly resigned and hard—the brittle hardness of those who have been disappointed in the world and cannot quite forget their hopes. Disillusion is not a comfortable thing to live with, though perhaps Miss Maudsley, coming from a more disciplined world, did not recognize it in her companion or wonder how far this subdued "correctness" hid the fires of an ardent nature full of passions that were alive and unsatisfied.

Such was my belief and my opinion of our witness. It was not Marion's. She saw Jane Birman as a more positive person who might take a lover but never lose her head over him, a cold individual of great determination with a quick, "noticing" mind, as was shown in her deposition. Here is a typical passage, and incidentally the vital one for us:

When I reached my room I went to the bedside table and put down the magazines I had borrowed from Mrs. Pye. I had switched the light on from the door. I remember looking in the long wardrobe mirror. It was then I heard the sound. It seemed like a door opening—the bathroom door—but I couldn't be sure. There followed a padding noise, like footsteps on the landing carpet—it was a thick pile Indian carpet.

I went to my door, leaving the light on, and looked out. There was a man going down the stairs. He was a big, burly man. He was walking fast but not running. His head was half-averted. I recognized him. It was the man known to me as John Maudsley, my employer's Australian nephew. I have never met him. I have seen his photograph often. There were snapshots sent from Australia. There was one portrait in particular that stood on the piano in the living room, at "The Towers." It was there when I first came. My employer took it down after receiving a letter from him that distressed her. She showed me the letter: it asked for money. It was immediately after this incident that the photograph was taken down. I don't know where she put it. But there was another portrait of him which she kept in her bedroom all the time, and it was there on the night of her death.

I recognized the accused clearly. He was wearing a darkish suit. I couldn't swear to the colour. Darkish, perhaps grey. Dark shoes, I think. He was bareheaded. He was carrying nothing in his hands. There was some light coming from my room and from the window above the stairs. It was dusk. It was dim on the stairs but I recognized the accused. I don't know whether he heard or saw me. He didn't turn round but went down the stairs, his face still half-turned from me, and went out of the front door into the drive.

Now that is reasonably definite identification and a prosecution cannot often hope for better. Jane, however, was the only witness. When considering the value of her testimony—and it was by all odds formidable—one had to bear in mind that on her own admission the light on the stairs was poor, the face of the man half-averted, and she had never previously seen John Maudsley in the flesh. Much could be made of this by a skilful cross-examiner, and I knew how Hesketh would have done it, drawing the net of doubt, step by step, over the testimony. Such an approach might well fail; perhaps nothing could turn so decided a creature; but it seemed to me the only chance, and I had assumed that Marion's mind also was set that way.

"There's something very odd about this deposition of Birman's," she said to me one day—she always called her Birman, for when defending it is no bad thing to be cool towards the hostile witnesses from the start. "Haven't you noticed anything?" she went on, seeing that I was looking blankly at her. "Read it again."

I did so.

"Just the old decided Jane," I said when I had done.

"Decided, yes. About some things. She identifies the *man* all right. What about the suit?"

I glanced down at the deposition again, though I knew every word of it by heart, and admitted: "A bit uncertain there."

"Darkish, she says, perhaps grey. She can't swear to it."

"It was dusk, remember."

"And darkish shoes."

"You couldn't expect her to notice shoes."

"She noticed the hands all right. He wasn't carrying anything. She noticed the face."

Marion paused and looked at me over the top of the glasses she used for reading, and sometimes in court when she wanted to impress people.

"Well?" I said, waiting. "What does it all add up to?"

"That Birman notices what suits her. It suits her to identify Maudsley." I tried to intervene but she held up her hand. "She could imagine *him* there, the man Maudsley, the man of the photograph. But she couldn't identify the colour of his clothes—*because she'd never seen them.*"

There was a moment of silence while I summoned the ghost of the idea that had once occurred to me, one of those fanciful ideas one sends to limbo.

"Whom did she see, then?" I demanded.

Marion replied at once: "She saw someone she *knew*, perhaps someone she knew very well."

"But that makes her an accessory."

"Oh, yes, she is. But I don't think she was reckoning on a murder. On a robbery, perhaps. Of course I don't know. She could have planned it and known everything; in which case the identification of Maudsley was cold-blooded. That's fairly in character. Or she could have planned one thing and found or suspected another. Or perhaps she returned unexpectedly, and interrupted the murderer and saw him going down the stairs—and guessed. In which case she wouldn't cry out. Oh, no, she wouldn't do that. She would have thought of the chance of her own body lying there."

"Now you're just being macabre," I reproached her.

She smiled at me and I could see that she was hugging herself over her own cleverness.

"Oh, it was all of that. Birman comes out onto the landing and there he is—her lover or what have you. Do they speak? What do they say to one another, the murderer and the witness? Or does he just go down the stairs unseeing? It's macabre, all right. She sees one man—so she identifies another!"

"But why? Why say anything at all? No one knew she was a witness. Why identify anyone?"

Marion looked me over sorrowfully. She must have seen that I was in revolt against her brain-child, but she was gentle with me.

"I suppose because it was the first thing that occurred to her: she may even have blurted out something irrevocable in those first moments to the cook. You must remember how vivid it would all have been. She couldn't *not* imagine the man: it was easier to transpose him. All the best lies shadow the truth."

"Taking a bit of a chance, wasn't she?" I objected. "Maudsley might prove an alibi."

She nodded. "Yes, that's a point. But if she stopped to think at all she'll have understood that Maudsley's alibis wouldn't be very good ones. That's so, isn't it? We've seen a sample. And there's another possibility. Suppose she *knew* where Maudsley was likely to be?"

"Oh, go on!" I said. I was really a bit short with her. "You'll be telling me she saw him at 'The Towers' that night!"

Marion took that on its merits. "Not inside, or she'd have been able to identify his clothes. But she may still have known in some way that he was coming there."

"So she arranges this of all times for her friend to rob the house!"

Marion said: "Perhaps Maudsley was to be the scape-goat: he was to arrive just after the robbery. But the *timing went wrong*. Perhaps Birman returned early. More probably X was delayed—by the killing, naturally. She thought the robbery was over and he'd gone, but instead she heard him still in the house. She was surprised. X was surprised—like the pedantic professor in the story. And Maudsley was surprised too. He came for his appointment, or whatever it was, and found the police. So rather naturally he didn't keep it. How's that?"

"Very fancy," I said.

"You don't believe me?"

"No."

But for all that, I was impressed. I had practised long enough at the Bar to know that the "long arm of coincidence" is not only a cliché but a fact. Besides, cross-purpose crimes of the Reichstag Fire variety have a respectable ancestry: do not some historians believe that there were two independent plots afoot on the night when Darnley died in Kirk o' Field? If Maudsley would admit to having been in the vicinity at the time, the case Marion had put would be half proved for me.

We went next day to the prison and Marion outlined the part that she believed Jane had played in the false identification on the stairs. He was full of admiration for the deductions she had made. "I bet that's the way it happened," he kept saying, with a few choice epithets on the side for Jane. Not that he appeared to blame her. He seemed to expect a high standard of duplicity from women. Beyond appreciation of Jane, however, he would not go.

Now as to the rest we were on delicate ground. An advocate cannot press a line of defence on a witness which may, for all the advocate knows, be wildly far from the truth. The witness knows the truth; it is his story and he must be left to tell it in his own way. Of course one can hint, but there are limits even here. Justice is a delicate plant. It was perfectly proper for Marion to cross-examine Maudsley closely about his alibi; she could ask him if he was at "The Towers" that night, she could make it plain that she believed he was. She could remind him that a lying alibi would be wrong and fatal. What she could *not* say was that his presence at "The Towers" had become almost a favourable point for the defence.

He again denied being there. He swore on oath, to which he was always appealing, that he had been at Mrs. James's. Either this was the truth, or he was so dense that he couldn't see what we were driving at. We all got so warm over it that some of his original suspicions must have revived, and he began to think we were against him. It was a very trying interview, the worst we had with him, and we were quite exhausted as we left the prison and travelled glumly back in the taxi. "The fool," Marion kept repeating. "He won't see it." I didn't say anything to her at the time, but the incident had made a great impression on me and decided me that her new theory was either mistaken or unworkable. I know that Mr. Clive agreed.

Next morning when I arrived at work I found Marion was already there. I sat down straight away at my desk and began to read one of my other briefs—it was a Harfield "black-list" case, but it made a change from

Maudsley and his tantrums and extrovert personality. I rather hoped we could forget him that day; certainly it didn't occur to me that it was necessary to make a formal interment of the corpse of Marion's bright idea —or very tactful, either, for I knew how disappointed she must be and I could see from the look of her that she hadn't slept much.

It occurred to me after a while that the usual peace of the chambers was being disturbed: there seemed a good deal of rustling and shuffling going on from Marion's side, and glancing up I saw that she was staring at me in an aggressive way.

"Why don't you say something?" she demanded, and got up.

I know that habit in women—I suppose we all do—and in some men too. They want to make an Aunt Sally of you; so will you please to perch yourself up there to be shot at!

"I don't think there's anything to say," I replied.

"Don't you?"

"Except that I'm sorry," I added most unwisely.

She pounced on that.

"Why are you sorry? Because Maudsley wouldn't fit in?"

I murmured that of course that was the reason.

She had the range now, however.

"And I suppose you're certain that my theory's wrong?"

"Not wrong," I said, soothingly, as I thought. "Impracticable."

"So my theory's impracticable? You always find the right word. The fact that it's true doesn't matter!"

"Now look here, Marion . . ." I began.

But it was too late for reasoning.

"I just want to tell you this," she said, throwing herself down at her desk. "That theory of mine, as you call it, is true. And that's the theory I'm putting up in court. Maudsley must say what he wants to say. But when I come to *Birman*"—her voice had hardened—"I shall put the case to her like that. That's how it happened. She shall be made to see it *as it happened.* And the jury shall see *her.*"

I don't think, looking back on it, that I ever admired Marion more than at this moment when all my professional hackles were up. It was a courageous idea, a magnificent idea. But fatal. Without an admission from Maudsley, which in itself might be a boomerang, there was no hope. No intellectual exercise is more dangerous than the cross-examination of a hostile witness. To browbeat one without breaking him down is to invite disaster. The jury becomes prejudiced against you: the judge may intervene. It is far, far better to coax people. All the best advocates are masters of this. They suggest, ever so delicately, that witnesses may be mistaken—through no fault of their own, of course. The light was bad: perhaps even worse than the witness thinks? The face of the man was averted: perhaps a little more than the witness thinks? The witness had never seen the man she identified before: so may it not have been possible that . . . ?

When such a cross-examination is done, one gets the impression that a mistake has *honestly* been made. "I know you're anxious to be fair, Miss Birman. But may it not be . . . ? A man's life is at stake, of course you appreciate that? You had just come out of the light into the darkness of the landing. It *was* dark, wasn't it? A greyish light? How far was the man from you? And below you, on the stairs, wasn't he? And his face half-turned away? How good is your sight? You wear glasses for reading, don't you? You only saw the man for an instant, didn't you? Just a glimpse? You were confused, weren't you? In a bit of a daze about it? Miss Birman, I know you're trying to help the court."

That was the line along which Hesketh would have taken her: one blunt, honest character to another. And here was Marion hoping with one blow to strike her down!

Of course there was a chance that she might succeed. Some witnesses can be broken. But not with such poor weapons as we had. And not Jane, I thought to myself, hearing in my mind the measured words of her deposition. She would gain the sympathy of the court. A wild, unprincipled attack, people would say, and it would rebound on us and on Maudsley.

"I wouldn't do that," I said, but I said it without much conviction, for I doubted my ability to turn her.

To my surprise, she didn't take me up in the impetuous way I'd expected. She was all sweet reason. "Now look here, Michael, there's no other chance. This woman seems a cool one, do you agree?"

"I don't know about that."

"All right," she said resignedly, "let's accept your view of her as a bundle of repressions for a moment, an analyst's case-book, though it's got its absurd side, you know, particularly as you don't accept my thesis of the Second Man. But do you grant me she's intelligent?"

"Of course I do."

"And no one's going to believe that she was *ignorantly* mistaken—that clever woman! But introduce malice, the deliberate lie . . ."

"She'll just deny things."

"All right, let her. Let's see her denying it. Let's hear her."

I could see that Marion really hoped to convince me. She was immensely plausible. But where she failed was in the fact that she was guessing, putting questions in the air. X was a theory, not a man. He might exist; indeed, such was Marion's power that at that moment I believed in his existence; but there was no proof of him, not a trace, not a "scintilla," as advocates are always saying in their speeches to juries, hoping that they will admire the sound of the word.

"Find that man and I'm with you," I assured her, but with the rather troubling knowledge that I would have to be with her anyway.

But where and how? Those were the problems she set us in those last days, or rather she set them to Mr. Clive. Poor Mr. Clive, he didn't like the theory any more than I did. "It's a bit dangerous, Mr. Irvine," he confided to me, but that was the limit of the criticism he allowed himself, for he understood that I must, as the junior, be loyal to Marion. He wasn't in a strong position *vis-à-vis* her, because he was between the devil and the deep, Maudsley being all for the new approach which appealed to his theatrical sense. "Well, the little bitch!" the latter said of Jane at my last meeting with him in prison before the trial, in tones which suggested that he was thinking rather the better of her. A lover; guilty caresses in the house of death—these were things he could understand, though they hardly matched Marion's conception of the woman. X seemed to become a very real figure for him. "I've got a bit of money left: just you hire a flatfoot and have that sheila watched," he instructed Mr. Clive, who had already taken steps in that direction, as we have seen. Clearly, either he expected drama or was giving a good imitation of a man who did.

But of course nothing dramatic happened. Jane had gone into a furnished flat about a mile from "The Towers" and was reported to be looking for a job in the same line, which showed an optimistic spirit, but apart from that she never stirred out. Nor were the deeps of her past easy to unravel. I have often wondered how detective agencies set about such things. They couldn't just go and ask her whether she had a past; Mrs. Pye was a friend of hers, an unapproachable figure; the day of the all-seeing, all-knowing servant was over.

It couldn't have been an easy job, and the results as we saw them proved it. There were, in fact, no results to speak of beyond the time-table of school, and army, the tea-shop, and companionings. Not that the agency wasn't trying. Once, passing "The Towers," I noticed a man of constabulary appearance hanging around. One assumes that the cook was asked more questions and that a great number of assorted tradesmen and taxi-drivers were probably bothered.

But to no avail.

"You see, it won't do," I said to Marion two days before the trial as the latest of these communications came in.

She read it, frowning a little. "Birman's a sly one," was all she said.

I could see that I was wasting my time trying to convince her: she had her fixed idea. I felt myself to be in a difficult position. Professional loyalty is a strong sanction, and there was also a personal loyalty which I owed to Marion. On the other hand, I was sure that she was wrong and that in nourishing these illusions she was endangering her own career and Maudsley's life. That last was probably lost anyway, for I could see no way round the evidence of Jane. But it must not be made more hopeless.

That afternoon, taking advantage of Marion's absence, I went to see Hesketh. I confess I was nervous, for we all went in awe of this brusque man, like the children of a Victorian paterfamilias; also I had the feeling that he must in some way be aggrieved at the lost brief.

Nevertheless I told him.

"Did Kerrison know you were coming here?" he asked me at once: he always called her Kerrison—I suppose it made it easier for him when he was regaling us at tea-time with his club-room jokes.

I shook my head.

"You shouldn't have come behind her back," was all I got for my pains.

But I knew all the same what would follow.

Just before the chambers closed that night he sent for her. It was only later that I heard the story. Apparently he didn't hesitate, but simply told her the oldest cross-examining maxim at the Bar: "Never, never, till the day of judgement (and preferably not then) ask a witness a question to which you don't know the answer in advance."

"But I do know this answer," she protested.

"No, you imagine an answer. You imagine X was there and Birman saw him."

She tried to argue but he swept her aside. "I wouldn't ask that question," he said.

And Marion came straight back to me and said that she wouldn't ask it either.

I remember that that decision gave me a queer little feeling in my heart.

Chapter Six

IT WAS RAINING ON THE MORNING OF the trial and the queue for the public gallery was getting a drenching as we walked into the Gothic hall that smelt of mackintoshes and wet worsteds. I think that nothing odder than our hall exists on this earth. There is always a choir practising "Messiah" or "Elijah" somewhere, and a library which is always shut, and a few of those rooms that the Victorians built, no one knows for what, though from the shape of them one assumes they were part of some crazy mathematical plan such as the Egyptians are said to have incorporated into the Great Pyramid of Cheops.

There are also two Assize Courts, probably put in as an afterthought about the time of Jack the Ripper. They seem cosy rooms until you come to sit in them. There is a good deal of panelling and red leather up on the bench, and blue curtains shield the judge from the wings, though not from the draughts which are very well drilled and persistent. Below, where the barristers and the press sit, there is a good deal of panelling also, but no leather at all. Galleries run round the halls half-way down their depth, and tiers of public seats rise up towards windows which are either very dirty or have armorial bearings on them—no one has ever decided which.

The case in front of ours on the calendar had lasted longer than expected. The Maudsley trial did not begin till after lunch, and these public seats were filled as Marion and I went in our wigs and gowns, with Mr. Clive behind us, and there was a tremendous banging and rattling going on, rather like a school of noisy children. Police stood around in the invertebrate attitudes that come to them when they haven't got their helmets on; clerks bustled to and fro, among them Jaggers, who gave the impression that he was a kind of steward of the meeting; and outside in the corridors hordes of lost-looking men and women wandered as disconsolately as characters in a Pirandello play.

There was a sudden hush as the judge came in, and we all bobbed up and bowed to him. He inclined his head at us and settled down quickly, not like some of his kind.

No judge in session can look altogether unimpressive. I have often been struck with a sense of anticlimax on seeing some of our Circuit masters out of their robes in the bar mess on a "judges' night," little dried-up men, before whom one had trembled in court only that afternoon. But you could see that Mr. Justice Lorne would look impressive anywhere. He was quite young, big, with a boxer's shoulders and a heavy neck and chin. His eyes were blue and "piercing," as reporters say.

"Not the man to quarrel with," I whispered to Marion, and I remember I was immensely relieved to know that Hesketh had talked the nonsense out of her. There was no sign of our man: the dock was empty.

And then suddenly I saw the top of his head as he came up the steps from the cells. He advanced to the front of the dock and clasped the rails, staring very coolly at the judge, who gave him the barest glance in return—Maudsley wasn't his bird yet.

The jury was empanelled. These formalities take a long time, and they are hard moments for barristers in their first big trial. As each juryman's name was called Maudsley inspected him—or her, for there were four women, three of them middle-aged, comfortable bodies, one somewhat younger, a dashing type, and I could see his look of interest.

They say that the Bluebeard, Landru, behaved all the time at his trial as though he were making assignations with the beautiful women who fought their way into the court and devoured him with their eyes. He waved and bowed, fluttering his white hands, and fixed that hypnotic stare of his on those foolish ones who might have been his victims. Maudsley was not of that Latin type, but you could see that he, too, was buoyed up with conceit and the excitement of it all. He was not in the least afraid. We had seen him for a few moments earlier that morning in the cells below the court, and his confidence had been something to marvel at—the magic armour of ignorance.

"Don't you worry," he had comforted Marion as we parted, and I think only the officers with him had stopped him from slapping her on the back. That was Maudsley. You couldn't help admiring him, though his self-control was almost the most exasperating thing I have encountered.

"You can bet *he's* not bothering," I said to Marion, with some vague idea of cheering her up, for I could see that she was as nervous as I was.

She gave me a wan smile and opened her brief; we didn't have much room at the table, for Kenyon had spread out a series of enormous plans and had walled in his juniors behind a barrier of law reports.

"Now for it," I said, as the clerk of Assize got to his feet.

Dead silence had settled on the court. No movement in the gallery where everyone was craning forward. Something must be happening, and here was a man in a wig to prove it.

"John Kelvin Maudsley, is that your name?"

"Yes, my lord," Maudsley said to the judge, who wasn't looking.

"John Kelvin Maudsley, you are charged on this indictment with murder.

"The particulars of the offence alleged against you are that you, John Kelvin Maudsley, on the tenth day of March at Langfield in the county of York, murdered Charlotte Kelvin Maudsley.

"How say you, John Kelvin Maudsley, are you Guilty or Not Guilty."

"Not Guilty," Maudsley said in what I had learnt to recognize as his "offended" voice. I thought for one bad moment that he was going to say more, and so, apparently, did the judge, for the blue eyes which had been resting in a bored way on the tails of the clerk's wig were suddenly raised and focused on the prisoner.

One of the attendants standing beside Maudsley made a slight gesture of dissuasion.

The clerk of Assize paused. He didn't want his own recitation of the sonorous ritual words spoilt by any cross-talk act. Then, seeing that his man was silent, he raised the paper close to his eyes, for his sight was bad, and turning towards the jury said:

"Members of the jury, the prisoner, John Kelvin Maudsley, stands charged upon this indictment with murder. Upon the indictment he hath been arraigned, and on his arraignment hath pleaded Not Guilty and hath put himself upon his country—which country ye are. Your charge, therefore, is to say whether he be Guilty or Not Guilty, and to hearken to the evidence."

The jury received all this with the look of attention all juries wear at the beginning of a case, though it wears off notably towards the end. "Yes, yes," they seemed to be saying, "it's all clear enough, except for some of the words. Just carry on." They looked disconcerted when the clerk sat down, for at the first stage in any new environment one gets a marvellous liking for the familiar. As one man they turned and stared at Kenyon as he emerged from behind his plans in his silk gown—they would have listened to anyone, even an usher, with the most strained and polite attention.

"May it please you, my Lord, Members of the Jury," Kenyon said, giving them all capital letters to begin with, "in this case I appear for the Crown with my learned friends Mr. Loader and Mr. Stein; and my learned friends Miss Kerrison and Mr. Irvine appear on behalf of the accused."

So the trial began.

It was a good opening speech. Kenyon was a first-class leader and Jaggers had been right to be afraid of him. He was of the modern kind that usually avoids rhetoric. He recited damaging facts against the prisoner in a voice which suggested that it was all a great pity, but duty had to be done and crime punished, and all sensible people—among whom, of course, the members of the jury were pre-eminent—would see that. He had won a lot of cases since he had come to the Bar in the vintage days of Carson, Simon, and Rufus Isaacs. I can't say he was a man I liked very much, for he was parochial in his sympathies and only really loved his clerk, his chambers, and his wife, in that order, but Hesketh, an old rival and crony, always spoke well of him in a disparaging sort of way, and he was certainly honourable.

He had a good case now and he made the best of it. "In effect what are we saying?" he asked in one passage which really summed up his case. "That this man was short of money, that he asked for money, and when he was refused money he uttered threats. We are saying that this man was seen in the house when the dead woman was newly lying there; that his fingerprints were found on the jewel box from which the valuables had been taken; that one of those valuables in the shape of a ring was found in his possession. And we are saying, members of the jury, that he lied about the possession of that ring."

"And really, what more can one ask?" the jury must have been saying to themselves. It is seldom in crimes of this kind that a murderer is seen in the act of killing. It is nearly always a matter of inference, or circumstantial evidence, which may claim to be the best evidence, the pointer of common sense.

Clearly the jury was impressed. They were good, sensible people; two housewives, a stenographer, a fashion journalist (the dashing lady), a tailor, a grocer, a chemist, an accountant, two company directors, a shop assistant, and a bookmaker's clerk to give a sporting flavour. Kenyon was just the man for them, like speaking to like, and I felt uneasily that they might not take so well to Marion and her illogical streak, the intuition that was so deeply a part of her character. They might not approve of a woman in her shoes, though they might make certain allowances, most of which she would all too probably disavow. And then there was the judge up there, that slumbering lion.

It was a damnably convincing case and I think only Maudsley couldn't see it. But he was sitting forward in a jaunty way, glancing round the court and relishing his position at the centre as he believed, though everyone else was watching Kenyon now as he built up towards the slight peroration he allowed himself:

"Well, members of the jury, that is the prosecution's case. Motive—we even have motive, though, as his lordship will direct, it is never necessary to prove it in a case of this kind. Can you doubt that he was in need of money? 'I must have money,' those are his words, his written words. Can you doubt that he found it, members of the jury, found it that night in that jewel case whose woodwork bears the mark of his hand? Well, I will leave it to you. You are the judges of fact. It is for you to say whether the prosecution has proved its case beyond doubt.

"So I will call the evidence."

The first witness was for identification of the dead woman, and it proved to be the cook.

Poor Miss Saunders, I can see her now. She was in deepest mourning. In the dead woman's will she had been left the sum of £1,000 and a choice of two of the missing rings. It was wealth to her, undreamed of. But hers was a sincere grief. "Poor lady!" she had said on the night of the murder, and she said it again now. It gave one a strange feeling to hear in those proceedings, so functional, so concerned with inventories and the mechanics of death, those genuine words of love. They made everyone uncomfortable. Nor was Loader, who took the witness with brusque efficiency, quite the man to handle her. When he was asking questions of what she had seen in the bathroom, and she was telling him, I got the impression that they were speaking of quite different people, he seeing the dead body, she the dead mistress and friend.

Even Maudsley seemed moved as her story was told, for he stopped glancing round the court and watched her quietly. She never looked at him; I suppose she couldn't bear to. They gave her a chair. You could only just see her white face peering over the top of the witness-box, and her voice was so low that several times Loader had to ask her to repeat her answers. But she created an effect such as no one else did in that court: a sense of the poignancy of life and death, the personality of the woman who had lived in that lonely house surrounded by the echo of past splendours, who had died so pitiably.

"Be very careful with her," I whispered to Marion as she rose to cross-examine.

But I needn't have been anxious. She was very gentle with the old woman, whose evidence was in no sense hostile to our case, since she hadn't claimed to have seen Maudsley that night, or his letters. There was only one daring question:

"Did your mistress ever speak to you of the accused?"

Miss Saunders hesitated and then said in a low voice: "Yes."

"What did she say of him?"

I could feel the anxiety of Mr. Clive behind me at

that moment, for there might be a damning answer.

Words came from the witness.

The judge cupped his ears, and the court stenographer, a harassed man, looked despairing. "I didn't catch that bit, my lord."

Lorne directed: "Please try and speak up, Miss Saunders, so that we can all hear you."

She gave him a scared look. You could see her making an effort and we could just distinguish the words: "She was very fond of him, she always said so."

"All the time? Even after he left to live elsewhere?"

"Yes, she was always fond of him. He was her nephew, you see."

I heard the sigh, the vast sigh of relief, Mr. Clive made as Marion sat down. But her intuition had been brilliantly justified—it was the first blow for the defence.

There was no re-examination. The witness stood down and Kenyon bobbed up again, booming: "I call Detective Inspector Kent."

The policeman marched into the box and took hold of the Bible in his right hand which he held well above his head. I suppose he had taken the oath a thousand times, but since they were holding up a little card to him with the words written on it, he focused and religiously read it out. Then he made a smart right-incline and faced Kenyon.

"Detective Inspector Reginald Kent?"

"Yes, sir."

"You are a detective inspector of the West Riding division?"

"Yes, sir."

"Do you remember the tenth March?"

"I do."

"Will you tell his lordship and the jury what happened on that night?"

"As a result of certain information," Kent began. . . .

He made it sound so dull. From what he said you couldn't picture the phone ringing in the police station, the humming activity, the cars tearing through the darkness. There is high drama in police life, and the proof of it is to be seen in the prosaic face the Force turns to the world, for if one lives on emotion one must protect oneself from it, just as actors do when they walk from some divine act of renunciation on the stage and in the twinkling of an eye are cursing their dressers in the wings.

Kent felt for Miss Maudsley. He was the most compassionate of men. But it was not his duty to show sympathy. He knew himself to be part of the machinery of justice, and the way the machine worked was for him to answer questions as precisely as possible.

"On arrival at 'The Towers' I went straight upstairs to the bathroom on the first floor," he said.

"Will you identify the room on the plan?" Kenyon asked, waving the enormous document at him.

Kent did so and the plan was passed to the jury who studied it with the deepest attention, glad, I imagine, to have something to do at last.

"So that was the room, marked A? I see. Yes, go on."

Kent continued: "The door was half-open. The body, identified to me at the time by Miss Saunders as being that of Miss Maudsley, lay on its back with the head towards the door and its feet extended under the bath."

"Under the bath?" Kenyon asked, seeing a look of

inquiry, or probably disbelief, on the fact of the dashing jurywoman.

"Yes. It was an old-fashioned bath. There was a scarf round the deceased's neck and it had been drawn tight and screwed up"—here he made a gesture with his hands as of a woman wringing wet clothes. "There were no signs of any struggle in the bathroom. Deceased was a frail-looking woman."

Those in the public gallery, who live on the strong meat of human passions, were obviously expecting a good deal more—a few details of strangulation at the very least. But Kent was not a doctor; what is more, I think he got a lot of quiet pleasure out of disappointing ghouls, and if he could have made a homicide sound like a sanitary inspector's report he would certainly have done so.

"What were your next actions?" asked Kenyon, who greatly approved of this witness, a sort of moral twin of his.

"I went into the bedroom next door to the bathroom." This, too, was identified on the plan. "There was a certain amount of disorder there. Drawers had been opened and the contents strewn around. On the dressing-table there was an open box with its hinges forced back. It had been opened—not with a key, I think, though that is only an opinion. There was no sign of any key. In the box were certain articles of jewellery." He enumerated them. "The box appeared to have finger-prints on its outer surface."

There was a pause, and everyone in the gallery must have expected the damning allegation that they were Maudsley's. Perhaps Kent lent himself a little to this illusion, for he had a sly sense of humour, but of course the truth was that he was not a finger-print expert—

that worthy was waiting outside the court in the corridor draughts.

"Will you tell his lordship and the jury what you did next?" Kenyon said. He was leaning back against the partition behind counsel's table, utterly relaxed, his silk gown bunched behind him and his spectacles on the end of his nose. He wasn't one of those advocates who are always pressing. Most of the time he coasted, but he could have his moments—in cross-examination usually—and then you saw why he was paid large sums for standing up there and beating in time with the orchestra.

"As a result of certain information . . ." Kent began again—he always liked that phrase which has infuriated generations of crime addicts.

So we came to the famous visit to Maudsley at the house of Mrs. James.

"I went to Number 7 Greenside Crescent at about ten past nine. I was shown into a bed-sitting-room. The accused was in bed, in pyjamas. I told him who I was and cautioned him. I told him I was investigating the death of Miss Maudsley, his aunt, and that I had reason to suppose that he might be able to assist my investigations."

"What did he say?"

"The accused said: 'Dead! My oath! The poor old sheila!' "

There was a burst of laughter. We in the well of the court were all expecting it and watching the judge. Lorne didn't raise his hand or threaten to clear the court or anything of that kind: but he simply stared into the gallery with those cool eyes of his, and the laughter died in the instant.

"Go on," he commanded, turning back towards Kent who had remained impassive.

"Yes, my lord. I then asked the accused whether he would care to give an account of his movements and other details relevant to the case."

"Was he willing?"

"Very willing," replied Kent, a trifle grimly, I thought.

"Did he make a statement?"

"Yes."

"Is this it? Exhibit J.K.M.1, my lord."

Kent examined it as though he had never seen it before.

"Yes, that's it."

"Is it signed?"

"Yes, signed in my presence."

Kenyon now read the statement aloud. It was the Maudsley version, the alibi. There was also a declaration of innocence with some details attached.

Kenyon fastened onto one of them.

"This statement contains the following words: 'I knew of the existence of my aunt's jewel box. I have never seen it. I do not know its contents. I have certainly never taken anything from it.' Now, Inspector, did you at a later stage search the house where the accused man was staying?"

"Yes."

"What did you find?"

"In a cistern the police sergeant working with me found an emerald ring."

"Is this the ring?"

"Yes."

"J.K.M.2," Kenyon intoned, and this was passed

up to the judge and from him to the jury, where I saw that the women were examining it with the closest interest.

The evidence of arrest followed, with Maudsley's closing words.

There was no laughter this time, for the gallery had taken the measure of the judge.

Kenyon sat down, and there was a stir as Marion got to her feet.

After a while you become sensitive to court atmosphere. There is the anxiety feeling among counsel and officials when some fledgling barrister rises; there is a tremendous sense of climax that men like Marshall Hall could create, the feeling one gets before the curtain goes up; and there is boredom, and malice sometimes.

I think disappointment was the key this time. She might have done well with old Miss Saunders but she didn't look as though she could make a fight of it against these cool, resolute men and their cut-and-dried case. They saw a young, small woman in a very white wig, a small woman at a corner of a table with a few papers in front of her, a young man beside her, and all the weight of the law and the prophets on the other side.

"How many keys were there to the jewel box?" was her first question.

First questions are very important, for it is at this moment that the witness is likely to be at his most nervous and vulnerable and the jury's attention at its peak. The witness has told his story in peace, and now for the first time that story is assailed. Cracks can be made to show in it; a witness's credit can be damaged; and even at the lowest a whole new line of thought can be opened up.

Naturally, Marion had no hope of knocking out so shrewd and honourable a witness as the inspector. But her question was cleverly conceived, a thrust at the weakest spot.

Kent seemed strangely unprepared for it and flustered, and I think for a moment he failed to see what she was getting at.

"I don't know as a fact how many keys there were," he replied, which was a fair answer too.

The judge looked a trifle sourly at Marion, but she remained unmoved.

"Perhaps not, Inspector," she said. "You don't know how many keys there may have been?"

"I'm afraid not."

"But you know how many you *found*?"

"Oh, yes."

"How many did you find?"

"Two. There was one on a key-ring which I observed was round the neck of the deceased."

"Yes."

"And there was another in a drawer of the dressing-table in Miss Maudsley's bedroom."

"Thank you," Marion said, and you could feel her pleasure at these answers—the power to communicate pleasure is no bad thing in an advocate, provided he can conceal the other side. "Now then, Inspector," she went on, "will you tell us whether the key was in one of the opened drawers you have described?"

"Yes, it was."

"The burglar, if I may call him so, the person who opened the jewel box, seems to have been looking for something, doesn't he?"

"I can't say. The drawers were certainly disturbed."

"Was the *key* disturbed?"

Kent glanced at the judge as though he expected a few thunderbolts to be launched at such a question. But Lorne merely looked at him.

"I can't say whether the key had been disturbed, as you put it, Miss Kerrison," Kent said. He was a good stone-waller, but so is Justice.

"But at all events it was in the drawer?"

"Yes."

"Covered by some articles of clothing?"

"Yes."

"The burglar might have been looking for it and missed it?"

"I can't say what he might have been doing."

"At all events you saw no key in the box?"

"No."

"And it appeared to have been forced open?"

"Yes."

"*Though there were two keys within twenty yards of it?*"

"Yes," Kent said. He had agreed with Marion five times in six questions, which certainly wouldn't have escaped the jury.

She began to turn the pages of her brief, preparing the new build-up, and I could feel Mr. Clive practically purring behind us.

"Are you aware that the accused lived at 'The Towers,' in his aunt's house, for six months or more?" she shot at the inspector suddenly.

He agreed that he had heard of this.

"Do you know that he is her heir under her will?"

"Yes."

"And that therefore she proposed to trust him with

substantially *all* her possessions after she was dead?"

"I suppose so."

"And do you really imagine that he was trusted like that and lived there so long *and yet didn't know of the existence of those two keys?*"

"The inspector may imagine all sorts of things," said the judge, tartly intervening. "Whether you should probe them is another matter."

Marion bowed to the bench and looked so humble that I felt sure she had another bullet in the gun.

"I beg your pardon, my lord, I can see that my question was badly conceived." She turned back to the inspector. "Let me put it like this. Would you be surprised to hear that the accused *knew* of the existence of a key in a drawer of his aunt's bedroom?"

"Surprised? Should I be?" Kent began rather airily, for I think he was looking for further judicial protection from the gadfly.

But this time Marion did not give way. "No, I am putting it formally to you, Inspector. Evidence will be given."

"He said nothing about keys in his statement," Kent was unwary enough to reply.

"Did you ask him?"

"No."

"Then let us turn elsewhere."

I could have hugged her: it was masterly. The implication of an "outside job" was firmly in the minds of the jury. The quick blow and away—no dangerous probings in the wound.

"Let us see now: you went down to the accused's house at nine-ten on the night of the murder," Marion was continuing.

"Yes."

"And he was in bed?"

"He was."

"Had you awakened him?"

"I couldn't say."

"But he was certainly in his night clothes?"

"Yes."

"You told him the news of his aunt's death?"

"I did."

"And you have told us his answer. Did it strike you as a flippant answer?"

That was a dangerous queston, but Marion knew her man and his innate honesty and decency.

Kent shook his head. "No, I don't think it was flippant."

"Genuine regret?"

"I don't know about that. He certainly seemed upset. He could have been upset for more than one reason."

"Quite. The fact remains that he was?"

"Yes."

"And you cautioned him. That's a serious thing, isn't it?"

"It's a normal thing in these cases," Kent said.

"A bit formidable, though, surely? He hears of his aunt's death, and he's upset, and you caution him, and then he makes a statement. I put it to you that he was still in the throes, still muddled and upset, when he made it?"

"Quite normal by then. He became quite cheerful," Kent replied.

"Excitable, mightn't he have been?"

"Cheerful, was my impression."

"Let us examine that statement. He said that he hadn't taken any jewels. And that wasn't true?"

"It certainly wasn't," Kent said.

"Do you know that he has admitted for some days now that he did take the ring you found at Mrs. James's house but that he took it some weeks before the crime?"

"That admission is news to me."

It was also news to the gallery which hummed excitedly, but I was admiring Kent. He also knew about the nuances of words, and "admission" was a well-chosen one.

"Would you accept it from me," Marion said, "that the accused was at 'The Towers' a fortnight before the murder?"

"Yes."

"And that he had opportunity then to take the ring?"

"How can the inspector say that?" demanded the judge in the hostile voice he had used towards Marion from the outset.

"I'm sorry, my lord, and I withdraw. Inspector, will you tell me this: there were finger-prints on the jewel box when you first saw it?"

"Yes."

"Maudsley's prints?"

"I can't say."

She rounded on him persuasively. "Oh, come, you *must* know. You are not the expert, we appreciate that, but you must have seen the prints under the microscope and made your own deductions."

Kent said slowly, looking at the jury: "So far as I was able to judge, the prints on the jewel box were similar to the accused's prints."

"Mightn't he have dashed upstairs on his earlier visit and with his bare hands used a key and opened the box—a quick theft which might pass notice?"

"Most reckless."

"Not as reckless, surely, as using bare hands on a box a moment after you'd done a murder?"

"All this is supposition," ruled the judge sternly. And he said to the jury: "I recommend you to put those two questions and answers out of your mind. They might figure in a speech for the defence, but not in cross-examination."

Whereupon Marion bowed again submissively. "May I with your lordship's permission return to the matter of the rings?"

It was certainly one way of putting it: you might have thought he'd been preventing her from keeping relevant.

"Now, Inspector," she went on, turning to him, "do you recall the contents of that jewel box?"

"I do."

"Let me test your memory. How many objects were alleged to be missing from it?"

He thought for a moment and replied: "Fourteen."

She made a display of checking with her own list and smilingly congratulated him. "Quite right. About what time was the crime committed?"

"I believe about six o'clock."

"And about nine-fifteen you saw the accused?"

"About that time."

"I take it that, after you left, a watch was kept on him that night and on the next day—a very discreet one, I'm sure."

"The house was watched," Kent said.

"Did he attempt to stir outside?"

"He did not," Kent replied grimly.

"And next day, as you have told us, about three in the afternoon you went down with your warrant and arrested him and took him into custody?"

"Yes."

"Later you searched the house and found one ring?"

"That is so."

"Fourteen missing articles and you found one ring!"

"Yes."

"Have you recovered any others since?"

"No."

"You've searched, I suppose? And you've made inquiries, full inquiries?"

"Yes."

"Full inquiries. And yet you found nothing. Fourteen missing articles and you found one ring!" She looked at him for a moment as though she expected that even at this late stage he must at least produce one from somewhere, and then she sat down.

Kenyon was up in a flash. He was a very good re-examiner, and no one could give you a stronger impression that you were getting back to the verities again after the irrelevancies and downright rogueries of the defence. By such means he succeeded in restoring a good deal of Detective Inspector Kent, framing his questions in such a way that Maudsley's lies and the shaky, improvised character of his second thoughts were given the maximum notice:

"In effect, Inspector, what you are saying, isn't it, is that when you saw him in bed that night you asked him to help your inquiries and he replied that he was willing?"

"Yes."

"You have told us that in his statement he mentioned the existence of the jewel box?"

"That's right."

"Did he say anything about keys or his knowledge of the whereabouts of keys?"

"No, he didn't."

"That story came later, didn't it, *after the discovery of the ring?*"

When he had gone through some more of this, Kenyon sat down, giving the jury a reassuring look as he did so, as though to say: "There, that's straightened *that!*" But I noticed that one or two of them were avoiding his eye, which is always a danger sign to an advocate or prisoner.

So far so good, for us.

The medical evidence came next: James Henry Herbert, divisional police surgeon.

This brand of evidence is obviously in its potential the most ghoulish of all. For this reason police surgeons, dedicated men of science even in their lighter professional moments, turn themselves when in the witness-box into supermen of science, so abstruse that only professionals can understand them, whereas barristers and juries and the gallery fail often by a notable margin and one catches sometimes a look of baffled wonderment, rather like that of a man who buys in the Charing Cross Road some book on sexual behaviour and finds that the emphasis is somehow on the lesser crustaceans and the nocturnal habits of bats.

James Henry Herbert was such a witness, and never was manual strangulation expressed more scientifically. You got the impression that a machine must have done it, which was all very helpful to the defence, for it seemed to put Maudsley and his great strangler's hands a thousand miles away.

But how to cross-examine a laboratory?

Marion rose unhesitatingly.

"I understand that the deceased was wearing a woollen scarf?" she said.

"She was."

"And this scarf, exhibit J.K.M.3, was in fact the weapon of death?"

"Yes," the surgeon replied, with a frown for the purple phrase.

"Isn't it a loosely woven scarf?"

"It is."

"Rather worn in texture?"

"Appreciably."

"My lord, may the jury see it again?"

The scarf was passed to the jury, whose members very naturally handled it as though it were infectious.

"Now, Doctor, the scarf is so appreciably worn, as you said, that there are little fluffs of wool on it, aren't there?"

"Yes."

"Of a kind likely to rub off under pressure?"

"They might."

"Threads might well adhere to any other surface touching them?"

"Possibly."

"Of course you examined this scarf under the microscope?"

"I did."

"Did you also examine the clothes of the accused? You did? And did you find on those clothes any traces of wool of such a kind?"

"No."

"Yet the murderer must have been in close contact with the deceased?"

"Not necessarily with his clothes," the witness said.

Marion gave him a look of gentle reproach. "But he might have been?"

"I suppose so."

"And his hands *must* have been in contact: according to your case"—and you could see that she was blaming him for the whole unreasonable prosecution.

"Yes," the witness said.

"Did you examine the accused's nails and hands?"

He nodded. "I did, but not till the following day."

She shook her head. "That is surely of no significance. Is it not a truism that the microscope can pick up, even days after the event, traces of what the eye has failed to see?"

"It can happen like that."

"When you examined the accused's nails did you find any trace of wool in them?"

"No."

"Though it was a loosely woven scarf?"

The surgeon did not reply.

"Yet you found nothing?"

"That is so."

"Nothing at all," Marion said, and sat down with a quick triumphant glance at Kenyon, who when at bay preserved an Olympian calm, just in case the jury happened to be looking at him.

So that was two ninepins down.

Of course, if you really thought about it there wasn't much substance in what Marion had won. It was all negative. The prosecution had the finger-prints on the jewel box, and the ring and Maudsley's lies, also they had Jane, whose shadow had hardly touched the case as yet. To answer to all this that Maudsley would probably have known how to open the box with a key instead of forcing it and that no bobbles of wool had adhered to him sounded, when analysed, rather like the celebrated efforts of Mrs. Partington. But the fact was that two prosecution witnesses had been made to appear to agree to almost everything that Marion had said. My confidence in her was growing all the time. She was behaving perfectly now, so perfectly that even the judge seemed to have accepted her, rather as lions in a zoo accept the public at siesta time.

It was now my turn, however, for we had agreed beforehand that the next witness should be mine. This was the finger-print expert, a melancholy-looking man, saddened, I suppose, by the infinite diversity of folk.

He deposed that the prints on the jewel box were Maudsley's prints, pointing out the sixteen similarities he had traced on two large charts which were passed to the jury, perfectly prepared, as we all were, to take the thing on trust.

"Were they very distinct prints on the jewel box?" I asked him when it was my turn to speak.

I heard a slight stir in the gallery and saw the reporters begin to write again, for a new voice in court always focuses interest.

The witness, of course, took me for granted.

"Adequately clear, quite distinct enough for identification purposes," he replied. More references to the charts and the sixteen points of similarity.

"Would you agree with me that the box prints, if I may call them that, are somewhat fainter than the finger-prints you took of the accused after his arrest?"

Witness replied that they might well be.

I gave him a nod of encouragement. "Quite. The prints are recognizable, as you say, but somewhat blurred?"

"A little."

"Appreciably earlier in date, I would suggest to you?"

The witness shook his head. "I wouldn't say that."

"Could those box prints have been made a fortnight before the date of the crime?"

"I doubt it."

"Can you say definitely that they were *not* made at that time?"

The witness looked at me. You could see that he very much liked to say everything definitely, for his was a scientific trade. But he was, like his predecessors in that box, a scrupulously fair man. "My impression was that they had been recently made at the time I examined them, but I could not swear to the precise age of those prints," he said, and clearly he found it a fault in himself that he could not. "It is a carved box and the surface is unfavourable," he added, excusing himself a little.

"Most unfavourable, I'm sure, and you have been most fair. Now as to the concentration of those prints on the jewel box . . ."

The witness looked relieved that we were back to questioning again, for clearly he found praise from the enemy hard to bear.

"They are mostly prints from the *left* hand?" I said.

"Yes."

"In such a position as a right-handed man would

naturally place his hand when opening the box *with a key?*"

"Or forcing it with some instrument," replied the witness promptly.

"Wouldn't he have to hold it more at the back for that?"

"No, I don't agree."

"These prints are chiefly on the lid?"

"Yes."

"And mostly the tips of the fingers?"

"Some of them, yes. But there are others indicative of a firmer pressure."

"You see," I said, "I am suggesting to you that the accused made these marks some days before the crime when opening the box *by key*. Would you agree with me that these marks are consistent with such an opening?"

"It is just within the bounds of possibility, I put it no higher than that."

I switched away at once to avoid pressing the witness on his own ground, for with each answer the jury would have seen things more and more with his eyes. The witness-box is a kind of X-ray machine and honesty, like dishonesty, manifests itself.

"The body was discovered in the bathroom on the first floor," I said. "Did you examine the handle of that door?"

"I did."

"Were there prints on it?"

"A great number."

"Did you find any prints of the accused?"

"There was a maze of prints."

"Perhaps you would care to put that differently—more positively, shall I say?"

"Very well," the witness replied. "I could find no distinguishable prints of the accused."

"Thank you, that is much better, much fairer." And reasonably content with events, I sat down.

"Jane next!" I thought and a thrill of excitement ran through me. I glanced at Marion, but she was leaning back, relaxed, as though she didn't care about Jane at all, and then I saw that Kenyon was screwing round to look at the clock on the gallery and that the court behind us was in motion. "Tomorrow at ten," came the voice of the judge. He turned to the jury, warned them against speaking to anyone about the case, and then he rose, giving us a curt nod, and vanished behind his curtains.

"That was grand of you both, grand," I heard Mr. Clive saying. I had never seen him so enthusiastic, for clearly he had been expecting the worst and could hardly credit the smooth way the day had gone. "You've only got to do the same with Birman, and you will. She'll slip up somewhere. It's the small failures and weaknesses that count"—a favourite maxim of his. "The client's asking for you," he added. Maudsley was always "the client" for him, which sounded so very much more respectable.

"Why?" Marion asked.

"He wants to thank you."

"He can do that when he's something to thank us for."

She was already hurrying towards the robing rooms and I think if I had let her she would have gone back to chambers and put in a couple of hours at another brief. I had other ideas, however. My car was parked near the side entrance, and after we'd changed I manœuvred her out that way. "We're off now: see you in the morning," I shouted to Jaggers, that slave-driver who was hovering near with a solicitor or two in tow, and I opened the door for her and drove off into the rush-hour traffic worming its way homeward to trim suburbias.

The morning rain had cleared. It was a fine night and it was pleasant to see the bright colours in the streets, the girls' summer frocks and the hats in the windows of the modistes'. There was quite a Parisian vista down Corporation Street, with the big stores on one side and the Library and the Civic Hall standing back primly on the other, behind a screen of plane trees and flowering shrubs. As we climbed by the arterial road and from the rim of the bowl looked down on the chimneys, towers, and the mountaineering streets of the southern escarpment, all blue-gold in the evening light, I felt a genuine pride and love of my town, not the affectionate disrespect in which we usually held it, the northern Babylon of the winds.

About six miles from the central post office the country began, a gracious park-like country, with big trees and a river in a valley, and far off across the plain a haze of hills. "You must let me take you there one day," I said, and I told her of the villages of grey stone, of Vanbrugh's great pile of Castle Howard (there was no other word for it), the ruined abbeys, and Coxwold where Sterne wrote *Tristram Shandy*, conjuring out of the staid Yorkshire air Corporal Trim, Uncle Toby, and all that gallant company that "swore so terribly in Flanders."

The traffic was still heavy, so we turned into the lanes, past farmsteads where the dairy cattle were coming home and geese hissed their dialectical dislike of us. In one village the cricketers were going out in their white clothes, and we stopped the car to watch the serious-minded men performing what a visitor from ancient Egypt or Sumeria would certainly have seen as a religious game, with goodness knows what horrors going on in the pavilion.

We drove for miles, and I have never covered the country in such an aimless, delightful way. We crossed the Wharfe, climbing out of the valley on the high track to Greenhow Hill where the deserted cottages of the miners squatted sullenly on the moor, and we went up the Nidderdale past Ramsgill, where Eugene Aram was born, and climbed the steep hill to Middlesmoor and drank there on a bench outside the inn while the light faded on the vista of the drowned valley, which less romantically is a reservoir of the Bradford Corporation water works. We retraced our steps to Pateley Bridge, a tiny metropolis of stone so black that I think it must have been specially imported by some rich exile from the Aireborough smoke, then rose to the escarpment on the eastern side under the lea of Brimham Rocks whose quaint silhouettes looked down on us like heads over the railings of a football field, and saw the vale of York spread below us and the Hambledons far away.

It was nearly dark when we drove past Fountain Abbey, sleeping among its great trees, to Ripon with its obelisk which ought to commemorate some vast event, and doesn't. As we circled the plain the lights came out. Once a hare, an enormous creature seeming the size of a young stag, came bounding down the beam till I had to stop and dip the lights. I switched on again but he was still there, crouching in the hedgerow, and behind, along the road, a cat came tracking purposefully.

"Shoo!" we cried at him, "shoo!" and Marion took my arm. We drove on more slowly, just touching, content with one another. The cutters were whirring in the hay fields, so quiet a note that you quite forgot the urgent men working against time in the headlights of the farmers' cars shining over the ground.

We didn't speak of the trial again, and indeed it seemed unimaginably far away on this night of high summer, with all the sweet scents of the earth around us and the galaxy of stars above. "On such a night . . ."

I fear my mind is much given to sentiment. I was always moved too easily: by the death of Steerforth, and the perplexities of James Forsyte, by Soames walking in his picture gallery at Mapledurham, Uncle Pio, Natasha at the window in the summer night, and the dying fall of the words that record the passing of Socrates. I know that this night in the country moved me very deeply, by contrast perhaps with the sordidness of the events we had been dealing with—the pedantic witnesses, the photographs of the dead woman which had been lying all day on the table before me. But I didn't kiss Marion till the very last moment of parting in the doorway of the house where she lodged, rather a fugitive kiss, as though in that moment we had remembered ourselves and Maudsley in his cell.

I didn't sleep well that night. I felt excited and full of the prospect of happiness, those thoughts lovers have that never define themselves until experience has blunted them. The dreams that followed were troubled and ominous. I awoke towards dawn and tried to recall them, but all I could track down was some presence which followed me at the tail of sight, like that dreadful apparition of M. R. James's story darting between the groynes on the lonely beach.

I drifted away at last and woke for the second time to hear nine o'clock striking from the St. Andrew's church clock at the bottom of the hill—diffidently, as though it knew that it was always too early or too late for someone.

I flung myself out of bed. How callous it seemed of my landlady down below to have left me sleeping on this of all days. In Cairo at the end of the war there had been a houseboy at my flat who would stand and shake the iron bed-rails at my feet slowly, ritually, as though rocking a Sultan, and I longed for him now. "My clothes, Abdullah, and my Sam Browne, then you might give the cap badge a rub and tell Hassan one egg and some coffee quick." "Mrs. Jones," I called, opening the door. A voice from the depths called back. "Mrs. Jones, I'm late." "Don't I know that, Mr. Irvine, and I expect you left your tea." There it was by the bedside, a cold and repellent chrome. "No time for breakfast, I'm afraid," I sang out, without much hope, for I could smell the bacon sizzling.

How hateful it is to begin the day as a debtor of time. My experience is that one never catches up. Of course, the car gave me trouble starting, forcing me to get help to push it over the crest of the drive till the engine decided to live, and the traffic was bad on the outskirts of the town and the parking places near the Assize Court were all taken, so that I had to chance a prosecution in a minor street. At three minutes to ten I burst into the robing room to meet Jaggers's disapproving stare. "You gave me a shock,

Mr. Irvine," he told me in his "serious" voice as he unfastened the wig box and handed me my starched white bands.

"I know. I'm sorry."

"And you didn't call at chambers," he said, gazing into the mirror behind me as though to judge what sort of condition I was in.

"All right, all right, I know. Where's Miss Kerrison?"

"In court."

"So what are you worrying about?"

Poor Jaggers, he was worried about a great deal more than my shortcomings, for he knew as well as I did that this was "The day." He gave me my wig, opened my gown and held it for me, then accompanied me down the corridor as though he were some Iron Curtain courier shepherding something very special in the diplomatic line. "You know what Lorne is," he said to me, putting all his fears into one bottle.

As it was, I scrambled into my scat just as the judge's clerk was appearing from behind the blue curtains like the little jungle bird that is said to accompany thc tiger. Lorne followed with his marshal, and the court rose very smartly and stayed up till he had settled himself in his red-leather chair with the sheriff's posy of flowers beside him, a relic of the old gaol fever days.

I had time to look around to see that Kenyon had got even more of the table to himself and that Marion was looking white and drawn.

"I gave Jaggers a shock," I whispered to her, for I felt this would be sure to cheer her up, but I couldn't get a smile out of her.

"THE QUEEN AGAINST MAUDSLEY," the clerk of Assize announced after a good deal of shuffling of papers, and next moment there was a clatter in the dock and there was our man between his attendants, as confident as ever, looking perfectly capable of asking the judge how well he'd slept.

"Yes, Mr. Kenyon?" Lorne said, with the barest perceptible glance at the prisoner.

Kenyon rose in a billow of silk.

"I call Jane Birman."

"Jane Birman!" you could hear the ushers shouting in the corridor outside, "Jane Birman!" Even on the stage one doesn't get such a build-up for an entrance, perhaps wisely, for the most glamorous actress might fail to live up to it.

Jane was very conscious that *she* was making an entrance, or so it seemed to me. She passed slowly through the crowd in the well of the court, where she was lost to view, and then suddenly she appeared in the little panelled witness-box with the testament in her hand, and everyone as silent as the grave.

She was dressed in black, soberly, the lady's companion, demure and somewhat frightened. There was a great deal of respectability in the black gloves, the old black handbag, and the face almost devoid of make-up. But for myself, from the moment she stepped into the box, the old suspicions revived. The dark clothes didn't altogether hide the fact that she was well made, slim, and almost elegant, and though her complexion might be pasty and her teeth bad, she had undeniably fine eyes and a mouth that the magazines rightly call "desirable." You got the impression that five years ago she must have been one of those disturbingly pretty though fading women who are said to make the most satisfying mistresses and the most tiresome wives—and might still survive a little on this level.

"A type," I murmured to Marion who was looking fixedly at the witness, rather the way you see a matador at the *barrera* studying a new bull.

She nodded, but I could see that "type" had another meaning for her and that the witness came exactly up to her expectations. She may have said as much to Clive, for she leaned back and they whispered together, till Kenyon gave them a sharp glance, perhaps imagining that this was some advocate's trick to spoil a good effect.

"Miss Jane Birman?" he boomed in a voice instinct with chivalry.

"Yes."

"Miss Birman, you are, I believe, by occupation a lady's companion, or secretary, and live now at 'Springfield,' Greenways Street, in this city?"

"Yes."

"I take it that my learned friend will not mind my leading the witness at this stage?" Kenyon said, extending his benevolence to Marion also, and a smile went with it.

"Lead by all means."

"Thank you. Now then, Miss Birman, is it a fact that in January of this year you took employment with Miss Maudsley, the deceased, at her house known as 'The Towers'?"

"I did."

"Were your duties to act generally as her companion—and friend, if I may put it so?"

"Yes."

"And did you occupy a room on the first floor of

'The Towers' next to the bedroom of the deceased?"

"I did."

"Do you remember the evening of the tenth March?"

There was a stir in the gallery, for here were the trigger words.

"Now then, did you go out that evening?"

"Yes."

"Where did you go?"

The witness tensed herself and replied:

"At about five, after we had had tea, I left Miss Maudsley in the drawing-room downstairs and walked to Mrs. Pye's house, she lives next door. I stayed there about an hour, talking. Just before six I started back. As I came up the drive I saw the lights were on in the drawing-room and I naturally assumed that Miss Maudsley was still there. I opened the front door with my key. In the hall I noticed that the drawing-room door was ajar and that the stair light was on. I was surprised, for Miss Maudsley didn't like waste, but I didn't take much notice and I went up, switching off the light at the stair-head and going into my room where I left the magazines Mrs. Pye had lent me and tidied my hair. Miss Maudsley was particular," she added with a faint smile.

Kenyon nodded, clearly delighted with this witness who answered so factually and in so pleasant and deferential a voice. It is useless to expect advocates to be machines. They may be the vehicles of justice the public expect to see, but they too might echo Shylock's impassioned plea before the court of Venice, for there are witnesses they hate and witnesses they nearly love, and how is it possible in the drama of a trial that they alone should remain indifferent to the effects and passions around them?

"Tell us in your own words what happened then," Kenyon was saying, leaning back as he always did when he was relaxed and happy.

Generally speaking, she followed her deposition closely. But naturally the tension in court gave it much greater significance. She never used any tricks of art as some witnesses do, but when she told of the footfalls on the carpet of the landing you seemed to hear them, and you could feel her curiosity as she listened, and went to the door, and opened it and peered towards the stairs in the grey light from the window.

There was not a sound in court beyond her voice. I looked at the judge who had only seemed to be with us as a "presence," and he was listening, watching her as intently as the rawest newcomer in the gallery. Just for an instant I felt for the witness. It couldn't have been comfortable to be the object of so icy a scrutiny, but she didn't seem to notice it. She gave him a glance occasionally, a dutiful glance, but for the most part she watched Kenyon, who stood there nodding his head as though calling the attention of everyone to these new tables of the law.

"You saw this man on the stairs, you were telling us?"

"Yes."

"Did you recognize him?"

"I did."

"Have you seen him again?"

She did not reply but merely looked at the prisoner. It was astonishingly dramatic. She just raised her eyes, and there was the accusation, and the eyes of everyone in court followed hers.

"Will you reply formally to my question?" Kenyon reminded her in the voice of one who is in duty bound to ask for rubber stamping even of a revelation of this transcendent kind.

She turned back towards him and said coolly: "I recognized the man on the stairs as the prisoner, John Maudsley, whom I see now."

"But had you ever seen him before?" he objected.

"No."

"How were you able to identify him?"

"By his photographs; they were very familiar to me. Even with his head half-averted I recognized him clearly. I would have known him anywhere."

"Having seen him," Kenyon demanded, "what did you do?"

The discovery of the body seemed to me pedestrian after that, though the colours in which she painted it were stronger. The witness seemed distressed. I see no reason to doubt that her distress was genuine, and there were sighs in court, the very human reactions to violence and death that do some honour, I think, even to the most ghoulish.

Kenyon's handling of the witness at this stage was masterly—sensibility itself. When they got to the scarf round the dead woman's neck and the witness stumbled over the words, the look of a rough man's compassion he gave her would have touched any juryman's heart—and it was certainly intended to; not that I blame Kenyon, for I think that he honestly believed in the witness and just had the actor's ability to pump up his emotions to heroic size. He was good all through, and nothing became him better than the end of the examination-in-chief, which is so often an anticlimactic moment. "There she is, poor soul, and she's yours now," he seemed to be saying to us before the audience of the court, and you got the impression that he was handing us some precious charge that we would ill-treat at our peril.

"For heaven's sake be careful," I whispered to Marion as he sat down, and though it was foolish of me and thoughtless to repeat the so-often repeated at that moment of stress for her, I couldn't help it, for I knew how the jury had been affected and that any sharp attack would be disastrous.

I don't think she heard me, as it happened, for at that very moment Mr. Clive pushed a folded slip of paper onto the table in front of her. She opened it, but I had the impression that whatever was in it had also failed to register. I know how she felt: the paralysis that can come to you at times of great public stress, when the mind seems to be fathoms down, like some poor land creature in the weeds of the sea.

For one dreadful second I thought she was going to break down, and I must record with shame that the first feeling through my mind was that it would fall to me to take the witness. I think I half-rose. I was aware of Kenyon looking at us and Stein's puzzled face peering round the corner of the law reports that divided us. It seemed an age. Certainly it was long enough to start a stirring in court, the rustling and shuffling of feet in the gallery, and then Lorne snapped "Yes?" in his most impatient voice, which I think was the kindest thing he did throughout the trial.

"Miss Birman," Marion said, "How long were you at 'The Towers'?"

"About two months," the witness replied, but I hardly heard her for the vast sigh of relief of Mr. Clive.

It had been a near thing, but Marion now seemed quite normal and assured as she faced the witness. "You are trying to be fair in this matter, isn't that so? You have told us that in that time you never saw the accused?"

"Only on the stairs."

"Yes, we will come to that. You saw his photographs. One was on the piano in the drawing-room? A full-face study, wasn't it?"

"I believe so."

"And there was one in Miss Maudsley's bedroom?"

"Yes."

"Which she retained there *even after* the quarrel we have heard about?"

"Yes."

"Was that full face too?"

"It was."

"Were those photographs good representations of the accused?"

"They were very like him."

"Would you care to look at him, perhaps?"

She did so. Maudsley stared back at her in his impertinent way, and if you'd been able to isolate them in time and forget the dead body between them and the accusation of blood you would have said that he was finding her a very fetching little piece.

"Now will you compare these two photographs of the prisoner," Marion said.

They were handed to Jane by an attendant. As she

held them up, something in her attitude must have struck Marion, who suddenly asked:

"Have you got your glasses with you?"

"Why, yes."

"So you *do* wear glasses?"

"For reading sometimes."

"Your sight is defective."

That was a mistake. It was a statement this time and the judge intervened sharply: "Miss Kerrison, oblige me by putting questions fairly to the witness."

"My lord, I am trying."

"That may be. The witness has said that she wears glasses for reading. One inference can be drawn from that, but you have drawn a very much wider one, quite unjustifiably, as the evidence stands at present. Do you wish to proceed?"

"My lord," Marion answered, "it is certainly not my wish to be unfair in any way. The witness has told us that she wears glasses for reading, and I willingly leave it at that."

Looking at Lorne, I saw a half-admiring expression on his face at this Fabian answer. She had retained something from the wreck: the suggestion of impaired sight, and that was the best we could hope for now, for short of absolute knowledge of defective long-sight (which we did not have) any pressing of the witness might have recoiled on us fatally.

"Please look at the photographs again—with your glasses if you would care to," Marion directed, and I could see from that delicate thrust that she was now restored to confidence. "Would you say that those photographs were taken at about the same time?"

"It's hard to say."

"But surely they are very different?"

"He is in a suit in one: in shorts and a shirt in the other."

"Oh, the suit and the shirt and the shorts!" Marion exclaimed, making great play with her S's. "The *faces*, I meant."

"He is a little older in this one, I think"—touching one.

"In the suit portrait, if I may put it so? The one that stood on the piano?"

"Yes."

"Would it be fair to say that these pictures might almost be of two different men?"

"I can recognize them," the witness said.

"Can you? In the other, the more informal study, he has a moustache, hasn't he?"

"Yes."

"And his hair is tousled?"

"I think he'd been bathing," the witness said.

"In the portrait, the formal study, his hair is brushed right down?"

"Yes."

"As he wears it today?"

The witness glanced at Maudsley again and admitted:

"No."

"Would you accept it from me if I told you that these two studies were taken respectively four and two years ago?"

"If you say so."

"Do you notice a change in him?"

"A slight change, yes."

"He's a bigger man now, isn't he?"

"Perhaps a little."

"And don't you find his hair much thinner?"

"No."

"My lord, may the jury see those photographs?"

She watched intently as the exhibits were passed along the jury benches. There were many signs now to tell us that these twelve good people had settled down. They no longer handled exhibits as unwary tourists do the postcards that get thrust into their hands outside the Moulin Rouge, but they looked at them squarely, and they looked at Maudsley and you could see that they were drawing sensible conclusions, by which I do not mean conclusions that were necessarily favourable to us.

"Is Exhibit J.K.M.4 (the formal suit study) the more recent of the photographs?" the foreman asked the judge, very rightly, for it was a matter which she had failed to make clear.

"Miss Kerrison?"

"My lord, yes. My information is that it was taken in Australia two years ago."

"And J.K.M.5, the beach photograph, four years ago, is that right?"

"Quite right, my lord."

"Thank you," the foreman said, as one reasonable person to another, and so much was he now at ease that he gave Marion a little nod as though to say: "All right, go on."

She nodded back at him and turned to the witness.

"So it comes to this, Miss Birman, does it not: you had no means of judging the appearance of the accused except by photographs, one of which was four years old?"

"I have accepted that."

"But you identified him?"

"I most certainly did."

"Though you only saw his face in profile?"

"I have said so."

"And for an instant?"

"Yes."

"And all but in darkness."

"Shall we recall the witness's words?" said the judge with dangerous mildness. He began to hunt back through his notes and after a while read out in a flat voice: " 'It was grey on the stairs. There was a light from my room. The door was half-open. There was the window. It was getting near dusk. There was a moderate, greyish light: you could see all right.' Those were the witness's words," he said.

It was a rebuff. Nevertheless, looking back on it, I am certain that at this moment Marion had all but won her case. The very repetition of the words Jane had used created an impression of shadow of conditions in which, with the best intentions, the witness could still have been mistaken.

But it is a truism that the fates of men and women often turn on trivial things—one joking answer of Oscar Wilde's destroyed him—and there happened now two incidents, both small, which in their impact on one another were to have strange results.

The witness smiled: one of those involuntary, nervous smiles. I don't think many people in court noticed it, for the judge was the centre of attention.

But Marion saw it. I don't know what she read in it: relief, perhaps, a shared relief, the suggestion that somewhere in that court other eyes were watching and rejoicing in the protection which the judge seemed to have accorded.

And in that same moment Marion must have

glimpsed again the paper which Mr. Clive had handed her, for she unfolded it for the second time, putting it on the table between us, and I read:

> *Private inquiry reports Birman visited an address in Fawcett Street last night at nine and met a man—identity not yet established. They spent an hour together in an upstairs room.*

"Of course she knew him, of course," I heard Marion say under her breath, but the words and her evident excitement made no impression on me, for I was obsessed with the note itself—the note as a fact, as a proof of the accuracy of her perceptions. I have often thought it ironical that I should have chosen this moment to think that and even to praise her, for I whispered: "You were right, then," without the least idea that I might be applying the match to a train long laid in her mind and heart.

She straightened up and faced the witness who was watching her—no smile now. The court had gone very still, and I think perhaps I was the only person there who didn't sense that some dramatic change was in the air.

"Miss Birman, did you know the man on the stairs?"

The answer came with a rush, the words tumbling over one another: "By his photograph, by those two photographs—I have already told you."

Marion said slowly:

"But did you *know* him? And do you *know* him now?"

"I don't understand you. I have identified the prisoner."

"Yes, you have identified the prisoner! Lies, I put it to you?"

Her voice had risen, shrill with bitterness and emotion. I could hear Mr. Clive shuffling anxiously behind me and I caught at her gown. She shook me off, and as our hands touched I could feel that she was trembling.

"It is the truth," the witness said.

"The truth! Isn't it the truth that you came out of your room and glimpsed in the semi-darkness a face you well knew?"

"The accused, I tell you."

"A face you had seen many times, not in photographs only but in the flesh—*and saw again last night in Fawcett Street?*"

"Stop there," said the judge, intervening so quickly as to deprive the court of any answer beyond the witness's start of surprise, which in any event was wonderfully controlled. "Miss Kerrison."

"Yes, my lord?"

"Do I understand you to be putting it to the witness that it was not the accused but *some other person* whom she is alleged to have seen on the stairs?"

"That is so."

"And that she suppressed that information?"

"Yes."

"Which amounts, does it not, to a charge that the witness was an accessory after the fact?"

"My lord, it does."

"I want the witness to understand this clearly," the judge said, "and to think carefully about her answer."

I saw suddenly that Marion had become painfully excited. I don't know whether she imagined in some way that the judge was going to protect the witness and rule that she need not answer; indeed, there is no knowing what she may have believed in the over-charged emotion of that moment. All I know is that to my horror I heard her cry out passionately:

"Let her refuse to answer, and let the jury hear her do it!"

Instantly a flush spread over the judge's face and he sat bolt upright in his chair. You could feel the power of the man, the truly formidable power.

"That is a most improper remark," he said. "In my experience of the courts I think it is the most improper I have heard. There can be no excuse for it: sex or emotion or anything. The witness had not refused to answer. She had waited because I was addressing her. Yet you have given the jury the impression that the witness was reluctant and false. You have prejudiced justice. You will now make a suitable apology to the court."

"My lord . . .'

"You had better sit down," the judge said, a little spurt of furious anger showing from under the façade of iron control.

"My lord, I am on my feet to oblige you."

"Oblige me, indeed! Let me tell you, since you do not seem to know it, that there are steps that can be taken in cases like this where professional conduct is so abused."

"Your lordship misunderstands me." She was still standing facing him, completely white of face. I think that she had meant all along to apologize, only the words got in the way, and that she was as appalled as I was and as Kenyon appeared to be—you could almost see the pious hands raised in horror at this intrusion of the female spirit.

"Your lordship truly misunderstands me. I must bear my part for what I have said, and I willingly submit. What I said was spoken in heat and misunderstanding."

"It had a malicious effect," said the judge.

"I regret that. I will do anything your lordship wishes."

He shrugged his shoulders.

"Yes, you will do that now, and what is the good of it? The harm is done." He wheeled round on the jury, whose members looked as scared as Marion—like small boys who have been caught listening to naughty words. "Appreciate this, please," he said to them with cold severity. "Comments have been made that should not have been made, and you must do your best to forget them. There was no reluctance on the witness's part. I was concerned to warn her of the very grave allegation that was being made, so that she should not misunderstand in any way. It is perfectly right that there should be full reflection at such a time. Is that understood?"

"Yes, my lord," replied the foreman, who seemed likely to have to learn all his confidence again.

It was a deplorable business. Nevertheless I felt sure that the result of it so far was more favourable to the accused than otherwise. The judge might protect the witness (as he was absolutely right to do) and he might direct the jury to do this and that, but the fact was that the point of the accusation and the slight hesitation of the witness had both been underlined.

I am certain that the witness herself appreciated this better than anyone, for she spoke suddenly, taking everyone by surprise:

"My lord, may I speak?"

"Certainly," he said.

"Then I would like to tell the court that I was always willing to answer. I have nothing to hide and the charges that have been made against me are wicked and wrong. The man on the stairs was the prisoner. Certainly I went to Fawcett Street last night, but I don't know why I had to be watched. It is a respectable street and respectable people live in it. I have friends in this world; though they are not murderers," she added, glancing at the dock.

There was no answer to that. Marion's question had been like one of those wild "haymakers" that either knock your man out or leave you helpless against a counter. That counter had been made and we were down from it.

"What did you want to let Miss Kerrison go and do it for?" Jaggers demanded of me as we rose for lunch at the end of the witness's evidence. He had a habit of being in court during one's failures, but he never seemed to be there for the good bits, though that didn't stop him from imagining them afterwards when he was giving clients the old commercial puff. "You should have watched her better," he asserted severely. "You know she's a woman."

"Well, my dear Jaggers . . ." I was beginning, but he cut me off.

"You know what they're like. Excitable! What started it? That note?"

"Yes, partly."

"Clive shouldn't have shown it her," Jaggers said, extending the area of blame. "Never spring a surprise on a woman. Clive should have known that. And she was doing so well."

"I know."

"And now she's bitched it."

All too evidently this was the opinion of the robing room, where a large company was assembled. Silence fell as I entered, one of those tactful silences that descend like a blight on the bereaved, and Kenyon gave me a fraternal look from the midst of his chambers' team which always gave the impression that it was about to swarm on him. "Bad luck," he seemed to be saying, "oh, what bad luck and not a bit of it your fault: but there!" A pleasant contentment reigned among them, as though the corpse they had interred had left the right sort of will, but you were left in no doubt that the solemnities were over, for the wigs and gowns were off, all the pipes were lit and Stein had brought out his snuff-box, a period touch which gave him the look of the young Disraeli.

"A very good tussle," he condescended to me, detaching himself from the hive.

"Yes."

"Where's Kerrison?"

"Lunching out—at the 'George,' I expect."

"How epicure of her," Stein said.

I looked round for company at the buffet lunch, which was not the least of our tribulations at Assize time, but only Serpell of our team was there, and he had the look of a man preparing to pass by on the other side. I was really grateful when Gilroy sauntered up, elegant as ever, with his beautiful linen and his bands starched by some magic genie of laundering.

"The *drama* of it, my dear fellow, the stark *drama!*" he exclaimed in his most fatigued voice.

"So you were there?"

His eyes opened wide. "Who would miss Portia in action? Now if only Shakespeare could have seen it! Think of it! A whole new conception of 'The Merchant.'"

"Have you joined Kenyon's chambers?" I said to him, for I was feeling hurt and dejected, and at such times one reverts a little to the simplicities.

He glanced across at them and you could see that he found them as provincial as he found me.

"No, no, you mistake me, Michael: this morning I took no sides, I was the disinterested critic. A better play than 'The Merchant'; a more subtle sense of hubris—in Portia, not in the Jew."

I turned away, but he followed me and sat down beside me at the trestle table where various desiccated sandwiches awaited their fate.

"Now I like Kerrison," he went on. "Kerrison has fire. She has the right sort of conceit, the conceit of the gods, and all the best dramas are fashioned out of that."

"Why don't you eat your sandwiches?" I said to him.

He looked at them with so eloquent a distaste that I couldn't help smiling. I think in his queer malicious way he was trying to cheer me up, and I certainly needed cheering as Kenyon and his minions sat down at the other end of the table and began to guzzle with an atrocious heartlessness.

"The trouble with you is that you're too pedestrian," Gilroy continued to reprove me. "This morning in court, for instance, you tried to hold her back, which was foolish. Do you think they tried to hold Hercules back when he threw himself on the pyre?

You don't understand the ways of heroes, or gods, or phoenixes—or young women, either," he added, watching me with his rather colourless eyes.

I didn't answer.

"Or do you think that you do, my dear chap?"

I went on eating—stolidly, as I hoped.

"Do you feel some special affinity? Or do I intrude there?"

"Impossible."

He gave a sigh, no doubt feeling that his perceptions and the way he was expressing them deserved better than that.

"Now that seemed like the expression of a prickly nature, Michael, and you are usually so placid. Was it a trying morning?"

"You saw for yourself."

"Not so easy, perhaps, dealing with the master race. Shall I tell you what I think? In Kerrison we have a rare creature. She has all the characteristics for a great play: fire and claws and passion and what-have-you. She has the makings of a celestial advocate (and I should greatly like her to represent me there, as will probably be necessary). But has she the makings of an earthly one? Like Kenyon, say?" he added with a glance down the table, as though to add, "and who could be more earthly than that?"

"I hope you're going to answer all these questions," I replied, glancing at my watch.

"All right, why not? Here is the test case with us now. Here we have an innocent man accused—or so it seems to me. You're very discreet about it, Michael, do you have doubts? And here we have this Justice, this infallible machine of Justice. Throw in a witness like Birman to taste, and get the devil to stir it, and what's the result?"

"You tell me."

"Ah, that's what I'm wondering. The balance is fine. One question too few, one question too many. . . . Perhaps she's already asked it."

"She was perfectly entitled to ask it."

He held up his hand.

"Quite, quite. Perfectly entitled. Would Hesketh have asked it, though? You see, people will be saying that."

The fact was that you couldn't be angry with Gilroy, for even when he was speaking most maliciously about people behind their backs he gave the impression that he would much rather be saying it to their faces and would put it a lot better too. Besides, he never descended to common tittle-tattle, and I knew that his voice wouldn't be raised among the pack that would fall on Marion if she failed, for he was fastidious, a lone wolf of gossip, and it was almost a privilege to be bitten by him.

I escaped, all the same, as quickly as I could, since the Assize lunch-hour was short and I wanted to see Clive and judge his reactions and have a word, if possible, with Marion before the afternoon sitting.

Outside the robing room I ran into Hesketh, coming with Jaggers from the Civil Court where they had been sitting late. I could see that he had already been briefed about our calamity. Some men, I suppose, would have stopped and offered a word of encouragement, but that wasn't Hesketh's way, and he gave me a nod, the sort of nod that Lorne might have given me, and passed on.

I don't know why I should have felt cheered by this, but I did. After you'd lived with Hesketh for a while you began to find your feet. You were brash and inexperienced, but he didn't treat you as though you were. If you were up against him in a case he didn't condescend or make a display of chivalry, but just beat the daylights out of you, and somehow you didn't feel bad about it, but grateful and a little more self-reliant. He had no time for gestures. He was a truly blunt man, not playing at it like Kenyon, but there was no cutting edge to him and the impact he made on you was salutary and good.

I know that I went from that encounter in a much better frame of mind, and I certainly needed courage, for Mr. Clive was distressed by the morning's events and in need of comfort. "It doesn't look too good, does it, Mr. Irvine?" he greeted me as soon as we met in the corridor. "And we were doing so well at one time." He didn't seem to imply "And now she's bitched it" (to remember Jaggers's words), for there was nothing censorious in his nature, but he just seemed sad about it and in the mood to blame his own unbelief. "The fact is, Mr. Irvine," he confessed to me, drawing me away from the door of the solicitors' room, "I didn't really believe Miss Kerrison; I hadn't her faith in the client—until I saw that last witness. She seemed to me a very clever woman," he lamented, shaking his head.

"Oh, Jane's that, all right."

"Do you think the jury believed her?"

"It's hard to say. Emotions act easily: indignation and injured innocence and so on. There's such a thing as overall truth. *You* suspect she's a liar now."

He nodded. "Yes, and I must say I didn't believe that once."

"And if she's lying, then Maudsley's not, and there's a chance of the truth showing through there."

This only had the effect of depressing poor Mr. Clive again. "Truth!" he murmured, and shook his head. "Our client's a very difficult man," was the way he expressed the old Adam of doubt that still survived in him. "Very difficult. He's so confident, Mr. Irvine. I saw him just now. He thinks he only has to say a thing and people will believe him. He's not a bit afraid of Mr. Kenyon, though I've warned him. But he has great faith in Miss Kerrison, and that's something."

"Why not tell her? It would cheer her up," I said to him, for I could see her white-wigged head in the corridor.

He took fright at once, being too honest to want to pay a compliment to her face when there were so many reservations in his heart. I thought for a moment that he was going to dodge away, but she was too close to us, and he couldn't do it without being seen.

"I want to wish you all the luck, Miss Kerrison," he said to her as she came up.

"Thank you."

"You lunched well, I hope? Surely better than we did? What service there is here!"

We turned towards court, Marion walking between us. Outside, the rain had set in again and was lashing the window-panes. It was stone cold in the corridor, whose benches were filled with resigned-looking people, plaintiffs, defendants, witnesses from the Civil Court, all with the appearance of being there for ever.

I remembered the first time I had walked there in wig and robes and how it had seemed to me that the eyes of the world were on me as I strode along with my small divorce brief under my arm. I was wiser now and knew the compelling nature of the fears and boredoms that people brought along with them. Sometimes I caught an inquiring glance turned towards Marion—it was usually a woman's—but for the most part they showed little interest, and it was strange to compare them with their brothers and sisters of the public-gallery queue which still extended in a shiny wet crocodile along the sidewalk outside. How greatly our own discomforts outweigh the tragedies of others! It was true of myself in the present instance, I thought as we went through the swing doors into the court, for in a sense it had been our setback, not Maudsley's, that I had been lamenting.

The room was filling up. We had hardly taken our seats before Kenyon led in his clutch of juniors, nodding at Marion, but rather coldly, for she was still under the threat of judicial interdict and he was not the man to contaminate himself. Their presence, and Mr. Clive's, made it impossible for me to say what I wanted to say to Marion, though I might have stayed silent anyway, for her action in choosing to lunch out alone, without a word to me, was a warning, and she seemed very cold and aloof from me now.

I know that these things hurt, for it is, I suppose, only human to be surprised at the way our friends visit their own failures and unhappiness on us. I watched her as she opened her brief and studied the notes she had memorized weeks before. I hoped that she might still turn round and give me one glance. But she worked on, and the minutes passed.

"The judge," I heard someone say.

I can still recall the oppression of that moment and the sense of fate around me as I thought of Birman, and Maudsley's evidence to come.

Chapter Seven

THE PROSECUTION'S FIRST WITNESS after lunch was purely formal evidence: the handwriting expert to prove the authorship of what Kenyon in his opening speech had called "The threatening letters." Marion did not cross-examine him, but reserved herself for Mrs. Pye.

This lady, Miss Maudsley's neighbour and oldest friend, was a little dried-up widow of about seventy, with dark, restless eyes. I am sure she was a good woman and regretted her friend, "dear Charlotte," as she called her, striking from the very first the personal note which always sounds so out of place in a murder trial. But for all that, you couldn't help suspecting that she had her fair share of *Schadenfreude* and that the various bereavements she had suffered had set her up wonderfully and given her a real interest in living. "I have known poor dear Charlotte for over forty years" sounded in her mouth almost like a claim she was making on the world's interest; yet, "I was with my mistress a long time," the cook, Miss Saunders, had said, and I had felt the presence of true emotion then.

Perhaps it was unjust of me not to have liked Mrs. Pye, and I am sure it showed a sad lack of understanding of the bleakness of her life in her great barrack of a house, alone with her cats and her radio set. I think what chiefly put me against her was her partiality for Jane—"A very nice, kind young woman," she told the court chattily. "She was so good to me, and so good to Charlotte."

"Do you remember the night of tenth March?" Stein asked, recapturing the witness under the spur of several black judicial looks.

"Why, yes, that was the night that poor Charlotte . . ." she was beginning, when sensibility overcame her and she substituted: "I remember Jane had come to me that afternoon."

"At what time?"

"At about five. We talked and talked. I gave her another cup of tea; she had had some with Charlotte already, you know. And I lent her some new magazines to take back home with her—she was *such* a reader."

"What time did she leave?"

"About five to six. She'd looked at the clock. I remember her saying: 'Look at the time! And I *promised* to be back for six.' She was *so* conscientious," the witness added.

"Confine yourself to answering the questions, if you please," directed the judge, who had obviously had enough of this.

"What was the state of the light, did you notice?" Stein asked hurriedly.

"Quite good, still fairly light, though the shadows were beginning to creep in."

"Right. Now will you take your mind back some

weeks. Do you recall Miss Maudsley ever showing you any letters?"

"Oh, yes,"—she was all eagerness. "Yes, she showed me letters on two occasions."

"Do you remember the dates?"

She wrinkled up her brow. "The first time was just after her nephew left her—the prisoner, you know," she added, but she did not look at him. "It would be early in February, I think. She had a letter in her hand and she said: 'It's from John. More foolishness. He wants money, he's a foolish boy.' Yes, it was a letter like that one you have there. She didn't actually let me read it, but I saw the writing."

"And the second time?"

"Was about a fortnight later."

"What happened on that occasion?"

"She again showed me a letter, saying it was from her nephew, John—it was like the one you're showing me."

"Can you remember her precise words?"

Mrs. Pye nodded vigorously. "Yes, I can, for they rather struck me at the time. Charlotte said: 'Money again. The boy's a nuisance. It's too bad pestering me like this.' I said how much I agreed with her, and oh I *did*, and she went on: 'I won't have it, Kathleen. I've told him if he goes on like that he'll get no money of mine.' "

"Did she say whether she'd told him by letter or face to face?"

"No, unfortunately," the witness said, and you could feel her disappointment at the shocking secretiveness of her friend.

"Did Miss Maudsley at any other time speak about her nephew, the accused?"

"No, never,"—worse and worse, and after forty years of devoted, self-sacrificing friendship!

"Thank you," Stein said, and bobbed abruptly down.

Marion rose, and as she did so you could see the little bright eyes of the witness dart in her direction like a bird's.

"Mrs. Pye, you were an old friend of Charlotte Maudsley's?"

"Oh, I was."

"You had known her in the days when she was one of a family at 'The Towers'?"

"Yes."

"A great family woman, wasn't she?"

"Devoted," the witness said.

"I'm glad you used that word. And indulgent, would you say?"

"Yes."

"She was the eldest of her generation, wasn't she?"

"I believe she was."

"Did she always play the part of an indulgent elder towards her juniors?"

"Yes, she was so good and kind."

"Was that in particular her attitude towards her nephew, John, when he returned to his father's home?"

"And very nicely he repaid it!" said the witness snappishly, and gave a sniff through her large and beaky nose. "Pestering her for money!"

"A very normal thing in families, surely?" Marion argued, with a glance at the witness, as though inviting her to laugh the whole thing off. She got no response from that little thrush of a woman and she went on: "You weren't in court, I think, when the opening speech was made, and the contents of the accused's letters were described as 'threats'?"

"No."

"Miss Maudsley doesn't seem to have taken them as threats, does she?"

"She didn't like them."

"Let's see what she says the first time. 'More foolishness. He's a foolish boy.' "

"Yes."

"Indulgent words, aren't they?"

"I wouldn't call them that."

"Wouldn't you?" Marion asked, and she looked at the jury and said "Foolish boy" again in accents so droll and resigned that you could see the response of humour in their faces.

"And the second time," she went on. " 'The boy's a nuisance.' Haven't you said that of someone before, someone you were fond of really?"

"No, I haven't," the witness said, and you certainly got the assurance that she herself would have chosen quite another word.

" 'It's too bad pestering me like this.' Wasn't that all part of the same resigned, tolerant, half-amused understanding?"

"It was not."

" 'If he goes on like that he'll get no money of mine.' "

The witness seemed to pounce on the words like a bird on a worm. "Charlotte said more than that: she said she'd *told* him he wouldn't."

"Did she?" Marion asked, watching her closely. "You see, I'm suggesting that you imagined those words."

"Imagined them indeed!"

"Because you have told us you had no way of knowing whether in fact Miss Maudsley *did* tell her nephew?"

"No."

"And in fact she didn't cut him off?"

"Perhaps she didn't have time," the witness said.

There was a gasp in court, but Marion took this reflection on her client with the greatest coolness. "You seem to make up your mind very easily," she said in a gentle voice. "Here we are assembled to try a man, and you have already done it and convicted him."

"I didn't mean that."

"Hasn't that always been your attitude?"

"No."

"Let me remind you of your words. May I have the shorthand note, my lord, of what the witness said about the second letter?"

Lorne nodded, and the little court stenographer got up and hunted through his notebook and read out in a rush: "Charlotte said: 'Money again. The boy's a nuisance. It's too bad pestering me like this.' I said how much I agreed with her, and oh I did, and she went on . . ."

"And oh I *did!*" Marion repeated, rising easily over him and giving the jury another eloquent glance. She turned to the witness. "Isn't it true that you have always been ready to believe the worst of him?"

"No."

"That you dislike him?"

"No."

"I put it to you that you have always had a prejudice against him."

"That will do," said the judge. "You haven't leave to repeat questions for ever."

"My lord . . ."

"No, they are the same questions and the witness is giving the same answers. There is really a limit to indulgence."

"My lord, with respect . . ."

"And I am reaching it," said the judge. "I recommend you bear that in mind."

"As your lordship pleases."

Loader was up on his feet now and we were very near to the bottom of the barrel.

"I call Police Sergeant James Duggan."

This was the officer who had found the ring in the cistern. He was a very ponderous, beefy man, and as he described his search, which in places seemed to have been as acrobatic as an old Fairbanks film, a pleasant humour seemed to pervade the court. "It was a very inaccessible cistern, my lord"—he pronounced it "inassessable." "The ring was in a very inassessable place—under water. I nearly fell in." There was a rumble of laughter which the judge made no attempt to stop. "But there it was, all right. Yes, my lord, that's it," he said, identifying the exhibit which looked absurdly small and unimportant in his hands.

It was fascinating to compare his treatment of it with that of the jeweller who followed him—an eyeglass and two white hands that caressed the gem. "This stone, my lord, is an emerald. It is a good stone, though by no means the most valuable in the collection. I have often seen it. The value of this ring is in the neighbourhood of £200."

"Wasn't it in fact one of the least valuable in the box?" I asked him, rising at once.

"The box?"

"In the collection, then?"

"Yes," the jeweller said.

"Wasn't there a diamond solitaire valued at £2,500?"

"There was."

"And another diamond ring at £1,000?"

"Both purchased at well below that price from my firm by deceased's father—who knew an investment," the jeweller said with a positively hypnotic stare at the jury.

"Those jewels have disappeared, haven't they?"

"Yes, but they would be insured, of course," the jeweller replied, emerging completely out of his witness's skin.

"At all events you have never been asked to identify them in this court?"

"Oh, no."

"Nor any of the other jewels?"

"No."

"Wasn't their total value over £8,000?"

"It was."

"There is just this one ring found in the cistern: value £200?"—I did my best to make it sound infinitely cheap.

"That is so."

"Thank you, Mr. Murray."

"And that, my lord, is the case for the prosecution," Kenyon announced, lumbering to his feet and looking at the jury as though to indicate to them that there might be something to be said for the other side for all he knew.

There was a pause while the judge shuffled his papers. Something appeared to be annoying him—a draught, perhaps—and he beckoned for his marshal and sent the young man off beyond the blue curtains. "Yes?" he said suddenly, looking up.

I confess that the abruptness of it disconcerted me. But Marion was already on her feet and she began at once:

"May it please your lordship, members of the jury:

"It is now the turn of the defence.

"You have heard the prosecution's story. At a later stage I shall address you in detail about that story and the gaps and inconsistencies which, in my submission, mar it beyond redemption. I shall say little now. But this I will say:

"This is a case that may depend on two witnesses. One you have heard: Miss Birman. The other you will hear: the accused himself. Their stories conflict: they conflict absolutely. Is one of those witnesses deliberately lying? Or is there the third possibility—that Miss Birman was not so much lying as mistaken about whom she saw in the half-light on the stairs?

"Well, I will put John Maudsley before you. You have seen him in the dock—'the prisoner,' as we have called him, 'the accused.' Need I remind you that he is still a man around whom the law in its wisdom has cast its mantle of innocence which only you can take away? When he goes into that box he is a witness, just like any other, no better, no worse; he will take the same oath. He is entitled to as much trust as you gave to all the others who preceded him there, for truth in England, as his lordship will direct you, is no prerogative of prosecutions but belongs with equal force to the humblest man or woman seeking justice before the law."

She looked at the jury for a moment, and then drew herself up and said in a resonant voice:

"I call John Kelvin Maudsley."

There was a rustle in court. I think that in the gallery they rather expected that the walls of Jericho would fall down and the prisoner pass before them over the heads of counsel and officials on some form of cloud and alight in the witness-box like Mahomet on Mount Pisgah. In fact he had to descend the dock steps towards the cells, and bob up in the corridor arriving through the press of solicitors and junior counsel in the well of the court.

As soon as he had reached the little pulpit of the box the official was there, proffering him the Bible and the card with the oath written on it, for all the world like a customs declaration. He looked huge there with his hand upraised, a strange and isolated figure. No one could help him. I suppose there is no lonelier place at such a time, and yet by reaching out his hand he could almost have touched the reporters scribbling below him, or the judge's marshal or the sheriffs on the bench above. He was not a dozen yards from me. I could see his tanned, leathery skin, and the small eyes, and the worn clothes which by night you may be sure the prison officers folded tidily.

He looked confident enough, glancing round the court from the new position in which he found himself, with the judge on his left now, and Marion to the right, and Kenyon facing him—the fat red face instead of the bobbing tails of the wig, which was all he had been able to see of his antagonist from the dock. I don't know whether many saw in him, as I did, something defenceless and pitiable. He didn't look the same to me as he had done during those interviews in prison: perhaps because I now believed in him a little more.

"John Kelvin Maudsley?" Marion said.

"Yes."

"Do you understand the charge of which you are accused?"

"I do," he said, "and I am innocent. I never killed my aunt."

"How long had you known her?"

"Since my arrival in England: for about eight months."

"Will you tell his lordship and the jury about that in your own words?"

So he told the story of that meeting and the life they had lived together. He was at his best in this. You truly believed him. There was a touch of humour in the way he described his arrival at the gloomy old house of his ancestors. "I hadn't reckoned on that sort of place," he said. "I reckon I didn't fit those old portraits and all that. I'd lived a different sort of life"—and you saw for a moment the plains beyond the Blue Mountains crossed by dried-up watercourses and dirt roads running to nowhere, clouds of dust, the good earth on its way to burial in the Tasman Sea, homesteads with corrugated-iron roofs, and the shafts of artesian wells.

"All this took a bit of getting used to," he told us, as though he *had* succeeded in getting used to our city and the clouds that seemed to be permanently attached to it. "I suppose *I* took a bit of getting used to, too," he added, and you could see smiles in court, those pleasant unforced smiles that respond to simple verities simply expressed.

"How did you get on with your aunt?" Marion asked him, taking her tone from him.

"Quite well at first, my oath. She was a good sort, she made me welcome all right. But you know how it is?—living together, people like us, different sort of people. She had her ways and I had mine. I don't say mine were good ways," he put in as an afterthought.

This time there was quite a burst of pleased laughter, and the witness went on to explain himself. He was extraordinarily frank. He was being tried for one thing and there was no need for him to have mentioned the minor prosecution in which he had been involved, though it fortunately had had a happy outcome; nor need he have dwelt on his woman trouble, omitting little except the lady's name. "I guess I was a bit lonely," he said in explanation, "and I said things I shouldn't have done and was a bit too free and easy all round. You get carried away sometimes. It was my fault, I reckon, but it landed me in a scene, and my aunt—she didn't like it, and well . . . she just said I'd better go."

The parting was touchingly described, without any false sentiment, and I am quite sure that every word was true. Miss Maudsley had had standards and she would not depart from them, since she was the guardian of something that was symbolized in her home, in those old albums of hers, and the jewels and the trinkets which she herself never wore. But her affection was another matter. From the moment this evidence was given, the real attitude of the old lady towards her nephew was made plain: she loved him, and that love put the trial, at least for me, onto a level of true tragedy.

"So you went to live in Greenside Crescent?" Marion said by way of epilogue.

"Too right. I had to go somewhere for my tucker and it was good and cheap. I reckoned ten miles away from the family was close enough."

"What were you doing for a living?"

"Whatever I could get: selling vacuum cleaners, mostly. I didn't sell so many, either—maybe I was a bit too 'Aussie from the Outback,' I don't know."

"Was your aunt aware of what you were doing?"

Maudsley smiled and you could see that at this distance of time he found the old lady's social prejudice amusing and pleasantly typical of the nation of caste-lovers among whom he had stumbled. It so happened that he had not told his aunt about his door-to-door experiences. But there was some other agency he had aspired to which seemed to him of a higher order, and he had asked her to advance him money to purchase that. "It was no go," he told the court with the same humorously resigned air. "It wasn't good enough for a Maudsley: as though I hadn't walked the roads like the swag-men you've heard about—kind of tramp, I reckon," he added, seeing the perplexed and slightly doubting expression on the faces of the jury, for "swag" sounded rather a piratical word.

It appeared that Miss Maudsley had had ambitions for him which had persisted even after the break-up of their life together. There was some secretarial job she had in mind for him which her influence could procure, but "Could I see myself in that!" he commented with a wry turn of the mouth.

He was making an excellent impression. It was almost impossible to believe that this large, friendly man was arraigned for a brutal murder, and you could sense the bewilderment of the spectators, the second thoughts that were passing through scores of minds.

"You preferred this agency?" Marion added.

"Too right. But it cost money to get it. I needed a hundred quid. So I wrote to my aunt. She turned me down. I didn't take that too hard for she was stubborn, just like my old dad, and *he* was so stubborn he lost every zac he'd got. I tried to see her. No go. So I wrote again. I needed that money. I reckon I'd got a bit stubborn too and a bit excited, the way you get when you want a thing badly and don't see why you can't get it. I'd have borrowed and paid her back."

"So what did you do?"

Maudsley said: "I went to the house and this time I saw her—it would be in February, some weeks before her death. I asked her again, straight, as man to man. She said there was this other job for me. So I went upstairs, to the lavatory as it were, and I went to the drawer in the dressing-table of her room and took out a key I knew was there, and I opened that old jewel box and I took that emerald ring."

There was a gasp in the court. You would have said it was the tribute of sorrow, of regret at the passing of something that was innocent and good. I suppose the fashionable crowd at the trial of Oscar Wilde felt much the same that day when Carson rose, and the shadows closed in on genius and on that bright, charming spirit, exposing the corruption of its Janus face. Of course I had known perfectly well what was coming, and yet the odd thing was that I felt it as much as anyone, so much so that for a moment I didn't want to look at him or at the people around me.

"You are not excusing yourself for that action?" I heard Marion ask.

He answered at once: "No, I'm not. I felt crook about it at the time and I've felt a lot worse since. I reckon I was mad at her for holding out on me like that. She could have helped me and she wanted to help, but she wanted to do it in her own way."

He went on to explain what had happened to the emerald. He had meant to sell it, but about that time he had received a windfall from a bet, and this with his commission had brought him so close to the sum he needed that he had made up his mind to wait a while on the chance of raising the money "legitimate": in which case he would have replaced the ring in his aunt's jewel box. The £50 found in his possession went some way to bearing this story out. Naturally he had denied all knowledge of the theft to Inspector Kent. "I was afraid," was his explanation of this. "I'd been in trouble of a kind, and here they were telling me of my aunt's murder and there I was with one of her rings in my house. Of course I did my block—panicked, I reckon you'd say," he added, interpreting the blank look on the jurymen's faces.

"Let us return for a minute," Marion said, "to the night in February when you took that ring. How did you get it from the jewel box? Was it open?"

"I should say not! She was a careful old soul."

"Did you force the box?"

"I used a key. There were two keys, actually: one on a string round her neck and the second in a drawer of the dressing-table. That was the one I used."

"Did you replace the key in the drawer?"

"Yes, sure."

"Did you use gloves?"

He replied with the utmost candour. "Tell you the truth, I never thought of that. Sort of impulse it was, the whole thing."

I began to breathe freely again. There was no doubt that Maudsley had come with remarkable ease through the first part of his ordeal. The jury, as you could see from looking at them, were shocked, but the thought occurred to me that they were shocked *about the theft*, and by this very reaction showed their belief in the story they were listening to.

Did I myself believe it? I think at this moment I came near to doing so. There was an extraordinary apparent sincerity in that man, and tolerance, understanding of others, an absence of self-pity. I have said that to me the trial was tragic, but the place that Maudslcy had conceived for himself within it was one of humour, of comedy, whose essence may lie in man's acceptance of the outrageous, just as tragedy may be the mirror of our protest against it. I remembered Jane and the impression of a calculating mind, so different from the evidence I heard now which seemed to fall with the accents of truth—truth that was not always kind to itself. I was almost in a mood of faith.

So we came to the alibi for the day of the crime.

We began with a morning with the vacuum cleaners, so vividly described that you could almost see the dismay of the housewives as they found this large antipodean figure on their doorsteps with his "demmo model." He had tried about a dozen houses. In one he had swept up the breakfast crumbs. In another he had been mistaken for an anarchist or a tramp or something to do with the "Government." There had been one sale.

On the strength of this, after the midday meal at Mrs. James's, he had gone to the pictures at the "Royal," where he remembered the girl in the box-office, apparently the sort of girl one did notice. The film had been all about big-game hunters and had bored him vastly—but he had paid and he came of a dogged race. Then he had walked home, arriving sometime between five-thirty and a quarter to six, after which he had stayed in with a book and a drink, retiring to bed about eight, being tired. He had not been near "The Towers." He had been dozing when the police arrived to tell him about his aunt's death. He had been cautioned and had made a statement—a true statement except in so far as the ring was concerned.

"Thank you, Mr. Maudsley. Is there anything else you would like to tell the court?"

He looked round at us, deliberating for a moment and then said: "No, I guess that's it."

"Thank you," she said again and sat down. There was a rustle and a sigh in the crowded room as Kenyon rose with a formidable slowness. "All the time in the world," he seemed to be saying to us and to the man in the witness-box. "It just needs time and we'll get to the bottom of all this." He hadn't his brief or so much as a note in his hand, but he just stood there waiting till the judge gave him a nod to show that he was ready, and even then he didn't hurry himself to launch thunderbolts but said in a mild voice:

"Mr. Maudsley, you came to this country as a stranger and without money, I think?"

"Yes."

"Did your aunt befriend you?"

"She did."

"She took you into her house. Yet you quarrelled with her. Acrimoniously, could we say?"

"We had our disagreements."

"Were you still pursuing your 'disagreements' when you wrote to her?"

"I wanted her help."

"You wanted *money*. 'I must have money': didn't you write that?"

"Yes."

"Didn't you write: 'When other people have made promises I have seen that they kept them'?"

"Yes."

"What did you mean by that?"

"That I was disappointed."

"Oh, come!" Kenyon said, and he looked at the witness as though this descent from frankness was a grievous shock to him. "It was a threat, wasn't it?"

"No."

"Were you angry with her?"

"I reckon I was a bit."

"Were you 'mad' at her? I think you used that word."

"Perhaps I was."

"You were 'mad' enough by your own admission to steal a ring—from your benefactress, from your blood relation?"

"Yes."

"Did you know you were her heir?"

"She'd often told me so."

"You admit that the emerald ring found in Mrs. James's house was your aunt's and that your fingerprints were found on her jewel box?"

"Yes."

"And you heard Miss Birman identify you as the man seen on the stairs on the night of the crime?"

"I did."

"Do you think she can have a grudge against you?"

"I can't say."

"Can you think of any reason why Miss Birman should have identified you if in fact it wasn't you?"

In these questions it seemed to me that Kenyon was only sparring. None was very pointed or dangerous; they were routine questions, the foundations, no doubt, for later lethal blows, very typical of an advocate who preferred unspectacular methods. But in the last question of the series he had blundered; he had given the prisoner the chance to repeat in much more telling form the suggestion Marion had thrown out in her cross-examination of Jane, and very well he took it:

"Yes, I can think of reasons. Maybe she was just mistaken in the dark. And maybe she wasn't. Since it wasn't me there, it was someone else. I reckon she knew that someone, too right I do! It's not more unreasonable than that I should bash an old woman I was fond of. . . ."

"Just a moment," Kenyon said, but the judge sternly interposed: "You must allow the witness to answer."

"Thank you, my lord. I *was* fond of her. They accuse me, but *I* accuse the witness. She wanted the jewels, I reckon. Why don't you look for them?"

You could see the reporters scribbling madly, though I don't suppose they can have imagined for a moment that their editors would let that one through, with threats of libel around as dark as thunder-clouds. Professional pride, I suppose.

Kenyon was put out, for he had made a nice fool of himself. Luckily for him, part of his *amour propre* was saved at this moment by Stein, who had received a note from the Crown solicitors behind and now handed it to his leader. Kenyon was able to engross himself in it. When he looked up his face was stern. "Propaganda!" I thought to myself. "All right, go on and make a play with it."

I was made more sure in my opinion when the cross-examination proceeded along the old lines:

"Mr. Maudsley, you come before us as a man who professes the truth, is that so?"

"Yes," he said.

"Yet in your very first statement to Inspector Kent you told a lie, didn't you, about the ring?"

"Yes, I have explained that."

"Oh, you have explained it, have you!" Kenyon cried, giving the jury an expressive glance. "Do you think lies are so easily mended?"

"I don't know about that," Maudsley replied, with the same admirably placid humour he had shown from the beginning.

"Why didn't you tell the truth about your possession of the ring?"

"I was afraid."

"Afraid about a mere theft when murder had been done!"

"It wasn't so much the theft. I was afraid people might think things."

Kenyon seized on that. "Because you had *in your possession* the *murdered* woman's ring?"

"Yes."

"But you have 'explained' that, of course! You took it weeks before . . . though no one saw you."

"That is so."

"We've only your word, isn't that right?"

"Yes."

"Just as we've only your word for your movements on the afternoon of the crime?"

"There's Mrs. James."

Kenyon stared at him, and you could see that the relationship between this witness and the prisoner was very perfectly understood in that suspicious, disenchanted mind.

"Oh, yes, there's Mrs. James, and we shall come to her in good time, but it was the *afternoon* I was speaking of. You went to the pictures at the 'Royal'?"

"I did."

"You remember the girl in the box-office. Did she remember you?"

"I don't think so now."

"And after the pictures you walked home. Did you meet anyone you knew?"

"No."

"Didn't you in your first statement to the inspector say that you had met a man by the name of Mathers?"

"Yes."

"Wasn't that a lie?"

"I'd mixed up the day before."

"Oh, you'd mixed it up, had you!" Kenyon said.

There was no mistaking the rising note of menace in his voice. I became somewhat alarmed and glanced at Marion, but she was watching the witness—perhaps for the jury's benefit—with perfect composure.

The advocate went on:

"Isn't it a fact that you have 'mixed up' a whole lot of other things that happened that day—the time you returned to Mrs. James's house, for one?"

"I got back, as I've said, soon after half-past five."

I saw Kenyon draw himself up as he glanced at the slip of paper Stein had passed him; and then he said slowly:

"Isn't it a fact that 'soon after half-past five' you were in a taxi *not more than one hundred yards from your aunt's house?*"

Sensation: you could see the reporters writing it; you could feel the deep surge of emotion in court, the kind of feeling you get at a bull-fight when the matador passes the bull close, close to his body in the cerise folds of the cape, and you hear the crowd cry out and the sound of a multitude rising to their feet.

I caught a glimpse of Marion's clenched hands and white face beside me. I think only the judge, Kenyon, and Maudsley remained calm.

"Absolutely untrue," the prisoner said.

I saw Kenyon glance at his man and I thought I detected a kind of unwilling admiration as he continued:

"Let us make quite sure what we are saying. You see, Maudsley, I am suggesting to you that at twenty to six you engaged a taxi at the central station—it was a blue taxi," he added, as though there might be some question about its colour.

"No."

"And the taxi dropped you some ten minutes later at the end of the drive. One hundred yards, did I say? Fifty might be better."

"Who cares if it was a mile!" Maudsley answered with truly heroic effrontery.

Kenyon cocked an ear and waited, rather like a knowing terrier who has treed a cat and has hopes that the quarry will imprudently descend. I think we were all holding our breath, when into the silence the judge spoke:

"Mr. Kenyon."

"My lord?"

"Mr. Kenyon, are you proposing to call rebutting evidence of all this?"

Our antagonist bowed.

"With your lordship's permission, yes. I will make the application, if your lordship pleases, after my learned friend's witnesses have been called. The evidence is certainly there," he added in a voice which must have chilled poor Maudsley's heart.

I could hear Mr. Clive making distressed clicking noises behind me. I suppose I had expected something like this all along, for I had never fully accepted the alibi, but the shock was none the less annihilating when it came. I couldn't think what we could say or do, and the length of the trial stretched agonizingly ahead—the grim farce of Mrs. James's testimony and the speeches.

"He's got firm evidence, all right," I heard Marion whisper—it was the first time she had volunteered anything that day.

I asked what she would do.

"Fight it, of course. Fight the admission of the evidence first and then fight the witness—the way he's doing," and she looked up at Maudsley, whose calmness was that of an immensely courageous or immensely stupid man.

The first part of his ordeal was ending.

That of Mrs. James began.

In a way it was the most macabre part of the trial. Everyone was concerned that she should understand her position and not perjure herself. She made a lonely and pathetic figure. You couldn't smile any more about her clocks. But she stood up there as I took her through her deposition and swore to Maudsley's alibi, and I never heard a more touching devotion.

In cross-examination, Kenyon was gentle with her. "Is that all?" she asked when he had finished, and she looked around the court as though still expecting the attack for which she had steeled herself. He nodded at her, but she made no move. She must have pictured the scene to herself many times, and was puzzled by the reality and by something strange in the atmosphere of the court. Expectancy—that was what she sensed. The court had been waiting for something and she had not provided it. There was much poignancy in her glance, in which you could read her fears for Maudsley and for herself and the sad little ambitions of one who for a bewildering instant finds herself before the footlights of the world.

"That is all, thank you, Mrs. James," the judge said, and as she made her way out she would have caught the hum of excitement as Kenyon rose again with a note in his hand.

"My lord."

"Yes, Mr. Kenyon?"

"My lord, I understand that there are no more defence witnesses." He looked at Marion, who nodded. "In which case, would this be a convenient time for me to apply to your lordship for permission to call a witness in rebuttal? He is a taxi-driver," he added in a studiously off-hand voice.

"Well, Miss Kerrison?" asked the judge. "Do you object to that?"

She was up at once, as the judge directed the jury to leave the court. "My lord, with respect, I do. It is surely an elementary principle that the prosecution must set up the case to answer before the defence is called upon; it must *initiate.* This witness was not called. We don't know what he has to say or how much his credit is worth; he may prove everything or nothing. But he wasn't called. Now at this eleventh hour my friend wants to produce him. The defence should not be taken by surprise in this way."

Kenyon rose, protesting in an offended voice: "My lord, I object to the word 'surprise'; it suggests that an advantage has been taken, and that is not the case. This witness has just come forward—out of the void, so far as I am concerned. It is no fault of mine that this evidence is late in the field. The delay may be a matter for my learned friend's comments, but it does not alter the fact that here we have someone who on the face of it has relevant matters to disclose to the court, and in my submission it is well within your lordship's discretion, and in the interests of justice, that he should be allowed to do so."

"Miss Kerrison?" said the judge.

Marion had gone very pale: I think "in the interests of justice" had been a bit too much for her, and she burst out:

"An advantage *has* been taken, no matter what my

friend may say. A crime was committed three months ago. Thousands upon thousands of words have been printed in dozens of papers about this case; scores of photographs of my client have appeared in the press; there were lengthy judicial proceedings before a magistrate; and for nearly two whole days we have been trying the case in this court. No one comes forward. My client goes into the witness-box. And when he has given evidence—only *then* is this convenient witness found."

I had watched Kenyon during this speech. His normally pink face had gone scarlet, and at the final words he could contain himself no longer but erupted:

"*Convenient!* Is my friend accusing me of *harbouring* this witness?"

The press men, who had been scribbling furiously, gazed at Marion, and behind the hard-boiled expressions you could discern approval, delight, and a vision of beautiful headlines.

"*Harbouring* is an unpleasant word," she said.

"You were accusing me."

She ignored him with a flourish of the gown that was provocatively feminine.

"My lord, I am making no accusations, for I respect the principles of my learned friend. But he mentions justice. Where is the justice of his submission? The effect he will produce is the same, however innocent his motives. My learned friend is fortunate, being above suspicion. But the circumstances are suspicious."

"You are using strong words," the judge said.

"Your lordship would be forced to use stronger if it should fall to you to sentence this man to death. I am defending a man on a capital charge and it is not my duty to be squeamish or to worry about the susceptibilities of my learned friend. I ask your lordship to say that there are limits to what may be done in the way of dredging up witnesses."

There was a gasp of astonishment in the well of the court.

"I fear there are no limits to your presumption," replied the judge in a voice of dreadful calm.

"Your lordship midunderstands me."

He shook his head. "No, I am afraid not. I should like to believe it but I think it would be naïve to assume that you express yourself so incapably or that you have not accused the prosecution of the most criminal suppression without the least proof." She tried to protest, but he motioned her down. "That is a matter between us and I may have to revert to it at the proper time and place. Meanwhile there is this matter of the calling of the witness, which is clearly within the province of my discretion. I direct that the witness be called."

The jury came back and Kenyon rose. Thunderbolts had been launched and you could smell the brimstone, but he hadn't flinched.

"I call Thomas Oldfield," he intoned, giving a ringing solidity to the name.

A short, wary-looking man went into the box. "Na' then, watch thisen!" his friends and his wife had undoubtedly instructed him, and to show that he was not nervous or disconcerted by the eminence in which he found himself he stared at us pugnaciously, as though passing this warning on.

"Thomas Oldfield?"

"Aye," he admitted with the native caution of the

West Riding, where you learn early not to give too much away.

"I think you live at Number 49 Back Wensgate Street and are a taxi-driver by trade?"

He nodded.

"Do you remember the afternoon of tenth March?"

Mr. Oldfield did. A slack afternoon, he had been at the station with his taxi and at exactly twenty to six had taken on a fare.

"Do you see that fare in court today?"

Very slowly his gaze travelled over us, still "watching" himself with the inward eye, and you could see that it would not have surprised him to catch the criminal down there on the barristers' benches or among the press men or in the jury-box. I choked back an insane desire to laugh, for it was comic all right, as comic as old Diogenes with his candle, and as tragic too.

"That's t'chap—theer," the witness said suddenly, discovering Maudsley sitting in the dock.

This time there was a titter from the gallery. Mr. Oldfield did not seem surprised by it, for it probably bore out his own—and the West Riding's—opinion of the queerness of folk, and he went on calmly to describe the time and place of the dropping of the fare, keeping his eyes firmly fixed on the prisoner throughout, as though afraid of losing him, and apparently unaware of what he was doing by his words.

"It amounts to this, then," Kenyon said, rubbing his hands over this model witness: "at ten minutes to six or thereabouts you saw the accused within a few yards of 'The Towers'?"

"Aye."

So much for the alibi!

It only remained to ask the witness why he had come forward so late in the day.

Mr. Oldfield was puzzled by that. I imagine his conception of justice was a foreshortened, simple one, and all he saw was today's trial with himself present at it in good order. Late, was he? Late for what? Only when the matter was pressed did it transpire that he was "no great one for reading" and had in fact only seen Maudsley's picture that morning in the papers, purely by chance, in between his studying of horses' "form"—he was a great one for that.

"In which paper?"

The *Star-Journal.* A copy was produced, and there was Maudsley in facsimile with one of those careful captions underneath him—"John Kelvin Maudsley: a recent study." You could just see part of the handcuffs and of a muscular and intrusive arm—Kent's, actually, since the "recent study" had been taken on the day of the arrest.

"I think that is all. Thank you, yes, thank you," Kenyon said, and sat down.

Silence fell on the court, everyone waiting for the impact of Marion's temper on the dour, canny man in the box. He gave her a surprised look when she got up, for I don't suppose his wife had prepared him for anything quite as odd as that, but you could see that he was willing to give her a hearing.

"Mr. Oldfield," she began, "you made this journey with this fare three months ago?"

He nodded.

"How many fares have you carried since?"

He gave her a look of astonishment.

"Hundreds, would you say?"

"Aye, mebbe."

"Do you recall their faces?"

"Some of 'em."

"Try and describe for us some you took—last Saturday, let us say."

Mr. Oldfield glanced at the judge, as though he had hopes that male freemasonry would at least protect him from absurdities like that. "It were a busy day, were Saturday," he objected at last, when this trust was inexplicably betrayed.

"So you can't remember?"

Mr. Oldfield thought again, producing from his memory one family on its way to the seaside, and a couple of "London chaps," and a bookmaker's clerk who had been evasive on the subject of winners.

The court smiled.

"Try the Saturday before."

More seaside families emerged, with an assortment of buckets and spades.

"Let us go back to March, or is that too much for your memory? Try and describe for us *one* other fare you picked up that month."

"Nay!" you could imagine the poor man saying to himself. "Nay, that's daft that is; I can't tell thee that"; and he shook his head.

"How is it, then, that you recall the prisoner on the tenth March, the time you picked him up, to the minute, and the place you took him to?"

"Because that were t'day of murder," Mr. Oldfield replied triumphantly.

"Oh, so you read of the murder?"

Apparently he had been told of it.

"And of course you remembered you had taken a fare near to the fatal house at the fatal time?"

He nodded again.

"Why didn't you go to the police then?"

"I weren't sure," the witness murmured.

"Oh, so you weren't *sure*—about what? Your fare's identity?" Marion said, looking significantly at the jury. "Did you know the police were making inquiries?"

"I heard tell of it."

"Yet you didn't come forward. You were interested in the affair, surely, a bit curious about it?"

"Aye, a bit."

"Are you telling me that in spite of that curiosity you didn't glance at the papers or see the photographs at the time of the arrest?" She paused. "Or at the time of the proceedings in the Magistrate's Court?"

Mr. Oldfield did not answer.

"You see, I'm suggesting to you that you *did* see those photographs?"

"Nay, I never."

"And that the reason you didn't come forward was the honourable one that you 'weren't sure,' in your own words, or that you didn't recognize the accused at all, in mine?"

"I recognized that last picture," the witness said.

She pounced on that. "Do you know that it was taken *three months ago?*" She conferred for a moment with Mr. Clive, who had been doing some frantic research in his files, and then she wheeled round. "Do you know that that picture was printed in the *Star-Journal at the time of the arrest?*"

Poor Mr. Oldfield! He shook his head again.

"Didn't you see it then?" she persisted. "Isn't it a fact that you saw it and it meant nothing to you?

You don't answer. But now you identify it! Now! Months afterwards when you can't recall another single fare you took!" She started to sit down, and then rose again and hurled these final words at him: "Isn't it a fact that this afternoon in that box you have betrayed the decent, honest doubts that kept you from the police these three months past?"

So we were in the melting-pot again.

It was time for speeches—Marion first, since she had called a witness in addition to the accused. It was one of her best jury speeches. She began quietly, dissecting the prosecution and with a fine scalpel:

"Here is an accused person, members of the jury. Observe the case against him. He is accused of threats. You have seen the letters he wrote to his aunt. Isn't it as clear as daylight that here were merely hasty words, perfectly understood as such by the relative and friend who loved him and continued to love him in spite of his faults? Remember Miss Saunders, the cook, a prosecution witness, and her tribute to the accused; also the dead woman's own words as reported by Mrs. Pye—words of half-humorous reproach: 'A foolish boy.'

"Observe the crime the accused is alleged to have committed, a crime of violence involving surely the closest human contact. Not a scratch on him, not a mark. Not a trace of the loose wool from the scarf on his clothes or in his nails or hair.

"Observe the motive: robbery. Eight thousand pounds' worth of jewellery disposed of. Where? And when? Is the accused alleged to have sold these rings? Where are the proceeds? Money—not a trace of it. Did this ferocious criminal naïvely believe in honour among thieves! Is there a fence or accomplice waiting somewhere to render account? Eight thousand pounds' worth of jewellery taken, and one ring found —the least valuable. Ask yourselves why he kept that. Isn't the possession of it consistent only with what he told us in evidence: that he took it weeks before, took the one ring he thought wouldn't be missed? A mean action, but we're not trying him for that.

"Observe the jewel box. How was it opened? By force. With what implement? None has been produced. None was found on the accused. Where is that implement? Isn't the inference that another man, the real murderer, took it and may have it still? The box was forced. Yet there is a key in a drawer not a dozen yards away. The accused tells us he knew that, and why shouldn't we believe him, since he had lived in the house? Yet the box was forced. Isn't the inference that the man who forced it didn't know about the key—the murderer again, a stranger?

"Observe the witness Birman. She had never met the prisoner. She identifies him by a photograph—by two photographs, and they're not alike. Here she comes and here in effect is what she says: 'I identify the accused by his photographs. Admittedly one was taken two years before the other. In one his hair is brushed up, in the other slicked down. In one he has a moustache, in the other he's clean shaven. Never mind: I identify the accused by these two photographs. Admittedly he doesn't look quite the same now. His hair has grown thinner while he himself has grown fatter. Never mind: I identify the accused. Of course I only saw him in the dusk, and for an instant and for the first and only time, and in profile (and the photographs were both full face). Never mind: I identify the accused.'

"Is this recklessness, members of the jury, a dreadful recklessness that is prepared to swear a man's life away? Or is it something more sinister? Suppose she *knew* the man she saw there in the half-light? Of course I have no proof. I don't accuse the witness. But is it not a possibility one should bear in mind when considering the value of this testimony? As such I put it to you. And doesn't it most strangely accord with much of the evidence, so suggestive of the presence of another man that night?

"Observe the witness we have just seen, the taxi-driver, Oldfield." Her voice had taken on a deeper shade of irony. "What astonishing identifications the prosecution relies on? First Birman and her identifications by faith—might one suggest, by prejudice? Then Oldfield. What kind of identification shall we call that? Guesswork? Identification between bets? Are you going to rely confidently on his memory? We had a sample of it and wasn't it a pitiful sample, the dim recollections of a mind concerned (as of course it was right to be concerned) not with the faces of fares but with Halt signs, traffic lights, and the maze of city streets—and perhaps visions of the 2.30 race at Pontefract as well? Can you safely rely on that? A man's life is at stake. I know you won't forget that when you consider the effects of the testimony of this witness who comes here at the last hour to give evidence from a past he has so evidently forgotten. What brought him here? It is not for me to say. Who knows what thoughts of notoriety can pass through men's minds? But can it be, do you think, that he is really telling the truth when he comes here with his cut-and-dried times and places and identification of one man out of that otherwise shadowy past? Do you really believe him when he tells us that he saw that photograph of the accused for the first time today, and never read a word about the murder before or saw those earlier photographs? Aren't those most unlikely chances, to put them at their best? Wouldn't it be safest just to remember the memory of Mr. Oldfield and leave it at that?"

She paused. There was no sound in court and I don't think there was anyone present not under the spell. I don't know what they had expected—the same indiscipline which had marred her relations with the judge, perhaps. What they had received was this pungent revelation of the weakness of Kenyon's case, and you could sense again the same surprise that had been present during the first part of Maudsley's evidence, the realization that the defence was not negligible. It was not the least humorous thing to see that change of heart suggested in the faces of the jury. "She's getting them," I heard Mr. Clive whisper to the young assistant beside him. "If only Mr. Kenyon wasn't following and she hadn't to mention the client's name!"

But of course that was precisely what she had to do.

"Members of the jury, now, last of all, consider the accused.

"The prosecution says that he went to the house of the woman who had befriended him; that he twisted that scarf around her neck, and killed her, and left her as you saw her in those photographs which you may not easily forget.

"Well, you have seen and heard the accused. Wasn't the sincere, unspoken affection between these two persons, aunt and nephew, one of the things that emerged most poignantly from the evidence? Do you think that he did that to her? He denies doing it, denies it utterly. You have heard that evidence. Didn't it seem to you that here was a man, admittedly with faults, but a candid man? Of his own free will be disclosed to you the details of his conduct which had led to his leaving 'The Towers.' He was not accused of that. He need never have mentioned it. My learned friend would not have cross-examined him about it, for it would have been against the high standard of fairness he sets for himself. Yet the accused disclosed those details.

"My friend holds it against the prisoner that in his answers to the police he said he had met a man on one day whom he had in fact met the day before. On what day of the year or century do you imagine Mr. Oldfield would have remembered him? Such trivial errors are surely easy to make. One untruth is brought to my client's door: he denied the stealing from the jewel box. He explained that—and even the word displeased my friend. 'I was afraid.' Is it so remarkable that in a moment of panic, hearing of his aunt's death and realizing what mistaken conclusions people might come to if they knew he had a ring, he should have denied all knowledge of rings? Foolish, yes, and his aunt had called him that. In a moment of folly he had stolen—one ring. Does not the absence of all the others speak for him louder than folly?

"Now the witnesses have all been called and you must choose between them. If the prosecution can point to a proven untruth on our side, I, for my part, can point to what I suggest are some of the wildest irresponsibilities ever put forward by a prosecution, and yet the witnesses who uttered them are the very core of the prosecution's case, which must be proved, as my lord will no doubt direct you, beyond doubt. Well, does the witness Birman satisfy you beyond any sort of doubt? Does the witness Oldfield? Add them together. Isn't it like adding nought to nought? Would you condemn a boy to a birching on evidence like that? And here is a man's life dependent.

"It is dependent also on your judgement of these things."

When she sat down I felt sure that Maudsley was saved. It wasn't an entirely rational feeling and I was not—nor ever had been—one of her converts. Perhaps the truth was that, adapting Brutus, I did not mistrust Maudsley less but Birman more. The feeling in court among the more emotional spectators may have been partly responsible: a climate of opinion as fickle as English weather.

Of one thing at least I was certain. "You were splendid," I whispered to her, and I know I felt so light-hearted that it was on the tip of my tongue to utter also the approbation "Bonzer!" which was one of Maudsley's better words. I restrained myself, for in spite of her triumph she didn't look at all in a receptive mood, and just at the moment Kenyon got up, spreading his black wings over my optimism like the Crow in "Alice."

There was the man for the prosecution's money! Undramatic, almost prosaic sometimes, no one was better at marshalling arguments and suggesting to the jury where its duty lay. He had a waspish humour, too.

By a clever inversion of time, he started with the Birman identification on the stairs, no doubt one of the "irresponsibilities" mentioned by his learned friend—and if prejudice were the prosecution's business he would know how to find a similar word, he said, to describe the wild attacks launched on this witness and the utterly unsupported allegations concerning the fictitious "Second Man."

It seemed, however, that that evidence of Miss Birman's was denied and the accused was not at "The Towers" that night. Very well. Let them go back a few minutes in time. Oddly enough, up turned the accused again. Another witness, Mr. Oldfield, identified him in his taxi near the house.

Mistaken again, apparently: another irresponsibility—and he might be able to find a similar word for the attacks made on this witness and his motives. Mr. Oldfield was mistaken too. Very well. Let them look around again. (You could see the jury relishing this as they discerned the rhythm of the speech, a clever parody of Marion's.) And what did they find? A ring! He held it up for their inspection, daintily, between thumb and forefinger. That piece of evidence couldn't be denied, for it had shape and size—existence. But of course there was no need to worry: it had been taken weeks before! That was the defence. The prosecution had only to prove something which the prisoner had denied—had only to prove that he had lied—and lo and behold, in some Gilbertian way this turned out to be a proof of innocence. So it was with the ring. So it was with the finger-prints on the jewel box. Both points for the defence!

Nor was this all, for a kind of "inverted virtue" surrounded all the accused's acts. Written words which some might interpret as threats were really endearments, it seemed, and the circumstances in which the prisoner left his aunt's house were somehow creditable and a proof of candour. Was it not better than anything Lewis Carroll had conceived? In this Looking-Glass world would not a prisoner be advised to plead Guilty and be sure of an acquittal?

There was some appreciative tittering at that in the gallery, which is the "gods" of the Assize, and the sound seemed to remind Kenyon that in his sarcastic flights he had rather overshot the bounds that modern prosecuting counsel set themselves in their desire to be fair and factual. I think Marion's speech and the bottled-up indignation of recent hours had goaded him to it. "You mustn't allow yourselves to take this matter lightly," he admonished the jury, naturally reproving them for his own misdeeds.

They looked suitably ashamed.

"For at the back of your minds all the time will be the victim of this crime, so cruelly done to death. What evidence connects that victim with the accused? Evidence, mark you: not prejudice or surmise. Rid your minds of all thoughts that stem from mere suspicion"—and you could see the example that he himself was setting in this regard. "The prosecution must prove its case beyond all reasonable doubt, as my learned friend has so rightly said.

"Consider the evidence, then."

He did so, setting an edifying example of dullness and detail, yet it was surprising how powerfully his case, and particularly Oldfield and Jane, emerged. "Nought added to nought," Marion had said, yet Kenyon made a very formidable total out of them, for, as he said:

"Both witnesses came here and both identified the accused. They were both definite: they expressed no doubts. Are they lying?" He paused and his glance ranged challengingly down the ranks of the jurymen. "Why should they lie? It is suggested that Miss Birman is shielding another man. If so, why did she identify *anyone at all?* Why didn't she just stay silent? Why take the chance of identifying someone who might have an unbreakable alibi?"

I glanced at Marion, for here in the open now was the problem which had troubled me for so long and had evaded all my efforts to solve in favour of the accused.

"Do you believe that Miss Birman took that chance?" counsel was continuing. "Is there a reasonable doubt in your mind? If there is, you must dismiss Miss Birman.

"But, even if she is lying, what of Oldfield? Is he the celebrated 'Second Man'? If not—and can you conceive of a more fanciful suggestion?—then why should he lie? What motive could he have? Love of notoriety, says my learned friend. Well, it could be that, for we must assume that there are people in this world who for a few head-lines would come here and send an innocent man to his death. Did Mr. Oldfield seem likely to be one of them? Is that a reasonable doubt in your mind? If so, you must dismiss Mr. Oldfield."

But there remained the ring, and the finger-prints and the letters, all making their second appearance, as the advocate turned them this way and that to catch the light.

"He's a clever fellow: makes the best of everything," Mr. Clive was sighing to the young assistant whom he was training in the ways of court.

"And the worst," Maudsley might have said to himself, as his alibi came in its turn under the review of that all-seeing eye. Yet Kenyon never once looked at him in the flesh. Perhaps he preferred to strike at the impersonal, since it is so much easier to become indignant over a lie or a heresy than over a man, whose suffering can be manifest, whose faults are always tempered by the knowledge of his mortality. Poor Maudsley! The odd thing about it was that throughout the speech I felt sorry for Kenyon too, a partisan doing his best to be fair but without doubts where the truth lay, and such absolute certainty of mind seemed to me a sad and chastening thing.

So we came at last to the judge.

We, the English, believing in the existence of an entity called Justice, do not readily discern the man behind the ideal. A whole canon of behaviour is built up for our chosen instruments: judges are reputed sober, aloof, impartial. They nearly are. Apart from his irritation with Marion, which was a personal matter, you could not have told from one word or gesture of Lorne's which way his mind was working, nor did the statue of Justice herself seem to hold the scales more nicely balanced than he did. It was a fiction, and I have no doubt that at the moment when he turned towards the jury he was no freer than any of us from the judgments that form spontaneously in the mind. He just knew their true value better than we did, and so he was on his guard against them.

"Members of the jury . . ."

They were all attention. You could read many conflicting thoughts in those faces turned to his: dread of the responsibility now so close, bewilderment, an assurance that guidance was on its way, and, above all, the independence of mind which is never far from the surface of a jury, though it seldom finds expression beyond the walls of the jury-room.

Lorne began slowly, leaning forward a little in his chair. You got the impression that he was conscious of them alone. Advocates might thunder for everyone's benefit, but the judge's voice was so low that people in the back of the gallery were hard put to hear him, and you could sense that immense concentration you get sometimes in the concert hall at the beginning of a symphony. It added greatly to the effect, though I am sure it was no part of Lorne's intention and that he was not concerned with us but only with the anxious, perplexed men and women who were his partners.

First, the evidence, which he reviewed in detail. He never had to pause for a word, but everything was in its place, clear and immaculate. Sometimes when dealing with the more intricate or important questions he would refer to his notes, but there was never any of the fussy searching which mars some judgements, but just the quick sideways glance and the almost uninterrupted flow of the voice, never emphatic, particularly at those points where counsel had used emphasis. You could see the relief on the faces of the jury; you could suspect they were speedily unlearning all that had been said before and were accepting words from the fount of Justice.

But where was it leading?

Back to the evidence of the witnesses, free of the interpretations that Marion and Kenyon had put on them. You heard again the officialese of Kent and the scientific doctor, Maudsley's bucolic humour, the militancy of Jane, poor bewildered Mrs. James and the goodness of Miss Saunders. And there emerged gradually a picture which was not pleasant to see, a picture of Justice as she is treated by men and women who pay lip service to her:

"Perjury, members of the jury. It is not a pretty word. We live in an age when the oath seems to have lost its value and whole philosophies are based on lies. Lies are not easy to penetrate. You can only judge by the demeanour of witnesses, the plausibility of the stories they tell and the way they match the facts around them. That is your problem. It is not the only one. There is also the problem of the recollections of human beings and the reliance you can place on what even the most honest say they have seen and heard. The trouble is that we do not all see the same things alike—even advocates in my experience seem to differ in their interpretations," added the judge with a melancholy smile. "There is a no-man's-land between truth and untruth where prejudice and error can operate, and blindness of the eye and dullness of heart. All you can do is to look at the individual circumstances and the men and women testifying before you."

For the next half-hour he examined them, three in particular, Jane and Maudsley and Oldfield, "the three controversial witnesses," as he called them. I do not think that we saw in this quiet analysis a true reflection of the judge's mind, for it was only in the occasional word that the personal peeped out at us: "A very assured witness" (of Jane, spoken in such a way that you could read "cocksure" from it); "A great appearance of frankness" (of Maudsley), and again: "Do not assume that because a man admits to one untruth this necessarily guarantees the truth of all the rest."

No one smiled more broadly than Kenyon at that ironic touch. He was participating still, glancing at the jury as though to underline a point made in his favour, nodding sometimes at the wiser passages, and doodling with elaborate unconcern in those moments when points were being made for the defence and Justice seemed to be tottering a little on her throne. Some might have thought such conduct more suitable to defence counsel but I did not blame him, for he was one of the certain ones, the believers, and could no more help himself than Maudsley could help his lies or Mr. Oldfield his celebrated memory, which now engaged the judge.

"I know you will consider the evidence of this witness most carefully," he was saying to the jury, whose attentiveness seemed to redouble at the words. "Certain charges were made against the witness Birman and you will no doubt give due weight to them. It was suggested that Miss Birman was an interested witness and was shielding someone, but I think you may take it that no parallel allegations were intended against the witness Oldfield. Either he is telling the truth, or he is a seeker after publicity who comes here with reckless falsehoods, or he is a man with so defective a memory that it cannot be relied on.

"Consider these three possibilities, first by themselves, and then apply them to the surrounding evidence.

"If you think he was telling the truth, then you may come to the conclusion that the evidence of Miss Birman is most powerfully reinforced, and, what is more, the accused's alibi is shown to be worthless.

"What of the second possibility? Do you believe it? You have only the witness's manner to rely on. Do you believe that we have here a clinical case, the press-struck person? It is for you to say, drawing on your own knowledge of probabilities, recalling also the factor of his late arrival on the scene. Are his explanations of that acceptable? You will of course carefully consider the suggestions made by the defence in this regard and so eloquently put by counsel.

"There is one other possibility I shall put before you: namely, that the witness was not so much seeking publicity as afraid of it, and that this shrinking from the limelight, natural to most of us perhaps, may have accounted for his delaying.

"Of course that does not explain his memory or lack of it," the judge added, probably feeling that he had leaned over too far the prosecution's way. "You will recall the questions in Miss Kerrison's able cross-examination and the answers to them." He read them again in a neutral voice. "There you have them: the doubts, the inability to remember, the very clear identification in the taxi. No witness deserves more of your attention. Compare most carefully what he says with what the accused and Mrs. James have to say. Weigh and balance them. There is an absolute conflict of evidence in this case, as was stressed at the outset. If you are in doubt—which is not a matter of definition but common sense—then it will be your duty to remember that accused persons in this country are deemed innocent until proved otherwise. There is not so much a benefit of the doubt to be conceded as a *right* to be *enjoyed*. Remember that and remember above all that you have sworn an oath as jurymen to return a true verdict according to the evidence."

He made a gesture of dismissal with his hand, and when the usher had been sworn to guard them the jury rose and filed from the box. Out of their shelter, they had a particularly lost and forlorn appearance, seeming to dissolve in front of your eyes into their component parts, so that instead of a tribunal with the powers of life and death you recognized the company director, the chemist, and the bookmaker's clerk.

As soon as the judge and the prisoner had also left the court we went outside into the corridor, where a few remaining witnesses and plaintiffs from the Civil Court still waited on the benches and the rain beat drearily against the panes. We came to the main doors and looked out into the street. The city was going home. The rain glistened on umbrellas, on the gaily coloured plastic mackintoshes of the shop assistants, and on the great double-decker buses sweeping past in clouds of spray. At the street corners they were selling papers and you could see the news-boards with MAUDSLEY TRIAL FINAL SPEECHES chalked up on them in almost as large lettering as YORKSHIRE ALL OUT, playing away that day in what must have proved a sunnier clime.

"Only a little while longer," I said to Marion with some hope that it might cheer her. I had never felt more conscious of my uselessness. It wasn't that I had expected to examine witnesses or play a great part in the trial, for I had only wanted to protect her and act as her watch-dog, but I had failed her even there and I think we were both glad when

Jaggers came bustling up with the latest rumours from outside the jury-room—about as likely and authentic as news from Lhasa.

"Where's Mr. Hesketh?" she asked him at the first break in the flow.

"Over at 'The King's Head.' "

"Was he in court?"

Jaggers nodded. I don't think he ever appreciated the relationship of trust and dependence between these two. "He was there all through the speeches and Oldfield and that bit of trouble you had."

She turned away from him.

He gave me a glance of reproach, for I could see that he had been reminded of my second dereliction of duty in failing to hold her back and that I was being blamed again—for his own tactlessness into the bargain. "Don't you worry about that, Miss Kerrison," he said in a voice full of foreboding. "It wasn't all your fault. Mr. Kenyon had no right to produce that witness."

"I'm not worrying about myself."

"Well, don't worry about him," Jaggers replied, meaning Maudsley, of course, a man for whom he had never been able to feel any great sympathy. "You did your best," he assured her. "You did pretty well. Mr. Fenney was saying how well you'd done."

We began to walk back towards the robing room. The corridors were more crowded now, for most of the people from the well of the court had left it and were sitting on the benches or strolling up and down. An air of subdued and growing excitement could be felt. There were many policemen to be seen, and once a whole posse of them debouched from one of the side rooms and marched towards the main doors with solemn tread.

In the barristers' robing room you might have been in another world and the atmosphere was pleasantly relaxed, like that of a railway carriage during a night journey. Kenyon was sitting by the unlit fire in the only decent arm-chair the place boasted, with his wig off and a plate of sandwiches on his knee, and the famous pipe, a companion piece to Hesketh's, reposing on an ashtray on the arm of the chair.

"Think they'll be out long?" he asked. "What does that Jaggers of yours say?"

Such affability was a bad sign and I was non-committal.

"My clerk thinks about an hour," Kenyon went on. "He thinks it's a quick jury. Ah, well!" He bit into another sandwich and you could see that he was prepared for the siege, no matter how long it lasted.

The conversation languished. There was a clock in the room, a most unreliable timepiece with a very loud tick-tock. Half-past six. The jury had been out half an hour and you could imagine them huddled around the table in the bleak jury-room downstairs. In the cells near by Maudsley waited. There were none of the prison amenities down there, they said: no cards, no dominoes, none of the small drugs to thought and memory.

Seven struck very loudly and jerkily, but Kenyon, half-dozing in his chair, Marion and Loader working at tomorrow's briefs, paid no heed to it. I could stand it no longer but got up and went outside, and there was Jaggers on the prowl also. No news, not a stirring from the jury-room, yet you could no longer doubt that within those walls a man's fate was being decided, for the atmosphere of expectancy among the people in the corridors was much greater now, a pulsation that was almost tangible.

"It'll be all right, you'll see: just take it easy," Jaggers counselled me. He must have attended a score of murder trials and had developed a truly professional aplomb, but underneath it I could sense that he too was painfully excited. Was he confident or fearful? I felt the greatest inclination to know, but I knew also that it was no use asking, for loyalty came as naturally to him as the propaganda he served out to clients and he would hardly ever admit defeat in advance—or often afterwards.

"How's Miss Kerrison taking it?" he asked as we began our walk.

"Pretty well."

"Ah, she's a good one, the right material, but reckless. That was a bad thing she did. Didn't I warn her about Lorne?"

"You certainly warned me."

"So I did, but I suppose you couldn't stop her. She could get into hot water. Nothing serious," he added, recollecting himself. "What matters is whether she wins, and of course she will. You could see that foreman was impressed."

As we passed the door of the robing room on our second circuit of the corridor we heard the clock strike its single chime for half-past seven, and through the open door we could glimpse Marion's head bowed over her brief. "I'll get her some sandwiches," Jaggers announced, though she had already twice refused them. He was feeling some reflection on himself in the fact that Kenyon was provided for and she was not.

"Don't bother her," I said.

He examined her for an instant and you could sense his admiration and approval for behaviour so like his own. "That's the way Mr. Hesketh was," he told me. "I heard from his old clerk about his first murder case, well before my time—him sitting there, working like that, and the jury out six hours. *You* could learn from that, Mr. Irvine," he said, appreciating suddenly that he could improve the hour.

"But what a time they're taking!" he was murmuring to himself as we came round again to the main doors and saw the streets almost empty apart from a crowd collected on the steps of the hall, watched by a solitary policeman from the shadows of the portico.

Eight o'clock struck from the steeple of St. Mary's church, the cracked chimes that were always good for a letter or two in the columns of our paper in the silly season. The people of our town as a whole were much attached to them. More stragglers joined the crowd staring up at us, and the large body of police inside the hall shuffled and coughed, regretting their lost suppers.

I went back to the robing room where no one seemed to have moved. As I came in Kenyon opened one eye as though he expected I was the bearer of news, and seeing that I wasn't he promptly shut it again and relapsed into agreeable dreams. The clock ticked on, giving a whirr at intervals as though preparing for something.

Nine, and still the same insupportable calm.

Half-past nine.

And then suddenly there was Jaggers at the door making gestures, an important Jaggers heavy with news.

"What's that? Coming are they?" Kenyon demanded, opening both eyes, though this apparition had made no sound.

"So they say, Mr. Kenyon," Jaggers said.

" 'They' will know: they usually do. Are you ready, Loader?"

Stein, who had been reading a detective story in a corner, now came up, and the procession formed and put on its wigs. All three men seemed eminently calm, but I know that I was feeling sorry for myself and Marion, also that I was troubled as I thought of Maudsley down there in his cell and the sudden telltale scurrying of feet he would have heard in the corridor before the summons came.

Outside the robing room, where three passages met, people were hurrying towards the court, and the police seemed to have been taken by surprise, so that for a moment there was a breakdown in control. I saw one large constable trying to bar the way, and on his face the most comically offended expression as he found himself engulfed and borne backward.

"Keep back, go slowly now!" an authoritative voice was exhorting. People began to smile, for it was so evidently a command which each individual in the crowd wanted to obey and the crowd itself did not. We continued to move forward, swaying from side to side. Marion was next to me and I took her arm and tried to clear a space for her, not very successfully, for one really needed Jaggers's frame, which I could see some distance ahead assisting the police with convulsive jabs of the elbow very distressful to his neighbours. We came level with the doors of the court and the double cordon of police drawn across them. Suddenly, magically, there was order; a path was being cleared for us and we were filing in.

Inside the court the lights had been switched on. A battery of them shone directly down on the judge's chair, brilliantly illumining its red upholstery and heraldic arms, and there were lights high up in the gallery, so that you could see the white faces peering down, seemingly more remote from us than by day. Only the dock, placed directly under the front tier of the gallery, was dimly lit, a place of shadow.

"Here they come now," I heard a voice exclaim behind me, and looking round I saw the jury, led by their foreman, filing towards their box. There was a pause, and then the judge came in taking his seat rapidly on the bench, and in the gloom of the dock I distinguished Maudsley with the officers beside him, all standing.

The clerk of Assize had risen. "Members of the jury . . ." They turned towards him and he called over their names. "Members of the jury, are you agreed upon your verdict?"

"We are."

"Will the foreman stand up?"

He did so: a small, nondescript man, like so many other travellers with destiny. In that instant I saw Maudsley clasp his hands on the ledge of the dock and his lips seemed to move, though I do not think he was speaking to his warders or indeed to anyone.

The clerk of Assize did not spare a glance for him. "Do you find John Kelvin Maudsley Guilty or Not Guilty of murder?" he asked the nondescript man, who alone had significance for him.

"Guilty," the foreman said.

I couldn't distinguish any more for the murmurous noise of the crowd, but when the usher had cried out for silence they put the black square of cloth on the judge's head, and he pronounced sentence, and the chaplain, whom I had not noticed before, stood up and added the word "Amen."

Chapter Eight

IMMEDIATELY THE FORMALITIES WERE over, thrusting our way through the crowds whose loud, excited hum of comment filled the hall, we went down to Maudsley, whom we found in a dark cubicle with a barred grating for a window, quaintly called "the interview room." There were two warders with him, and you could see that his importance in their eyes had greatly increased now that he was a convicted man. They had a special watchfulness and care for him—you might almost have called it tenderness.

He came across to us at once, seemingly little altered, though he was certainly paler, almost as pale as Marion who was deeply affected. "I can't believe it," were his first words to us. He was obviously greatly shocked that twelve people could have been found to doubt his story, and he seemed more angry and contemptuous of them than afraid for himself, exclaiming over and over again: "They believed that bitch rather than me!"

We didn't answer, for it was certainly not the moment to mention Mr. Oldfield and the alibi that had destroyed him.

"I thought you had Justice in this country," Maudsley said, not showing at all the spirit I had expected—the mixture of heroism and heroics which Jaggers had assured me was typical of men who have been condemned. What we were seeing wasn't the old Maudsley but someone shriller and with less shine to him, a less likable person, though I think I felt more truly sorry for him then than I had ever done.

"What next?" he wanted to know.

He was told that appeal would be made to the Court of Criminal Appeal.

"We'll show them how that bitch lied," he answered, half to himself, striding up and down the tiny room. "They'll straighten it out and see it the way it happened. They *must* see it—they're sensible men, aren't they? Not a flock of sheep like we had today watching her sheep's eyes. Isn't that right? And will you be there to make them?"

"Yes, if you want me," Marion said.

A little of the old Maudsley came back and he halted opposite her, cocking his head on one side. "Too right I do! But you'd better win this time. Don't you ride too close a race." He must have imagined that he'd offended her, for he came still nearer, as though to touch her, and added: "But I've great faith in you—great faith."

Neither of us spoke as we went back up the stairs into the corridors, empty now except for a few policemen. When we reached the main doors we saw that it was nearly dark outside—a cold night with leaden clouds and a wind rising, rustling the papers and refuse in the gutters.

"Better let me take you home," I said, as we went down the steps on which the crowd had waited that afternoon.

She didn't say yes or no, but followed me to the car. I didn't like her silence or tenseness of manner. I saw that she had played herself out in the weeks of effort, but though I could recognize the approach of the reaction I had no idea what form it would take or whether it might be wise to provoke it now, while she still had me to talk to.

"Why don't you relax?" I said, as soon as I had her safely inside and we were driving through the deserted streets in which the traffic lights continued their vigil, winking busily at one another.

She didn't answer.

"You won't help Maudsley by brooding," I said to her as severely as I could. "It's foolish; does no one any good. Don't you see that?"

She was looking out of the window at the streets of back-to-back tenements and the waste land on which some children were still playing, stooping over the pools which the rain had left among the mud and tufted grass.

"Marion," I said, "do answer. Say anything. You can say anything you like: that I'm a nuisance to you and you don't want to be here."

"That wouldn't be true. I'm very grateful."

"But I want to be of real use, and I could be if you'd only let me. Don't you want to talk about the case?"

She shook her head.

"Why not?" She remained silent, turned away from me in her corner of the car. "It's a bad thing to brood. We're both thinking of Maudsley, as it's natural we should, but we can't afford to 'personalize' him too much. It's not good to get too close to a case. I don't know why I'm reading you a lecture like this. Do you mind?"

"No."

"I mean you can be sorry for Maudsley—that's one thing. But anyone would think that you were blaming yourself for what happened."

She didn't answer or give any sign, but though I had spoken at random, hardly realizing the sense of the words, I saw now that they were true. Perhaps it would have been better to have ignored that knowledge, but men are seldom wise in these things, or merciful, and I slowed down and drew into the side of the road near other cars parked on the waste land, the cars of lovers, strangely forlorn.

"Ah, that's foolish, Marri," I said to her. "He damned himself. No one could have saved him."

I said much more—in reassurance, as I thought—and then I fell silent and we stayed there in the warm darkness, close together, hearing sometimes the sound of voices and laughter borne on the wind. It made one feel very solitary somehow, even more when the moon came out from behind the storm clouds and lit for us these little islands of content in the desolation around us, and the walls of warehouses, bleak as the prison in which Maudsley lay.

That night when I got back to my lodgings I found again that I couldn't sleep. I was troubled with memories: Birman in the box; Maudsley's hands as he waited for sentence; the clerk arranging the black cap on the judge's head—fussily, like a milliner. I found myself wondering if Lorne were sleepless too and whether he could follow the prisoner, as I did, into the cell where the warders sat with the checker-board on the table under the shaded light. I found it strange that Maudsley should obsess me now, at the moment when we had all but done with him, but it certainly wasn't the possibility of his innocence that disturbed me, but rather the conviction of his guilt. It was a paradox that a verdict which others had declared on my behalf should have enlarged the victim in my mind, but so it was, and I found that although I had cared very little for the supposedly innocent man whom I had known for so many weeks, I cared very much that the guilty Maudsley should not die. It seemed to me that at last I was at one with Marion in this: and on that thought I fell asleep.

Next morning—comedy, as one expects of life.

There, by my plate at breakfast, was a paper folded open at the picture page, on which you could discern two figures in the act of going through a door. It is always a shock to recognize ourselves as the world may see us, but Mrs. Jay, my landlady, had no doubts. "There you are, Mr. Irvine, and just fancy!" she greeted me, as she brought my tea, and I could see her looking from the paper to me and back again in an awed way. "Is that Miss Kerrison?" she asked me, pointing to the other figure which walked a pace or two ahead.

I nodded.

Mrs. Jay looked doubtful, for like most landladies she was a mother to her guests, with all a mother's prejudices. "I expect it's not a very good photo," she said, making allowances. It certainly was not, though no doubt the paper had done its best, providing a proper rogues' gallery of us, including Kenyon, a burly figure taking his confidence home with him, and Maudsley arriving in court, with a coat thrown over the handcuffs and a smile on his face not altogether agreeable to behold.

"Who'd ever think he'd done it, grinning away like that!" Mrs. Jay said with a sniff, not appreciating, I think, that I had defended the man, for she naturally assumed that any lodger of hers would be on the side of the angels. The kindest-hearted of women, she was filled that morning with the warm, comfortable sense of righteousness which a "good murder" always induces in the law-abiding. "He's got what he deserves," was how she expressed this, applying the code of automatic rewards and punishments on which she had been brought up.

I found something very compelling in this certainty which was not the result of cocksureness but of a profound moral sense. Mrs. Jay did not invariably believe her neighbours, still less her lodgers—she was not as simple as that—but she had a regard for truth and practised it herself and had a tendency to look for it in others—a refreshing attitude after those with which I had lived for the last two days, and I took care not to bruise it in any way, which was all the easier because I think that I agreed with her in my heart.

The wind had dropped in the night and I drove down to chambers on one of those limpid summer mornings, with big ballooning clouds washed as white as sheets in a detergent poster, and birds singing as though it were still May.

There were no queues outside the Assize Court where a particularly dull company swindle was to be tried; the police were all back at their traffic duties and lurking in the squares to impose the parking regulations on the unwary; and on the steps where the crowd had stood the previous afternoon the corporation dustmen laboured, sweeping up the litter into the finc modern vans emblazoned with the gold arms of the city which shone brilliantly in the sun.

It was so hot and beautiful a morning that the windows were open even in our chambers, and the light poured in on the briefs with their gay pink ribbons, on Jaggers's watch-chain and Belle's summer frock printed with petal shapes of large exotic flowers. She gave me a special smile as I came in, and held up her paper behind Jaggers's back for me to see, pointing vigorously. No smile from the great man himself. He looked depressed and I think it more than likely that he had already visited a few of my sins on that blonde and innocent head. "Seen yourself, I suppose?" he inquired of me, following me into my room.

I expected an attack if not on the publicity, at least on the *kind* of publicity I had been subjected to. But he didn't seem to have the heart for it. "It hasn't turned out at all well," he lamented instead in a lugubrious voice.

"Did you think it would?"

"Why not? I thought she'd be able to do it. I thought she'd do well."

"She did," I replied coldly, moving away from him to my desk.

He saw that I was angry, but he wasn't the man to

spare the rod—and with every stroke you got the impression that it hurt him more, as I believe it truly did.

"You were both all right up to a point," he conceded. "A well-prepared case, and I know you worked hard at it. But *you* didn't watch her and *she* didn't watch the judge . . . and between you . . ." He gestured with his hands. "It was her being a woman did it," he announced, summing it all up.

"What nonsense!"

He gave me a pained look. "All right, Mr. Irvine, but *you* know, for you saw it. No self-control—wasn't that typical? People fasten onto things like that."

"What people?"

His eyes opened wide. "Clients, of course. D'you think I worry about anyone else? They can think what they like over there"—with a rude gesture towards Kenyon's chambers, which could be seen from ours—"but when solicitor clients think it's another matter. She's done herself no good."

He went on and on, and I could see that he was genuinely upset and grieving for her, for his own lost faith and the uncertain future. What he didn't know was that she for her part was concerned only with Maudsley, but when I tried to tell him this he couldn't see it. "Maudsley! But that's done with. And he was Guilty, anyway."

Nor could I make him see that, holding this, he was being illogical in blaming her. "It was the *way* she lost it, Mr. Irvine," he explained. "Getting excitable like that and brawling with the judge! D'you think Mr. Hesketh would have done it? Or Mr. Fenney?"

There are few greater temptations than the desire to play the candid friend. Jaggers was always giving way to it, out of the best of motives, need I add; but for this morning he had to be prevented. "Now just keep off it," I warned him. "Don't say a word to her. She's upset and you must let her settle down." For an instant the awful analogy of killing the goose that laid the golden eggs flashed into my mind and I all but put it to him as an argument; which would have hurt him deeply, for the commercial was never his guiding interest. Fortunately, I held off, receiving for my pains a few grieved reproaches, to the tune that he knew when to be tactful and didn't need reminding.

So far, so good. There were other gauntlets to run, however.

At half-past ten Marion came in. At a quarter to eleven there was the usual morning tea in Hesketh's room. I didn't want her to go. I imagined Serpell at his most wounding and the anxious amiabilities of Fenney which would be worse, but I couldn't think of a reason for preventing her without showing my own doubts. Of course they had all been talking about us. You could see it in the elaborately casual way they looked up when we came in, and Fenney, who always excelled himself on these occasions, was up at once fussing over her, pouring tea for her and rescuing the chocolate biscuits from Serpell's clutches—I could cheerfully have kicked him.

"Bad luck," Hesketh said, intruding some sanity into this atmosphere so strangely charged with malice and knight-errantry. But even he seemed to feel the need for sensibility, and met it in his own way, by trotting out some rude stories he had picked up on the train—they were bluer than usual and you could see Fenney being shocked by them and Serpell's watchful appreciation of what was going on. I kept expecting the thrust, but it never came. Perhaps Serpell was finding enough entertainment in me and my anxiety, which must have been obvious enough; perhaps he was still at heart a little afraid of Hesketh; but in any event he got no credit from me for holding his tongue.

It was an immensely embarrassing ten minutes and I know that at the end of it, when we'd got back to our room, I was up in arms about them. I resented their patronage and clumsiness and even their good intentions. It was an unreasonable indignation, as protective feelings so often are, and what was really at the bottom of it, I suppose, was that I wanted to take Marion in my arms, there in that room among the law reports, the briefs, the litter of our professional lives, and comfort her and tell her that I believed in her; also, far more important, that I loved her.

But routine and doubt are powerful masters. There was Marion at her desk, her head bowed over the papers of the Maudsley brief, and I couldn't be certain that she wanted me to say or do these things. I became aware of how ridiculous it would be if in the middle of it all Jaggers were to come in, or Fenney with his condolences. I would make *her* ridiculous.

At that moment she looked up. She did not seem much changed by the events of the last few hours. There were dark shadows under the eyes and you could guess that she had slept wretchedly, but she seemed very assured and calm—the daunting calmness that was in such contrast with the side of her nature that the trial had revealed.

I felt even my indignation against our colleagues ebb away. I found it natural that I should talk only of the work ahead of us and of Maudsley, not of those other things whose presence I could not detect in her heart.

And the moment passed.

For the next four days we worked together on the Maudsley appeal with a transcript of the judge's summing up before us. It was on this document that the prisoner's hopes now rested. He didn't know it. He would be thinking in terms of an appeal in the sense in which the word is used in everyday speech—as something emotional—but the law is not ordered like that. The time for emotion had passed with the speeches. No court was going to weigh the probabilities again, or Jane's evidence or Mr. Oldfield's memory, for a jury had done this and had pronounced a verdict—so sacrosanct a thing that I think those twelve good people and true would have been surprised to know of it, and as greatly distressed.

Not they but the judge was our target now, though even in his case we could do no more than read what he had said and compare his words with the evidence which had gone before, in search of inconsistencies between them, the so-called misdirections of law and fact. It was not an easy or, on the surface, a very hopeful quest, and as I went through those pages I found myself admiring Lorne, who had achieved a true simplicity. He had wasted no words. There was no forcing or attempt at colour but only a statement of the case and the law in the round, with all the defence arguments clearly set out.

And yet as I put the typescript down after the third reading I found myself wondering if it was only the prejudice his treatment of Marion had aroused in me that was telling me now that all along he had disliked and distrusted Maudsley. I hadn't noticed it at the time, for the spoken word acts as camouflage for thought. But if Lorne had disliked Maudsley, could one isolate, I wondered, the ingredients of that dislike and bias of mind? There were vulnerable passages—one where he had been dealing with the evidence of Oldfield and had advanced his own explanation of why the man had stayed silent for so long.

I pointed these out to Marion who saw their relevance at once, and their weakness too. "What are you saying? Is bias misdirection?" she asked me, with that direct glance of hers.

I replied that if communicated it could certainly amount to that.

"Communicated to whom, Michael? To the jury? Or to you?"

It was really very clever of her to have guessed that the distrust of Maudsley I professed to find in Lorne might be no more than a reflection of my own, and though I believed I had found more solid ground, could I be so sure that I was right? "Read it again," I urged her, and showed her the passage I had marked.

She did so and was full of praise, the most generous I ever received from her. Yet all the time I was conscious that something was wrong. I felt quite certain that she wasn't laughing at me secretly, for that wasn't her way, and I think I can best describe what I felt by saying that there was something perfunctory about it in spite of the apparent warmth, as though she wasn't really interested in what I had to say and regarded it as an irrelevance—which it certainly was not.

"After all, what else have we got to work on?" I said to her to test her out.

She shook her head. "Nothing—except the witnesses."

"What do you mean—witnesses? Have you unearthed some new ones?"

"No."

"Well, what do you mean? Not Birman and Oldfield, surely? You can't call them."

She gave me a glance, the meaning of which I certainly didn't fathom. I think, looking back on it, that the idea that was to guide her future had already occurred to her.

"No, I can't call them, Michael. Of course you're right."

Only a day or two later, however, in the course of a conference with Clive, she used similar terms again as part of a general review of the case. I don't think our friend noticed them particularly—he had seemed strangely abstracted, as though listening to some inner voice beyond her words—but when it was over and I was showing him, as was my custom, to the outer door, he paused, so obviously seeking my confidence that I went back to get my hat and rejoined him on the stairs.

He gave a sigh and remarked what a worrying time

it had been. When I agreed—"And very worrying for Miss Kerrison," he went on. "She's taken it hard, you can see that."

"She was upset."

"You might almost think she was blaming herself," Mr. Clive said suddenly, as though the possibility had just occurred to him. We had reached the bottom of the stairs where the lift attendant was standing, and he didn't add anything more till we were out of earshot in the street, when he turned to me and said with great earnestness: "I don't care what people say, I don't believe that a good fighter ever truly failed and I'd tell her, only you know how it is, she wouldn't let me. She won't be told things. I'm afraid she's very severe."

"I'll be sure to tell her *that*."

He began to smile. "Good, good, only you'd best be careful," and I could see that although he had spoken jokingly he really meant it and had been struck, as I had been, by something in Marion's manner, a kind of repressed emotion, as though you were watching the workings of a clock that was ever so delicately overwound.

"Women take some understanding," he resumed after a moment in an undertone, trying to explain it to himself. "With all respect, they're so personal and take things so much to heart." He paused and I caught sight of his face, full of puzzled concern for her. "She has such trust in the client, Mr. Irvine. Of course we all have in a way. But with her . . . faith, you might call it. You might think she *knows*."

He was clearly uncomfortable with the word.

"She believes in him," I said, helping him down.

"Yes . . . belief . . . a very good thing. Do you think she believes in his chances, though?"

This was so unlike the cautious Mr. Clive that I turned and gazed at him with astonishment.

He gave me an uneasy smile. "There! Think nothing of it. Perhaps I'm knowing things too."

I began at once to defend her against this charge of loss of heart, and Mr. Clive, already repenting of his lapse in discretion, was only too anxious to meet me half-way. It was a "difficult" case now, however one looked at it, he said, which was the nearest he would come to admitting the extreme danger in which Maudsley stood. Naturally Miss Kerrison had to take account of difficulties. All the rest was just an idea he had had—mistakenly, as he could see.

I was left in no doubt, however, as to Mr. Clive's real feelings and fears, which so closely matched my own. Nor were we alone in this, as I was soon to discover. Returning after a hurried lunch, I found Belle by herself in the outer office, perched on the inside sill of the window, dangling her thin and rather pretty legs.

"Better not let Mr. Jaggers catch you like that," I advised her, smiling, for, as I have said, I liked Belle.

She jumped down into the room. "Oh, him! He's out, anyway. And just let him talk!" For some reason I always seemed to have the effect of awakening the Jacobin in her, and though I am sure it was bad for discipline, I must say that the emergence of that spirit always pleased me—besides, Jaggers's dignity was beyond the power of mortal puncturing.

"Is there anyone with Miss Kerrison?" I asked, nodding towards the door of our room.

"No, she's all alone." She gave me a reproachful

look. "You should have taken her with you, Mr. Irvine. She can't get a proper meal like that. Sandwiches again. She'll starve herself."

It so happened that for some time, on and off, I had been waging a campaign against the sad little cafeteria meals that Belle herself indulged in, and I felt justified in retorting: "Well, *you* should know."

"I don't think men notice much," Belle said in a contemptuous voice, ignoring this.

"What should I notice?"

"What I've told Mr. Jaggers. Only of course *he* can't see it either."

I clasped my head in my hands. "Belle, dear Belle, for pity's sake! What did you tell Mr. Jaggers and what couldn't he see?"

She stared at me for a moment, weighing me up. "You know all right," she said. "And you want to look after her, Mr. Irvine, and see she's not worried with this case, and stop people talking about her the way they do."

"You can't say women expect much!" I thought to myself as I went in to Marion, but I was touched by this display of sisterly feeling which is one of the most charming and tender of emotions. I felt a warm regard for Belle and respect for her intuition and for the warning implied in her words—a very just warning, though I could see no way of profiting by it.

Next morning, accompanied by Clive, we went to see Maudsley. I hadn't seen him since the night of the trial but in person he looked exactly as I remembered him, for apparently he'd been eating well and prison life hadn't had any effect on a complexion which had always been sallow, with the leathery tinge that comes of years of exposure to the sun. And yet there was a difference in him. You noticed a certain detachment, as though he were an onlooker standing aside from a problem that didn't concern him.

Not that he was rude or offhand in any way. I think he had always liked Marion—after the first astonishment at a type he had not met before. He had got used to her. I am sure that it pleased him that she had dressed for this meeting with such evident care, in a lighter suit than usual, with a gay red scarf. Certainly he was attentive and kind to her: but it was to the woman he turned, not to the advocate who was explaining the grounds of appeal in which he had shown such passionate interest on the night of the trial.

Only slowly, as she went on, did his mind come back to his own case. He began to ask questions—routine ones at first. What was the date fixed for the appeal? Would he be there in person to hear it?

Assured of this, he became thoughtful. Probably he had suffered more than we had imagined at the hands of Lorne and Kenyon and the jury he had professed to despise. I have often noticed that in such cases the urge towards resignation is surprisingly strong, since defeat is a drug that wears off only gradually, till we taste its true bitterness at the bottom of the glass. I think Maudsley shrank from the idea of another trial and the whole dreadful process of torture by hope. The measure of his courage was the way in which, in the course of a short interview, he turned his back on illusion and faced the future.

It was a gradual process. We didn't lead him in any way. We went in detail through the grounds of appeal, which were quite long enough to impress any layman. All the points I had taken from Lorne's judgement were made, and he seemed pleased with them at first, nodding his head as I read them out, with an occasional glance at Marion to see how she was taking it. She was sitting very still, watching the wall above him where a grey square of daylight filtered in. "Sounds good," he commented at one point. I have seldom hated anything as much as that recital of arguments whose weakness became more and more evident to me. I felt it might be better after all to tell him the truth. Looking up, I saw that he had already begun to learn it. But, "That's good," he said again.

When I had finished there was a long silence. We were all on the defensive against this man whose courage and realism we had misjudged. Mr. Clive was clearly aware of this and of the trend of the prisoner's mind. It was very rarely that he intervened at all at these meetings, but now I was surprised to hear him declare in his weightiest and most professional voice: "You may not know it, Mr. Maudsley, but Miss Kerrison has put in a great deal of work at this case, a great deal of work. And of course Mr. Irvine has also."

"I know that," he said. "I'm very grateful to them both."

He was watching Marion, who had gone very pale.

Perhaps Mr. Clive misinterpreted her reactions or Maudsley's words and thought that sarcasm lay behind the latter, but instead of withdrawing, as all his sober instincts must have hinted to him, he plunged on, revealing, as he did so, the grievances he had done his best for so long to hide:

"It's not been an easy case from the start. There was a lack of candour. You were warned about that. You must understand that everything possible has been done for you, and of course will continue to be done. You owe a great debt to Miss Kerrison. No one could have worked harder. It was under difficulties, though."

"What difficulties?"

Mr. Clive had risen from his seat. Perhaps with his vast experience of criminal work he had caught echoes that Marion and I couldn't hear, and had seen possibilities that I for one had never seen.

"Do you want to know?" he said. "Your alibi, for a start. Think of the two stories the jury heard. They couldn't believe that *both* Oldfield and Birman were mistaken. They couldn't believe that they were *both* malicious. Perhaps they might have dismissed Oldfield. But they couldn't see how even a criminal Birman could have dared identify you unless you'd been there on the stairs. You might, for all she knew, have had an alibi—I'm going to say a real one. How did she *dare*?"

Maudsley hesitated for a second, and watching him I saw in his eyes a flicker of the old smile.

"I suppose she dared because she saw me there that night, the bitch," he said.

Chapter Nine

THERE IS A DRAWING OF THURBER'S somewhere of a middle-class family: mother and father and a small oblong child with downcast, cynical expression. "All right then," the father says. "You're disenchanted. We're *all* disenchanted." That drawing springs to my mind because it represents something of the half-amused, half-contemptuous anger that came over me at this revelation of Maudsley's, destroying the small reliance I had placed on his word. I found him incorrigible, a man who saw moral values as animals see the world around them, in neutral shades, and of course I was right, though it was strange that I should have been so sure of it at a moment when a tale I had always doubted was denied and something was substituted which clearly was nearer to the truth.

But how near? The more I thought about it, the more I found myself accepting it as a confession, or at least as the nearest we were going to get to one. The man was a murderer.

The new story he had to tell naturally made little impact on me in this mood. I listened because I had been paid to listen and it was my duty to continue to represent him as best I could. I began to take down his words. It was true that he had been at "The Towers." He had arrived in Mr. Oldfield's taxi, he said, at ten past six, not, as the witness had thought, at ten to—he had known this because he had looked at his watch. Why, in particular? Because he had come by appointment to see his aunt and he was almost "on the dot."

"What do you mean, appointment?" Marion demanded suddenly, from her place beside me.

"An appointment. You know—by telephone."

"You'd telephoned your aunt?"

I caught the note of excitement in her voice.

"Yes, I'd phoned her—about money, actually—and she asked me over."

"Go on."

Dismissing the taxi in the main road, since the gates into the drive were shut, he had walked towards the house. The front door was open and there were lights everywhere. "I thought it a bit queer," he commented, "seeing the old woman wasn't one to waste a zac. So I went prospecting for a bit. That's when Birman may have seen me. I saw her—right by the window looking out. And a policeman with her, too."

"What was the time?"

About six-twenty-five, he reckoned, though he hadn't checked. "What did I do then?" he went on, anticipating us. "Well, I remembered a thing or two" (he meant the ring he claimed to have stolen and perhaps other peccadilloes of which we hadn't heard). "I thought they'd found out something and maybe I'd been asked round for a reason. So of course I acted shy."

"Did you enter the house?" Marion asked him, looking at him steadily.

"Oh, no."

"You weren't on the stairs?"

"Never—not that night, I mean."

"Did you see anyone hanging about or anything suspicious?"

"No."

"You saw the police officer. Did other possibilities occur to you?"

He shook his head. "Not at first. I thought that copper was there for *me*, my oath I did. But I listened and I heard things—it was the old cook, chiefly, carrying on, the poor old sheila. I guessed then."

"That your aunt was dead?"

"Too right. And murdered, by the sound of it. You can bet it didn't look so hot for me."

So he had gone home, walking to the bus station and then taking a crowded Number 10 which dropped him about 7.30 near Mrs. James's house. There had been the ring to hide after that, and some persuading to do to get the alibi confirmed, and you could guess from his manner the form it had taken; indeed, in all this part of the story you noticed a reversion to type in the suggestiveness, the slang expressions, and the plausible manner that somehow gave you an impression of deceit.

One thing was clear, he wasn't ashamed of his lies, which no doubt had seemed to him necessary, though he was a little uneasy about the effect they might have had on us. "I don't know, I just couldn't tell you at the time," he said, reasoning with us.

"Looked too black for me that way, I reckoned. Was I so wrong?"

I expected the thunderbolt, for I saw from Marion's manner how excited and troubled in mind she was. But all she said was: "I'm afraid it wasn't very wise."

"Maybe not. Anyway, I've told you now."

"An extraordinary person!" Mr. Clive said as we settled down in the taxi to return to town. I was glad that he'd spoken first, for I was brimming over with comments of the kind that you know are foolish before you utter them. "Extraordinary," he repeated. I waited for more. But Marion hadn't spoken—she was sitting far back in her corner—and Mr. Clive's demon of discretion speedily took charge of him again. "There's no doubt it sets a problem," he said to her in his most wary and official voice.

"Yes."

"Though what kind of approach precisely . . ."

"I don't see *any* approach," I broke in.

He gave me what seemed a warning look. "No? Well, it won't be easy, of course. We must go cautiously. There's no denying, though, that what we've heard today is, on the face of it, quite rational."

"It's about the only rational thing we've had from him," I burst out. "And he's told us now! Part of it."

"Quite, quite," Mr. Clive replied soothingly. He took out his watch and looked at it and I saw that he had given me up as a useful proposition for the moment. "Are we going to have a conference about this, Miss Kerrison?" he asked.

"Yes, most certainly."

"Tomorrow perhaps, if it would suit you, when

we've had time to digest it"—he meant when I'd calmed down. "It's important. Wants sleeping on."

"You might think he'd seen a new day dawning!" I said to Marion as soon as we were back in our room. I was in a sour mood. I had never had any faith in Maudsley or his alibi, and I had been right, and yet far from getting any credit for my good sense or my heroic resistance to the urge to say "I told you so," I had been snubbed by Mr. Clive. That was another grievance to add to the knowledge of weeks of wasted time. But I was annoyed with Marion too: for being gullible, and over-gentle, and mistaken in her judgement. I couldn't make her out. Her silence in the taxi had suggested suppressed excitement rather than the despair I had expected to see in her and to comfort with reassuring words. That was perhaps another reason for my irritation with her. "I don't know what he was thinking of," I grumbled, using our good friend as a stick with which to prod her into activity. "He seems almost to believe that story."

"Yes," she said.

"You could sound more surprised."

"But I'm not."

"You don't mean *you* believe it, Marri?"

I suppose I had known from the start, only I hadn't cared to recognize it. I didn't like to think that perhaps all the things they said of her were true and she was no more than emotion with a clever tongue.

"But you can't mean it!" I cried, arguing as much with myself as with her. "It's not reasonable. Sentiment's one thing. You can feel sorry for him. . . ." I broke off, for I could see from her expression that she guessed the thoughts passing through my mind.

"He's just a liar," I said hotly. "He lied to you and you took it."

She was looking at me, her head slightly tilted to one side, and I realized that these words had lost all power to hurt her. "You don't deny that?" I went on, puzzled by this reaction.

"Of course I don't deny it."

"Well then?" I paused to let her explain, to excuse herself perhaps. "Look here, Marri," I told her when she didn't answer, "we've got to take the man as he is. There's no point in having illusions about him. First he never took a ring. Then a ring's found in his house. But he was still never at his aunt's that night. Now he admits it. But he wasn't inside. Where's the end of it to be?"

"You tell me, Michael."

"Oh, no, I'm not going to say he did it. That goes too far. What I do say is that he's a liar by nature who doesn't understand what truth is, utterly unreliable. . . ."

"Even when the facts fit what he says?"

I stared at her. "Facts? What facts?"

"The telephone call, for one," she replied promptly. "Don't you see that it explains things?"

"I certainly don't."

"Suppose Birman had overheard that call? Then she'd *know* that Maudsley was coming soon after six that night. Suppose she planned the robbery that way —so that ten minutes afterwards there'd be a convenient suspect in the house?"

"Suppose, suppose!" I burst out in irritation, and disappointment too, for she always had the power to fire my imagination and make me over-expectant.

She didn't let that divert her but went on just as

though I hadn't spoken: "Only, you see, it became *more* than a robbery, Michael. No wonder she was looking out of the window for him. She couldn't be sure he hadn't seen something—the other man, or worse. I expect she dithered for a bit, uncertain what to do, a bit afraid of setting the constable on and starting the hue and cry. But by the time Inspector Kent had arrived she's made up her mind. So she identified Maudsley to him—*to be sure of being first with her story.*"

"*If* there ever was that call," I objected. "You haven't proved it." But my words sounded half-hearted, even to me, for the fact was that I was almost inclined to believe her. There was logic in it, and it was true that it explained the problem of the identification that had bedevilled our thoughts from the beginning. "The call can be checked anyway," I said.

"Not directly. It was from a call box. But there were incomings that morning, remember? The telephone records showed two."

"Unaccounted for, ycs, I remember. And the rest fits in. Fanciful, but it fits. So why the false trail? He must be the biggest fool."

"That's *much* better, Michael."

I went over to her and took her hand. "You know, you're a perfect devil, Marri," I said. "You nearly had me sorry for you there."

"I know."

"You know too much; you're too clever by half. You know me too well."

It was true. Maudsley and his problems were beginning to seem shadowy to me, but she for her part still had room for nothing else, and gently she withdrew her hand.

"So long as you really believe all this?" I said, a little doubtfully again.

"Yes, I believe it."

"So what will you do?"

"Do? Not much with the court, for they won't listen. Let's have a look at the reports on X and Birman."

I took them out of their folder—a series of day-to-day summaries by our detective, Fox, and his assistant. The daily routine of Jane was there for our inspection, from the early days before the trial: it continued to achieve a most purposeful monotony:

Female Subject visited employment agency in the morning. Lunched alone. Returned early lodgings. Morning at lodgings. Went to the Forum Cinema at 2 p.m. Returned for tea.

Subject visited agency again. Went shopping in city centre. Met no one. Returned for lunch and remained indoors.

X seemed to be more socially inclined. We had a name for him now—one Berg, a Pole with a good war record, now naturalized and in business as a general dealer, with a small store behind his lodgings at Number 19 Fawcett Street, a rolling stone, living no doubt in the no-man's-land on the far side of respectability, but without a police record that Fox could trace.

On June 22nd, for instance, while Jane was at her agency, this "Male Subject" (as the Report sternly called him) attended a sale in the city, took part in a mock auction, visited a public house, and followed this activity with an afternoon in his store and an evening at the "dogs." One of the "wide boys," you would have said. But his photograph, caught for us by Fox in a sly moment, hardly bore that out: a smallish, quietly dressed man, clean shaven, more like a bank clerk than anything else.

There was a contradiction here: and another between the man's trade and Jane, the army officer's daughter, the companion of old ladies. Of course one had to take account of the legendary magnetism of this attractive Polish race—there might be more to Berg than met the eye in a photograph, something irresistible and of a kind to appeal to the sheer sexuality in Jane, of which we might not have taken sufficient account. It was a contradiction which Fox, when we sent for him, resolved by a suggestion that did him honour (seeing that it might have spelt the end of his commission): "Do you think, Miss Kerrison, that perhaps the meeting between him and the Female Subject was—how shall I put it?—just random and accidental? Maybe she called on business. There's no other connection I've been able to trace between them."

We considered this very seriously—as seriously as people can treat a suggestion which contradicts every preconception they have made. I found it hard to believe that any casual thing could have brought Jane to a man's room so late at night: the idea of a conspiracy of some sort between them was too strongly implanted in us. And yet, if they had conspired, where had they met to do it or to get into bed with one another? I quite discounted love—it seemed alien to them—but that the sex motif had played some great part at least with Jane I did not doubt, and were we to assume that she had only indulged it once? No, they had met before; they had met many times, I thought, remembering Jane in court, the thin, feline look of her.

"Have you tried his landlady at Fawcett Street?" I asked.

Mr. Fox shook his head. "Too dangerous, Mr. Irvine. It would put him on his guard."

"The neighbours, then?"

"Ah, yes, I've tried them, but they don't know anything beyond some gossip about a woman they've heard sometimes late at night, but it could be anyone. He's a sly one, and if they've met . . ." He paused for a moment, thinking it over. "They'll have spread it out—sometimes at Fawcett Street, sometimes down at that shed of his in Vincent Square, where it's quiet at night, and hotels now and then. It's almost impossible to check."

There was now little time left to us before the Appeal. We had still a great deal to do and had other work as well, though it was noticeable that the flood of briefs for Marion had dried up somewhat and Jaggers was gloomily watching his prophecies come true. It was an anxious time for us, during which the first flush of our new belief in Maudsley died. It had seemed simple to point out how the pieces of the jigsaw puzzle fell into place once you accepted that Birman had known of Maudsley's visit to the house, but on reflection we saw that we could never call the man to swear on oath that all he had sworn on oath before was nothing but a pack of lies. No court would listen to him or even permit him to be called. There were also Fox's words to be digested, the leaven of which worked uncomfortably in us, with its suggestion that the whole basis of our theory was wrong.

It was on a Tuesday, a week before the day we expected the Appeal, when Jaggers was already busy with our London reservations, that I received another report from Fox. I had returned from lunch to find the familiar envelope on my desk, and opening it, with the distaste I had come to feel for it, I read:

Last night at 9.30 Female Subject proceeded to the house, No. 19 Fawcett Street. Was admitted by Male Subject. Soon after ten, Male Subject was observed drawing the curtains of an upstairs room. A light was observed to be switched on. At 11.35 Female Subject appeared at the street door, alone. She let herself out and proceeded homeward to her lodgings.

"Take a look at that," I said to Marion when she came in, handing her the note. She read it and her face lit up. "You see!" she exclaimed triumphantly. She was excited, as I was, by this news after the weeks of failure. It was like watching a curtain go up—one of those gauze curtains beyond which we see in the gradually increasing light the figures of dancers on a stage.

"You see we were right. We *were* right, Michael. I knew it."

While she was speaking I had taken up the envelope in which the report had come, and it seemed to me that there was another note inside it.

There was: an appendix to Mr. Fox's discovery that had so greatly pleased us, an apologia, written in a much smaller hand:

This morning at 9.5 Male Subject left the house, proceeding on foot to the tram stop at the corner of Grange Road. Caught a Number 3 tram into the city and proceeded to the Piercey Street arcade. Subject had manifested a certain restlessness and suspicion. He commenced to walk fast. At 9.34 he entered Grace and Perrott's store. At 9.45, since he had not re-appeared, inquiry was made for him inside. One assistant recalls seeing a person answering to his description near the back premises of the shop. There was no trace to be found of Subject, who must be reported as having temporarily evaded observation.

"The buffoon!" Marion cried, when she had read this. I suspect that she was thinking less of Mr. Fox's failure in the difficult conditions of the arcade than of the phrasing of his report, the last sentence of which has always been a favourite of mine. "We've lost Berg now."

"Only 'temporarily,' " I said. I felt as bad about it as she did but I couldn't see any good in getting worked up about it and devouring poor Fox, who had tried his best and had brought us some real news into the bargain. "The fact is, Marri, it was too big a job. Berg was bound to get wind of him. You need the police for a job like that."

"So you do," she replied, sitting up in her chair. "And why shouldn't we have them?"

"We can't go to the police," I objected.

"Bar etiquette, you mean? Well, perhaps we can't. Why shouldn't Clive go, though?"

"I suppose he might."

Mr. Clive was apparently perfectly willing; he was

a man of great persistence and tact. I thought he would need it with Kent, an excellent man but cagey, as policemen have to be.

Clive found him on the Thursday in his office at the police station—a little bare cheerless eyrie full of graphs put up by the statistical department to prove the sinful state of our city. I think the preliminaries of that meeting must have been amusing: the perfect discretion of two old friends meeting in the no-man's-land that divides the opposing parties in a law-suit. But at last, when Mr. Clive had refused his second cigarette and the inspector was puffing away at his pipe, the onus will have been squarely laid on our champion to begin and he will have outlined our case—the proved and secret meetings between Birman and Berg, the suspicious behaviour of the Pole in evading poor Mr. Fox.

Inspector Kent seems to have listened to this with his usual courteous attention. "What it amounts to," he said at last, "is that you want me to find the fellow?"

"Yes."

"You know we checked up on him after the allegation made in court?"

"I thought you would."

"Well, Berg has no record, not even a parking offence, and *you* can't say that for yourself, now can you?"—for Mr. Clive, most law-abiding of men, had been one of the victims of the unending war of attrition waged by the police on the motorists of our city and had been wounded to the tune of ten shillings and costs. "No," the inspector had continued, "he may be a foreigner, but you can't hold that against him. He's quiet, not like some; his business is well conducted and there's no suggestion of receiving stolen goods or anything like that. Mind you, I don't say we're infallible."

"But you believe he's innocent?"

So direct a question appears to have inspired Kent with that mixture of canniness and candour that was peculiarly his own.

"He hummed and hawed a bit," Mr. Clive said, repeating the conversation to me next day. "He reckoned he didn't know how much he ought to say to me, or me to him for that matter. But then he came right out with it. 'I'm going to be straight with you, Mr. Clive. To me, Berg isn't only innocent; he's irrelevant. He doesn't come into it. I've got the right man in gaol there. Did you know Maudsley had a record of violence Down Under? Street brawling—what the Aussies call "bashing," and it sounds the right word. He was drunk at the time. And that's another thing. He was never at the cinema that afternoon: he was in the pubs down by the arcade.' "

Nothing could have been clearer than that the inspector was convinced by his own case, but Mr. Clive seems to have borne up very well.

"You never found any more of the jewels, though," he objected.

This was a sore point with the inspector, who had a tidy mind. He was forced to admit that the police were "not fully satisfied" about the jewels, which, being translated, meant that they were puzzled to death by them.

"What do you think Maudsley did with them?" Clive asked, rubbing salt into the wound.

The inspector seems to have suggested that they had been "disposed of."

"Free, gratis, and for nothing?"

"Well . . ."

"You found fifty pounds on him, no more and nothing extra in his bank account. Do you think he's a philanthropist?"

I dare say that Kent was regretting by then his admirable frankness. He could do no more than suggest that Maudsley had hidden the jewels or the proceeds or may have been working with someone he'd come to trust. In any event the police net was cast for the jewels and they would be found, though such operations by the nature of things took time and patience. There was a check on jewellers and "receivers."

"But not on Berg?" Mr. Clive said, intervening.

"Because he's not a jeweller or 'receiver.' "

"So far as you know?"

"So far as I know."

"Though he's connected with the case through Birman?"

"So are a great number of people," Kent said, and went on to read him a lecture on the respectability of Jane, who had long since been canonized by the Crown. "We've nothing against either of them, and nor have you," the inspector declared, feeling no doubt on firmer ground, and ended with a Parthian shot: "Your Pole's no more than a name and a guess. Would you dare subpoena him?"

There was really no answer to that, nor did we attempt one. The more we came to think about it, the more clearly we saw that Kent was right, for there was no "lead" to the suspect, nothing to connect him to the case, no question we could ask him that wouldn't be blocked by a simple denial. Yet what else had we? Only the grounds of appeal I had drafted—a kind of shadow-boxing, as we knew in our hearts, a polite fiction of argument which the court, also with politeness, would reject.

Gradually, as these thoughts became clearer, a mood of despondency settled over us, helped no doubt by the nervousness of counsel due to appear for the first time in the Court of Criminal Appeal. Jaggers naturally did his best to help us. "Don't let her try any fireworks, Mr. Irvine," he counselled me, impressing the gravity of this advice by smart taps on the arm. "The Lord Chief Justice won't stand for it. Logic's what you want to aim at. Reason. Give them the *facts*."

There was to be a dinner in the bar mess that Friday night, Grand Night, as we called it, when the judges on Circuit came as our guests, and the thought of the noise and the wine and good fellowship seemed at that moment an attracive one. "Come on, I'm with you," I called to Ross, who happened to come through the office providentially, hat in hand, sporting the carnation he always wore to grace these occasions.

He led me first to the wine bar where I had taken Marion on the night I heard of her entry into the Maudsley case. The same patrons seemed to be there and they gave us the same challenging stares, cheerfully returned by Ross, whom nothing discomfited. I had feared that he might try and pump me or say something about Marion I should be forced to resent, but I needn't have worried, for he was concerned as always with his approaching marriage, and the continued obduracy of Vivienne which was always implied, though never directly referred to now that there was an engagement on record in the columns of the *Yorkshire Post.*

Time passed agreeably and I found I had forgotten what an absorbing topic Vivienne could be. At seven, restored to our old intimacy, we drove down to the mess. Almost the whole galaxy was there. I saw Kenyon and his myrmidons, the London contingent, Gilroy, Hesketh, and Fenney, Stein, the Circuit "junior" whose duty it would be to propose the loyal toast, the leader of the Circuit, Arthur Hillary, and in a corner, talking with his "brother" of the Civil Court, Mr. Justice Lorne in a suit as immaculate as Gilroy's, with a pearl-grey tie and a watch-chain with a beautiful gold fob.

I suppose that judges see Banquo's Ghost at every dinner they take with the Bar: the reflections, in the familiar faces around them, of murderers long since condemned and rotting in their prison graves. It is certainly not callousness that preserves their appetites, though it is possible when you are very close to such events to imagine this, and I know that I was watching Lorne in no friendly way as he sat down at table, spreading his napkin and waiting for the wine to be poured into his glass.

"What's the matter? Expecting it to choke him?" Gilroy said, having descended several places in the hierarchy just for the pleasure of being near me.

I gave a sigh, for there was no Vivienne to distract this keen observer of the foibles of others.

"You can take it from me that Lorne *always* dines well, particularly towards the end of an Assize," Gilroy assured me, looking at the soup now set in front of him with the same doubting glance he used for witnesses.

At the first mouthful he began to cheer up. "Say what you like about Stein," he said, "and practically everyone does—but you've got to allow the food's better since he took over 'junior.' You seem to be going a bit slow, however, Michael. Lost your appetite?"

I tried to engage Ross, but he was involved in a story someone was telling farther down the table, and Gilroy was soon able to recapture me—all the more easily because I half-wanted to hear the worst that was being said about us and knew that no one would put it better. I had to wait for his most artistic efforts, however.

"Pity Kerrison can't come to these little dinners," he resumed with the roast, getting into the rhythm of the thing.

I made some non-committal answer.

"Perhaps she wouldn't want to," Gilroy said, circling the wine in his glass. "Over-sensitive. Or maybe she just isn't convivial? I'm asking you because you know her so well."

"I think that must be it."

"Well, don't you? You've *experience* of her, haven't you?"

"In the pure sense you mean it, Gilroy—yes."

He nodded his head and I felt sure he was giving me more credit than he had done for a long time.

"I expect she'd be too busy for us, anyway," he said. "Working on that *cause célèbre* of yours. When are you off?"

"Pullman—Monday."

"You say that very calmly. Has the drama run down a bit?"

"There isn't any 'drama.'"

He looked at me over his glass. "What's the matter, Michael? Your cocks won't fight? *She*'ll find one that will, don't worry. Something or someone. Your game is only just beginning."

I was hardly listening. The hum of voices around us had greatly increased in volume. Cosy red-shaded lights shone down; the port decanters were being brought in, each with its chain-necklace and date; there was a rich gleam of mahogany and silver; and even with Gilroy there to pester me I felt relaxed and happy, part of a pattern that had been old when Sergeant Buzfuz was a junior and Dodson and Fogg innocents whom even their mothers could take in.

"I don't think you were with me," Gilroy was saying, without rancour, for he was always prepared to be patient with his listeners. But he couldn't make much headway against Ross and some of the other juniors who, after three or four glasses, were inclined to shout "Shop!" at him on principle, and mentally jostle him. "All right: later," his expression seemed to say, and he sat back in his chair, raising his eyes till he resembled a missionary dining al-fresco among the aborigines. The noise grew louder. You could hear the clink of coffee cups being carried from the kitchens and see Stein looking anxiously up table, judging his time for the toast, with one eye on the waiters to make sure that the glasses were being charged.

This was the part of Grand Night that I liked best. I loved the sudden silence before the Queen's health was drunk, the first curls of cigar smoke drifting under the lights, the port decanters passing. It gave you a warm and companionable feeling to be among so many people whose thoughts, at least in these moments, were tuned to your own—in silence, in the renewed burst of voices, and silence again as the leader of the Circuit got slowly to his feet.

Hillary's party piece. I have heard many imitations. Every music-hall comedian thinks he can do the dialect of our town, and does it at the drop of a hat. But Hillary *was* our town while he was speaking: its blood and sinew and its inward thought. There was no condescension about it, no sense of parody. You didn't laugh at him, but through his eyes at the comedy of life—rather a grim comedy, with the hearse just round the corner and the bailiffs moving in. "Maudsley would have liked that," I found myself thinking as I listened, recognizing the same mixture of tragic fact and the madly banal word. Since he was seldom out of my mind it was natural to think of him at that moment and to remember his humour and fatalism as expressed at the crises of his life—valedictory thoughts, for I didn't doubt any longer that he was lost and that the next occasion would be the grimmest of all.

A dead case: I knew it and everyone else knew it too. Only Gilroy had felt free to indulge his fancy at my expense by imagining the opposite—in words, only the gist of which remained to tease and anger me a little, as we are angered by a joke at the wrong time.

I remembered more clearly when I got back to my lodgings late that night to hear that Marion had rung me several times. It was something of the utmost urgency and importance—so the message went.

Chapter Ten

ALL THIS TIME MR. FOX HAD BEEN "pursuing" (as he would have put it) his inquiries. The disappearance of Berg had been a help in a sense, releasing his energies into other necessary channels. Every second day, alternating with his assistant in the watch on Birman, he had been visiting the jewellers and antique shops of our city, spreading his net as far as the grimy fringe of inner suburbs where the pawnbrokers resided, so many sentinels on the pockets of the poor. Nothing of interest resulted from all this, but Fox was not discouraged —he was doing what he felt to be a necessary job, and he was being paid for it, which is a marvellous encouragement.

On the Thursday before the Appeal, on the morning that Mr. Clive visited Kent, Fox reported himself at the usual time at the end of the street in which Jane Birman lived. A routine had become established. Jane would emerge soon after ten, turn right towards City Road, take a 15 tram, descend at the Technical College, and walk to the agency, emerging again about 11.15 for a brief jaunt into the shopping centre and a snack-bar lunch.

On this morning, however, Fox, watching desultorily from his street corner, was astonished to sec the quarry emerge from the house and come at a brisk pace towards him. He had to dodge out of the way, probably not too well pleased if the truth were known, for routine imposes its own charms.

Jane proceeded up the hill, caught a tram in Grange Lane, going northwards away from the city, and got out on Birton Moor (which is a desolate waste at the end of the tram tracks).

Fox, trailing purposefully in his little car, guessed her destination then. She was going by bus to Wakeby, a smaller companion-piece to our city, ten miles away, all blackened Gothic towers and pinnacles.

The purpose of the expedition, however, remained obscure, for there seemed no method in Jane's wanderings. She had a cup of coffee in a big store in the town centre, visited the market, and then wandered out along the Manchester Road among the mills and factories with their sprouting chimneys, as much a matter of competitive pride to Victorian builders as campaniles in Tuscany.

At one o'clock she returned and lunched at a snack-bar near the main cinema, a focal point from which you could watch the solid citizens of the town going about their business with that peculiarly West Riding look of keeping down appearances, all caution and good sense.

Fox was now satisfied that this was a rendezvous, and was anticipating at every moment that his second suspect would appear. But time passed and nothing happened. At two, Jane, who in the words of another of his reports was "manifesting a certain restlessness," went out and took up her seemingly aimless wanderings, backwards and forwards across the town. Had she come by appointment? Fox began to wonder. Had Berg fought shy of the danger of the meeting, or was it no more than a speculation on Jane's part, an attempt to find her elusive partner?

At four, after tea in the same bar, with its plate-glass windows overlooking the street, Jane gave up the quest and caught a bus back to the moor. Fox, however, remained behind, telephoning to his assistant to take up the watch next day. He spent the night in Wakeby (running up a modest bill at a commercial hotel), and first thing on the Friday morning, acting on his conviction that Berg was in the town, he began to tour the jewellers' shops, of which there were more than you would have expected at first sight, reticent shops that lured you in with a few cheap watches and wedding rings and then displayed in their show-cases gems of a surprising brilliance.

Just before tea-time, Fox arrived at a shop a little way from the town centre, the most modest he had visited, in whose windows were exhibited placards announcing: GOLD AND SILVER COINS BOUGHT, ALL KINDS OF JEWELLERY FOR SALE OR PURCHASE, while even the pieces of jewellery themselves had little tabs attached to them—UNIQUE PURCHASE, NOVELTY BRACELET, SUITABLE WEDDING GIFT, and so on.

Fox went inside. There seemed no one there, until there suddenly emerged from behind a high partition of the kind one sees in chemists' shops a bird-like man with a magnifying glass still fixed in his eye.

This was Mr. Marcus Green, proprietor of Marcus Green & Rayner (long deceased).

Fox, a man of wide experience, had varying techniques for dealing with the people he encountered in the line of duty—affability, abruptness, admiration, and downright curiosity. He seems to have dealt gently with Mr. Green, asking to see samples of jewellery—rings and necklaces; "nothing expensive," he explained, with just a hint that he was more substantial than his clothes would lead one to suspect.

An assistant had come in, presumably from an early tea, and Mr. Green, overcoming a natural caution, opened his showcases and took out a gold chain set with emeralds and a turquoise ring. Fox examined them, saying all the right admiring things. He expressed himself as flattered at being shown these gems, which must be of high value.

"Bargains, nevertheless," the jeweller said.

That might be so. But were there, perhaps, other pieces of the same or higher quality? Diamonds, now? He was interested in diamonds, and sapphires also. Were there, perhaps, diamond rings or pendants, which always attracted the ladies?

Mr. Green nodded. He must have placed Fox now as one of those elderly admirers whose activities are always helpful to trade, and he went behind the partition at the back of the shop, returning with a black box which he opened with a key.

These rather secretive goings-on aroused Fox's interest. He had in his pocket the list of the missing jewels, with a photograph that had been taken for insurance purposes, and one can well imagine the eagerness with which he scanned the offerings now laid out for his approval. He saw, at once, however, that his optimism had been deceived. There were diamonds there, but comparatively small ones; even a pendant, but it was an over-ornate and bad piece of workmanship which no jeweller would have dared to show to old Mayor Maudsley, that connoisseur of the solidly respectable.

He gave a sigh, regretting his wasted time.

But he had said diamonds, and diamonds he was to see. Mr. Green became insistent. He brought another box, lined with wool, full of small unmatched stones, some of them mere chippings, and when these too were rejected the assistant was sent into the window to ferret out some of the bargains displayed to public view. They were brought back in handfuls and placed on the glass-topped case in front of Fox.

Sadly, a trifle warily, for he had become conscious of his own false colours, our man examined them. Marked with a tag, UNIQUE VALUE, and priced at fifty pounds was a pair of diamond ear-rings which he recognized at once.

It was on his list.

Chapter Eleven

FOX'S ACTIONS IN THE MOMENTS succeeding this important discovery which his own vision and hard work had made possible were beyond praise. It requires tact of a high order to disappoint salesmen who have entertained hopes of selling you diamonds, yet Fox seems to have managed it with some aplomb. He became at once the trained investigator, so official that Mr. Green, perhaps imagining that he had the police to deal with, was co-operative, remembering all sorts of useful things about how the jewels had come into his possession three days before. Fox took all this down, obtained a signature, together with an expression of the jeweller's goodwill which was not the least remarkable thing in the whole proceeding, and returned in triumph to Mr. Clive, to whom he made a full report.

Clive himself hastened over late that same night to Wakeby to see the witness, telephoned his news to Marion, and next morning called on us in chambers in a state of some excitement. "It's all quite true,

Miss Kerrison. He'll give evidence. He seems a willing man."

"Not too willing, I hope," I said, remembering Maudsley's evidence.

He turned to reassure me. "I don't think you need worry, Mr. Irvine. He seems a very cool, competent sort of fellow."

"Certain of his facts?"

"Oh, quite certain. It happened so recently, you see."

Of the potential value of the witness there could of course be no doubt at all, for if the court would allow us to call him, which seemed likely on the face of it, we were now armed with evidence wholly favourable to our case. For all that, I confess to have been a little apprehensive at first. It all seemed so providential, so exactly the kind of thing we had been hoping for, and I suppose my experiences at the trial had made me unduly suspicious of witnesses and the vagaries of fate.

Mr. Clive's word and the witness's statement were enough to dispel that feeling after a while. It was clear that there was no mistake about the jewels; indeed, there was a directness and certainty about the words of the man's statement that carried great conviction. The tide was turning, and it came as no great surprise to us when late that day we heard that Berg was once more back at Fawcett Street, where we could reach him if we wanted. After some debate on the tactics of the matter we determined to subpoena him—and there we rested, content for the first time since the collapse of Maudsley's alibi.

Two days later we left for London on the morning Pullman. I didn't greatly care for it as a train, for I preferred more room for my legs and luggage, but it was the professional and business train and Jaggers had insisted on it. As we pulled out we could see him near the barrier in his dark coat and grey striped trousers, looking smaller than usual, as people on platforms somehow do. I don't think he really trusted us out of his sight. "Don't think you're going on Assize," he had warned me, handing up the brief cases and the woollen bags in which barristers keep their wigs and gowns. "If you're in doubt, play safe. You've got the hotel reservations?"

"Yes."

"And you know the address of chambers in the Temple? Fairley will look after you; I hope you'll soon get used to him." Fairley was the clerk who by arrangement "stood in" for Jaggers whenever any of his barristers were in town.

"Jaggers was having Doubts again," I reported to Marion, who had been down the coach talking to a woman she knew.

"About the case?"

"About us getting lost and not loving Fairley. I'm afraid we've been a trial to him."

The train emerged from the station into the sunlight. You could see the rows of houses, their outlines softened in the haze, so that they fitted into the mosaic bowl of the city rimmed by the distant hills. The sky was so blue that even the canals and the little ruined rivers we crossed had a countrified and innocent look, and soon there were fields of a sort around us, cows grazing in the shadow of factories, and hen-runs full of shifting patterns of brown and white.

The train ran rapidly on and there was exhilaration

in its movement, the sense of endeavour that attends the beginnings of journeys. All the unpleasant fears that had troubled me for so long seemed to have vanished, so that I felt in myself a stirring of excitement that would probably have surprised and alarmed Jaggers very much.

"Only a few more hours now," I said to Marion.

"Yes."

"How do you feel?"

"Much as you do, I expect."

"Well, I feel good, Marri. Such a beautiful morning. Do you remember how it rained for the trial?"

"Yes."

"And the queue out there in the rain, and the damp smell everywhere?"

"It was a sad beginning," she said.

"But it all feels different now, don't you agree? The whole feel of the case is different since Green came in. Of course he may need careful handling."

"I've thought of that."

"And Berg?"

She opened her brief case and brought out the file, with the photograph clipped to the top page. We looked again at the small tidy features, the neat suit, the thoroughly commonplace *petit-maître* appearance of the man. You could believe that Jane had been the leader and instigator of the plot: if that were not so, then this mild appearance of Berg must be a pose, something deliberate, the suppression of a personality that had aroused in Jane the will to defy the law, conscience, caste, and the natural compassion of women. Such a force must be strong indeed, as strong as the bond that brought Ethel le Neve to the shadow of the gallows for one puny, ineffective man. Could one, I wondered, have inferred so much from the photographs of Crippen that filled the papers at the time? Should one infer it here—the magnetism that had drawn her to brief moments of passion in that upstairs room, the shadows on the blind?

"I don't know about Berg," Marion answered slowly, and I have no doubt that the same thoughts were passing through her mind. "We know so little about the kind of person he is. We mustn't have preconceptions about him because of his race or what we believe may have happened between them."

"Love?"

"Such a wide word, Michael! Who knows what she may have felt for him? Desire? Fear, perhaps? Or he for her, for that matter. The one certain thing is that he'll be *our* witness, sitting there behind us."

"If he obeys subpoena."

Her face hardened. "He'll come all right: it would be madness not to. But he's a clever fellow, Michael, as we should know by now."

"What can he do, though?"

She shrugged her shoulders. "Put it this way: what can I do? What can I ask him? In effect we're calling him to do no more than admit that he's the original of the snapshot, and that's a long way from the confessional. He's our witness. I won't be allowed to cross-examine him."

"Perhaps he'll volunteer something," I said.

"That's our hope. If he talks."

"As Maudsley did."

"Yes, just like that. The chance word; the small failure or weakness, as Clive keeps putting it."

"I think he will," I said, feeling the sudden conviction that it would be so. "You can win this, Marri."

"You think so?"

"All you have to do is to believe it."

She looked straight at me. "Well then, I do," she answered, and there was a light in her eyes that I hadn't seen before.

I sat back in my chair. There seemed no need to say any more. The papers were on the table before us: the Appeal, the depositions of the witnesses, all the familiar things, a little sad and tattered now. As the train raced on through the early afternoon and the wide Midland fields gave way to the market gardens and golf courses of the London suburbs I thought of Maudsley, and tomorrow's case that had seemed lost and now gave hope again. But I had my personal reasons for happiness.

Chapter Twelve

WHEN I WAS A PUPIL AT THE BAR, doing my year in London chambers, I used often to go across the Strand from the Temple and spend the day in the Law Courts, that curious pepper-potted building near the site of Temple Bar. The story goes that when it was to be built, and a competition was held to find the best design, two plans in particular commended themselves—so equally that no one could decide between them. The outside of one was therefore chosen and the inside of the other, and they were told to get along together.

I believe that story. There is a pleasantly crazy touch about it that helps to humanize the all too logical things that go on at the heart of the labyrinth through which you could wander for ever unless rescued by an attendant, or clerk, or registrar, or the Lord Chief Justice himself. It is a ridiculous building, but it is ridiculous in the grand manner. It grows on you. It has a perfectly useless hall as large as a cathedral. It has a room called the Bear Garden, full of furious litigants, where Dickens would feel himself at home. It has vast numbers of Gothic rooms. And, on another and more transcendent plane, it houses the Court of Criminal Appeal.

We robed in the Temple, the rookery of lawyers' chambers that lies between the Strand and the river. Our host for the day—a very nominal one—was Parks, Q.C., Hesketh's old master, whose name appeared at the head of a list of counsel on a dirty board on a dilapidated staircase; but it was Fairley, Jaggers's *vis-à-vis,* who adopted us, lending us his office, out of which he turned a typist (male) and a pimply junior clerk. He could hardly have done more with his furnishings to make us feel at home, I thought, looking round at the same "Spy" cartoons we had hung over Jaggers, the cobwebs, and the stacks of briefs in varying stages of decay.

Marion, all woman on such occasions, even on a morning like this, was examining the place in detail. "They've got a spare set of 'Halsbury,'" she announced, discovering the books in a corner under what appeared to be a budgerigar's cage. "The carpet's a good one—I'll have to tell Hesketh that and try and shame him over that frightful thing of his. But will you just look at the curtains!"

"Here, steady on!" I protested, as a small cloud of dust escaped into the room.

She began to laugh. "It doesn't surprise *you,* naturally," she said.

"Why should it? If Miss Egerton and Belle, and you for that matter, can't sweep our little home . . . and you certainly don't. . . . Besides, I like it here. Don't you?"

"Perhaps. If I could only find a mirror."

We hunted around and ran one to earth in a corner,

took it to the table, and set it up against a pile of books. The light was immediately above her as she stooped down to arrange her wig, and I saw her pallor, the sensitive and graceful lines of jaw and forehead, the curve of the neck above the prim little black frock she wore.

"You'd better not take too long about it," I said in a voice whose roughness surprised me.

She gave me a puzzled look. "Rather ungallant, isn't it? What's the matter? We've ten minutes yet."

"Fairley may want the room."

Clearly she didn't accept the reason I'd given. "Doesn't do to get over there too early and have to sit around," she said. "And I don't think Fairley will mind so much." But she had left the mirror and was standing, half-turned from me, with her hands clasped in front of her.

I saw that she was afraid and had been trying to compose herself, and that I had shown a dismal lack of understanding. "Forget it," I said, furious with myself. "Stay as long as you like. Here! Is my wig on straight?"

"You'd better look."

I went to the mirror. I had got the thing cocked over one eye, as usual. It was a very white wig and I found myself intensely disliking its newness and the air of inexperience it gave me. "I don't know why we have to wear these things," I was grumbling as I straightened it. "Making a pageant of the law, and a damned ugly and uncomfortable one!" I turned round. She was standing just behind me—white against darkness, a touching and tender beauty that caught at my heart. "Well, Marri?" I said.

"Well?"—and we looked at one another.

"You know what I want to say?"

"Yes," she said.

"I've said it before. Not in such a queer place, though."

"It was in your car."

"But I thought perhaps it might help now, as I know it helps me. There's a lot of comfort in loving."

"I need that, too, Michael."

There came a discreet tap at the door and she started away. "Even Jaggers wouldn't have timed it quite like that," I muttered as she called out that we were almost ready and would be with him in a moment.

"Hold the mirror," she commanded.

I held it up and she came close to me again, examining herself, her head tilted in the way she had. "That was the nicest thing you said."

"No, Marri."

"And you mustn't spoil it or let me spoil it either with foolish thoughts. There!" She reached up, and before I could guess what she was going to do she had kissed me and was away again. "Now are you ready?"

She was already moving to the door and I followed, bewildered by the rapidity of her change of mood. The ease of manner with Fairley which I vainly enjoined on myself seemed less desirable when she practised it. I should have known her better, but I was deceived: I couldn't help suspecting a certain lightness of nature.

We came out of Middle Temple Lane into the Strand. There was a lot of traffic and many passers-by on the pavements. I thought with trepidation of what would happen in our town if barristers were to walk out robed from the Assize Court into the streets: but here, apart from a few curious ones—provincials, probably, like ourselves—no one took the least notice of us: we were part of the day-to-day life of London, ranking along with buskers, guardsmen, Chelsea Pensioners, and American naval ratings in cute little white caps. The Law Courts clock was showing twenty-five past ten as we entered the great hall and followed Fairley up the steps that led to the court of the Lord Chief Justice of England.

I hadn't been in it for years. It struck me as smaller than I remembered, though it was a pleasant, well-proportioned room, neither grand nor sordid as some Assize Courts are. There was a good deal of board-room panelling and the usual uncushioned seats for counsel and solicitors. Facing you, under the Royal Arms, was the bench, with three chairs for the judges: below it a table for the Registrar and his Assistants; in the wings a dock, a witness-box, and assorted curtains to keep out draughts.

The place was already fairly full. Kenyon was in his seat in the front row: he had brought an air cushion which his clerk was inflating for him, and he had Stein and Loader busily at work behind him arranging the Law Reports in the order in which he might require them.

Seeing us come in, he shuffled along the seat towards us, all urbanity and condescension, though I noticed that his eyes strayed occasionally to the papers that Fairley was laying out for us and then back to us again—he was intrigued about the new witness, of whose existence he had naturally been told, and he wanted to gauge how much reliance we placed on him.

"Shall we finish today, do you think?" was the nearest he allowed himself to come to so vulgar a thing as curiosity.

"I think so, yes."

"Even assuming that leave to call fresh evidence is granted? Have you seen who's sitting? The Lord Chief with Drew and Manning. A strong court. I don't think we could have wished for better."

"Meaning *he* couldn't," I whispered to Marion as our opponent returned to his air cushion and his lozenges and other aids to "character." But I was encouraged by this foray on the part of the enemy. It augured a certain lack of confidence, and I was still savouring the taste of it when I heard the rustle of a crowd rising around me and, looking up, saw that the judges had entered the court.

I remember very little of the first stages—the voice of the Registrar, the arrival of Maudsley in the dock —for I was too intent on the bench. As a pupil I had often seen Lord Chief Justice Benson in court and I had cherished admiration for this most formidable yet chivalrous of men, combined with the fervent hope that I might never have to appear before him. Manning I knew also: he had been on Circuit to us in the previous year, a witty man who had convulsed everyone on Grand Night, though on the bench he had one of those dour expressions that challenge you to find anything funny in the world. Mr. Justice Drew was therefore the only stranger to me, a comparative new-comer to the bench, an intellectual from the look of him, thin and bony—in fact, the impression you got from all of them was much the same: high cheek-bones, Roman noses (though Manning was reputed to have got his at football as a boy), an abundance of chin. Informality and lack of fuss was another impression they gave you as a group. Kenyon's habit was to settle himself with a rustling of feathers like an old bird on the nest, but these men, having politely noticed us, sat straight down in their tall-backed chairs, suffered the preliminaries, and were immediately ready to begin.

"Miss Kerrison," Lord Benson said.

She rose.

"Miss Kerrison, this is an application to call new evidence?"

"Yes, my lord." She was on uncertain and controversial ground, but you would never have guessed it from her manner which was now wonderfully assured. "My lords, the onus of showing cause in this matter is squarely on me. As I understand the law, the Court of Criminal Appeal will not usurp the functions of a jury where the trial below has been properly conducted, and it will not therefore hear further evidence unless it can be shown that this proposed evidence was not *available*, or could not *with reasonable care* have been available, in the court below.

"Will your lordships be so good as to look at the depositions which have been provided."

They did so, and after a while she continued in the same conversational voice: "The first witness is a private inquiry agent who will prove the taking of a certain photograph. The second is a jeweller from Wakeby, who will testify to the receipt of certain articles of jewellery brought to his shop last Tuesday. None of this evidence was available at the trial for the best of reasons—that it had no existence then. It is, in my submission, clearly material evidence such as would have been admissible at the trial.

"The third witness (whom I propose to call out of turn for convenience's sake) is the Maudsley family jeweller, if I may call him so, who will formally identify the Wakeby gems and a photograph of the missing jewels. The fourth is a gentleman by the name of Berg who may be able to assist the court in various ways. I understand he is present," she added, looking round behind her to where the witness sat. "I should add that all this evidence was disclosed within the last few days, which gives an appearance of short notice—unavoidably, I ask you to accept."

"Mr. Kenyon?" the Lord Chief Justice said.

He rose billowing up with a paternal smile for so much youthful persistence. "My lords, who would dispute the accuracy of that? It is established that the leave of the court is necessary and that it may be granted in the proper circumstances."

"Have you views about the propriety of the circumstances, then?"

He smiled a deprecatory smile. "What do your lordships wish me to say? The notice has been short—through no fault of my learned friend, I hasten to agree. As I understand the practice of this court, the calling of evidence on appeal is jealously regarded and is not to be looked on as a natural and everyday thing, nor must there be any invasion of the rights of the jury. The onus of convincing you that the evidence should be called is squarely on my friend."

"Yet this is new evidence," Lord Benson said. "Do you dispute that?"

"No."

"It seems to satisfy the tests."

Kenyon bowed to the bench with a humorous gesture of submission.

"My lords, it does. Let me make it clear at once that personally, if I may be permitted to say so, I welcome the witnesses, provided they have something new and relevant to say. I am greatly in favour of hearing them."

"And we are greatly disposed to agree with you," the Lord Chief Justice remarked dryly. "Miss Kerrison."

She had remained seated during Kenyon's statement, but she got up again at once.

"Miss Kerrison, we are going to allow the evidence."

What in fact now happened was that the court clothed itself with the statutory powers to hear the witnesses and we were launched on the appeal: but there was no visible hiatus or indication that we had moved from one plane to another, and the judge continued almost without a break:

"There are now witnesses to call and no doubt submissions you will wish to make—on the heads of appeal, the alleged misdirections," he explained in a voice that hinted all too clearly what he thought of them. "Now will you call the evidence, and then address us."

"Yes, my lord."

"Very well, then," he said, sitting back in his chair.

Marion gave a hitch at her gown.

"I call Thomas Fox," she said.

Our friend appeared, looking constabulary and spruce in a dark-blue suit with a tie to match. He was not of the type that is diffident about his calling, but announced himself and the name of his agency with confidence and more than a suggestion that those in court might as well take note of it for future reference. Clearly he was pleased with his own part in the affair; though it was his fate to be cheated of all the heroic bits, being confined by Marion to the taking of the photograph.

Shorn of its context, this evidence was pedestrian—a matter of time and place and condition of light—and the court appeared to slumber through it; nor did Kenyon even bother to cross-examine the witness. "I'm sure I accept the photographs," he was heard to murmur, casting a look of distaste at poor Fox, who descended a trifle crest-fallen. "*And* your 'family jeweller,' " Kenyon added, as our old acquaintance from the first trial, Mr. Murray, took Fox's place under my direction and identified a photograph of the missing jewels which Miss Maudsley had prudently had taken some years before.

When he had done, Marion rose again, announcing amid a sudden stir of interest in the court: "I call Marcus Green."

The witness went into the box, taking the oath on the Old Testament. Then he glanced round the court and at the three formidable personages in phalanx near him. He was small, with a dark jowl and spectacles, and on one hand he wore a ring—one of the heavy, ornate kind one sees sometimes on bookmakers making their way in the world and rich old ladies who have had theirs made for them.

"Mr. Marcus Green?"

"That's right."

"You are a jeweller trading under the name of Marcus Green and Rayner, with premises in Old Dean Street, Wakeby."

"I am."

"Do you specialize in the buying of old jewellery and plate?"

"I have a large business," said Mr. Green.

"I am sure you have. Now then: were you in your shop on Tuesday last?"

"Yes."

"Did something particularly memorable happen on that day?"

"It did."

"Please tell the court about it in your own words."

He swivelled round in the box to face the judges.

"My lords, it was like this. About one o'clock I was alone in the shop, my assistant having gone off for lunch, when the street door opened and a man came in."

"We will leave the description of him for a moment," Marion said. "Tell us, rather, what he did."

Mr. Green nodded. "What he did—yes, certainly. What he did. He came up to the counter and asked if I bought jewellery. There are three notices in the window about *that*," the witness said, feeling perhaps that his own business acumen was in question. "I told him, yes. He then unfastened an attaché case he was carrying and took out of it a white box. There was cotton wool inside, and from the cotton wool he took two articles: some ear-rings and a necklace."

The jeweller's voice had taken on a sharp edge and his eyes seemed bright behind his spectacles. The connoisseur was alive in him.

"It was a beautiful necklace," he said reverently. "Or rather I think it must have been."

"What do you mean by that?"

He considered for a moment.

"Because it seemed to me that the gems—they were rubies of fine quality—had been given a chain that was hardly up to them. Not common, I don't mean that. It was a good necklace still. It was just an idea I got"—here he raised his hands as though reproving his own fancy. "I seemed to see another and finer chain with them."

"The artist's eye?" suggested Marion.

Mr. Green looked pleased and nodded his head. "Exactly. I would have expected something more delicate and finely worked."

"What was the value of the necklace?"

"Hard to say. I might have offered £200."

There was such a suggestion of reticence and canny dealing in the way the word "offered" was pronounced, that a ripple of amusement passed over the court and even Drew was seen to smile.

"One has to think of margins, my lords," the jeweller said, smiling also. "One buys and one has to sell. The value to *me* of that necklace would have been, as I have said, £200."

"Did you in fact purchase it?"

"I did not."

"Why?" Lord Benson asked, leaning forward in his chair.

The witness returned his glance with something less than perfect equanimity. "My lord, the chain did not attract me. Resetting would have been necessary, which is often costly. Even at my price—and I was not offered it at my price, my lord—it was expensive. Besides"—here the witness shrugged his shoulders—"it is not often you see jewellery like that. You will appreciate that I had never seen the man before."

"You were suspicious of him?"

"Not then. Cautious, I might say. Yes, I was cautious."

"So you refused to purchase?" Marion said, taking over the witness again.

"The necklace—yes."

"You bought something?"

"I did. A pair of ear-rings—a pretty piece, though of no great artistic merit. Cheap, too," he added. "Thirty pounds. They were small chips, you understand."

"Would you identify them?"

The small glittering objects were carried to the witness-box where Mr. Green examined them, handling the stones with about the same amount of reverence one shows to a pocketful of change.

"Yes, those are the ear-rings I bought. I paid cash for them—pound notes. Mine is a large business," he explained in an apologetic way. "Perhaps I should have asked more questions but there seemed no need. It was a very small thing I was buying."

"Having bought them, however?"

Mr. Green swung back towards her. "Having bought, I made a note of the purchase and decided on a price. I got my assistant to write out a ticket and I placed them in the window. Three days later . . ."

"Yes, go on."

". . . last Friday, that is, another man came in—ostensibly to purchase jewellery," added the witness, who had probably recovered from his admiration for Fox. "I showed him the ear-rings among other articles, and he said . . ."

Marion held up her hand.

"Don't tell us what he said, please. Oblige me, instead, by examining this photograph of certain jewels. There is a necklace shown there, a ruby necklace, is there not?"

The jeweller examined what was handed him and nodded his head.

"Yes. The one shown me was of that kind, though the chain was rather different. And here are the diamond ear-rings in this distinctive pattern." He was pointing to the exhibit in his hand. "It was a bad buy, that of mine," he added in a rueful voice.

"Bad?"

"I shall have to give them up, that's why. They're the Maudsley jewels all right."

"They're the Maudsley jewels," Marion repeated slowly, looking at the bench. "And this first man had brought them on the Tuesday. Did he give a name?"

"He said his name was Levett—perhaps it was."

"An address?"

"Number 15 Collins Street. He didn't live there."

So we came to a description of the mysterious stranger: if "description" can be said to have a useful meaning. Though the witness did his best, you saw how incapable words are the moment we match them against the so-called real world, the world of everday things. Even words as familiar as "a brown suit, a raincoat, a snap-brimmed hat" only imperfectly translate the objects themselves as they exist to our sight and touch; tallness is relative to our size, and Mr. Green was very small; "a white, long face, full lips, brown eyes, a prominent nose," are no more than so many nouns and adjectives that conjure up a vague miasma of a man. Only the moustache struck a more positive, though fanciful, note: "I got the impression it might have been a false one," the witness said.

Kenyon was heard to murmur, inexcusably, that he presumed this was "the artist's eye" again.

"It was just an idea, an impression," Mr. Green replied, obviously put out by this interruption and by the titter of amusement it caused at the back of the court. He gave the Crown lawyers and the policemen behind them an almost scared look, as though he had realized that there was another side to all this and other interested parties beyond those gentle creatures Fox and Clive. "You can't be sure of such things," he went on haltingly. "Besides, it was a dull day outside and the shop lights weren't on—" Apparently a certain measure of economy was the rule with Marcus Green & Rayner. "It was no more than an impression."

"Will you please look at this photograph?"

It was the one which Fox had identified in his evidence some minutes earlier.

"Will you look closely at that photograph?"

The jeweller did so.

"There are certain resemblances," he replied at last. "The general shape of the face. Of course this man here is clean shaven. It is not altogether a clear photograph. There are similarities in the nose and mouth, perhaps, so far as one can see."

"Do you identify the subject of this photograph as the first visitor to your shop or as someone very like him?" the Lord Chief Justice asked, after a long pause during which we had all expected the witness to continue.

Mr. Green was seen to be shifting unhappily in the box. "Not exactly," he said.

There was a murmur of astonishment in court.

"What do you mean?"

"I mean there are resemblances. The mouth and the nose are not unlike."

"Not unlike!"

"That is so, my lord," the jeweller said, apparently quite unaware of his own change of emphasis. "The general outline is not altogether dissimilar. Of course this man in the photograph is clean shaven and the print, as I have said . . ."

"Is it the print that worries you, Mr. Green?" Marion asked, seeing his hesitation, and you would never have guessed the terrible doubt that must have sprung up in her heart.

"Yes, it does, Miss Kerrison," he said.

She gave another little hitch to her gown. "Well, that can soon be remedied. Will you look around the court?"

She got no further, for Kenyon rose with a whirr like a partridge from the stubble. "My lords."

"Yes, Mr. Kenyon."

"My lords, a photograph was put to this witness. No identification followed. But my friend will not accept that. The witness does not identify the likeness of the man, so he is to be asked to identify the man himself. Is that my friend's intention?"

"Yes," she said.

"That is a form of cross-examination, I suggest. Almost invitation to the witness to have the right kind of second thoughts."

"Is not that a trifle strong, Mr. Kenyon?" Manning asked in his gentle voice. "A reflection on counsel and on the witness too, who has been very frank, it seems to me?"

"Yes, my lord, and I am asking the court to accept that frankness as it stands."

"Without hearing what more he has to say?"

"Come, Mr. Kenyon," Lord Benson intervened, seeing that our opponent was still on his feet. "You would surely not wish to rely on technicalities in a case like this? They are not well-founded technicalities either, to my mind. I do not say Miss Kerrison has acted perfectly in this matter and the photograph is certainly an irrelevance if the original of the photograph is here. But if he *is* here . . ."

"From my friend's words I am assuming it."

"Then I think we should not prevent the witness being asked to pick him out."

"As your lordships please."

Marion rose again and turned towards the little jeweller, who had listened to this exchange with downcast eyes.

"Mr. Green," she said, "will you look around the court? Do you see present here among us the man who brought the ruby necklace and the diamond earrings to your shop?"

Silence had fallen, as profound as I have ever known in a court. The jeweller looked up. He seemed to be quite uncertain what to do, staring in front of him, where his gaze rested on the Crown benches and the gallery behind. Then very slowly he turned towards us—the little dark eyes, bright with a sudden perception.

"I see the original of this photograph," he said.

"Where?"

"On the fourth bench from the front." He was pointing now, and the eyes of everyone in court followed to where Berg sat.

"Let him stand up," the Lord Chief Justice said.

A rustling sound was heard—that thrilling emanation of a crowd caught in the moment of emotion: then Berg rose.

I saw him properly for the first time: a neat, pale man, with hands as white as a woman's and fair, thinning hair. It gave one a very strange feeling to see him standing there in the flesh, the cypher we had talked and dreamed about. Well, we had him at last, our "Second Man." I felt an oddly possessive feeling towards him as though I had always known him and he belonged in some way to the deepest and most personal part of me.

"That is the man of the photograph?" I heard Marion say.

"Yes."

"Well?" I caught the note of impatience in her voice. "Do you identify him as the man who came into your shop?"

There was no answer. Turning back towards the jeweller, I saw that he was no longer looking at Berg.

"Mr. Green," the Lord Chief Justice said.

He swung round at once to face the bench.

"Did you hear the question? No one wishes to hurry you. Yet it is simple enough. Is this the man who brought the rubies and diamonds to your shop? Do you see definite resemblances to that man?"

"In a way." He caught the calm, patient expression on the judge's face and added despairingly: "In the ways I have already told your lordships—a suggestion here and there."

"No more than that?"

"My lord, I thought so yesterday."

"You *said* so yesterday," Marion burst out passionately.

Benson turned towards her, gentle still. "I understand," he said. "I know you have acted in perfect good faith, but you must take the evidence as it stands. The witness is on oath. I don't know what he thought or said yesterday—I am concerned with what he says *now*, after full reflection."

He turned to the jeweller who had been watching him with awed fascination and said slowly: "Is there anything you wish to add?"

Mr. Green answered unhesitatingly: "No, my lord."

"You got no more than a series of impressions—similarities, I think you said first—of nose and mouth? The general shape of the face, you said later, was not altogether dissimilar. Is that the way you wish to put it?"

"Yes."

"Is that your reaction still, now that you are faced with the original of that photograph?"

"Yes, it is," he said, "and I am more than ever certain now that this is not the man."

I have never been quite sure what caused this change of front in a witness who had made so confident an identification in his deposition. Perhaps he had never been truly convinced and was one of those persons who are always open to the last suggestion made to them. I feel, however, that there was another and more compelling reason. We had accepted him as honest but he was probably a "fence," a receiver of stolen goods. He had thought of Fox as a representative of the police and had been helpful to save his skin, though of course he would have found out soon enough how the matter lay and how immensely "hot" his jewels had been. And then in court when Kenyon rose, hostile, formidable, with the Crown and police behind him, Green must have sensed that his evidence, so far from pleasing authority, was in fact anathema—for so it will have presented itself to his sharp, suspicious mind.

That was Marion's belief and she must have felt it even at the moment of betrayal, for she rounded on the bench at once—"My lords, there is an application I must make."

"Very well."

"It is for leave to treat this witness as hostile and be allowed to cross-examine him."

But the Lord Chief Justice, having glanced at his colleagues, was slowly shaking his head.

"No, Miss Kerrison," he said.

"But there is the witness's signed deposition in my hand, and I need hardly explain that it tells a very different story."

"That may be."

"Your lordships have seen the demeanour of the witness."

"Yes, and we are not going to deduce from it any dishonesty—perplexity, perhaps. Even that was resolved when he saw the original of the photograph face to face. He had no doubts then."

"Think of the contradictions, my lords."

"No, Miss Kerrison, no. You must accept the witness."

She made a gesture of resignation, and interpreting it, Berg, who throughout this exchange had been standing calmly in his place, sat down. As he did so

I saw him look at Marion: it was the merest glance, veiled and fleeting, yet one seemed to catch in it an extraordinary suggestion of malignity and power. I drew in my breath, for I knew that I had glimpsed the real man, the man whom Jane had known on the stairs outside Miss Maudsley's room, negative and indistinct no longer but a vital being, potent, formidable.

I turned to Marion: and she had seen it too. She had gone very pale, not with fear, I think, but with a sudden resolution—indeed that glance, so challenging, was to play its part in our story. She looked quickly round the court, probably surprised as I was that no one else had recognized the man for what he was. But the judges had turned back to the witness, Green, and Kenyon was on his feet to give a little admonitory crack of the whip where none was needed.

"Really this man—whoever he was—seems to have mistaken you for what is vulgarly called a 'fence'?" he remarked pleasantly.

Mr. Green blushed a little and was heard to reply that it might have looked like it.

"Fortunately we are not concerned with his impressions but with yours," the advocate went on. "What were you concerned with, Mr. Green? The jewels?"

"I am a jeweller: that's my trade," the witness answered with an uncertain smile.

"Exactly!" You could hear the satisfaction in Kenyon's voice. "Exactly, you are a jeweller. You were shown some fine rubies, weren't you? Your professional instinct was aroused, to put the matter at its lowest. What was the man to you?"

"Very little," Mr. Green answered in accents of truth.

"Of course: very little, hardly anything at all. You asked some perfunctory questions about him—name, address, and so on—but you paid very little attention to the man himself. You don't identify him, do you, as the person who stood up in court just now?"

"No, I don't. I don't think it was him after all."

"Mr. Green," Kenyon said, almost purring over the witness, "there isn't the least need for me to detain you another minute. Wouldn't it be fair to say that, so far as you were concerned, that visitor of yours could have been almost anyone—almost anyone in the wide world?"

"I suppose so."

"He could have come by the jewels in a dozen ways? From the hands of Tom Smith or Jack Jones or Harry Robinson—or John Kelvin Maudsley?"

"Yes."

"He could have come by them last week or the week before—or on the night Miss Maudsley died?"

"So far as I'm concerned," said Mr. Green.

"Thank you. Thank you very much."

I believe that at that moment, when Kenyon sat down, most advocates in Marion's place would have despaired. The case, of which we had had so great hopes, was in ruins. She could not even call Berg now, for after Mr. Green's refusal to identify him there was no point in going any further, no question we could ask. But there remained the pair of ear-rings which lay now on the table in front of us, and after I had recalled the family jeweller, Murray, to identify it definitely as one of the missing pieces, she rose with a promptness that showed that there was at least one unwearied, undaunted spirit to speak for Maudsley.

First the misdirections. I think she was wise in this: it was fresh and not highly controversial ground, though even so she was interrupted several times—chiefly by Drew, who showed himself to be unimpressed, to say the least, by our arguments. "Where is the misdirection in *that?*" he asked on one occasion with a bewildered glance. "Where is your point of substance?"

We were to come back to it soon enough.

"My lords . . ."

Kenyon, who had been sitting comfortably in his place, with his arms crossed, suddenly leaned forward. His alert ear had caught the change of tone.

"My lords, it may be that in this case I have greatly tried your patience, as I fear that I tried that of the learned judge below, and I am sorry. I will not offend further with a jury speech—it would be out of place, and yet the paradox is this: that your lordships must now project yourselves in some sense into the minds of jurymen and consider whether a reasonable jury, knowing of this new evidence and properly directed, would have come to the conclusion they did, or whether the doubt cast upon the case is such that they might have decided otherwise.

"Let us, then, look at the case as it was presented by my learned friend. A murder is done. No marks of a struggle on the appellant's person; no traces on his clothes of the woollen scarf Miss Maudlsey wore. No footprints. No finger-prints in the bathroom, the place of the crime. No trace of the stolen jewels—one ring excepted, one of the least valuable."

While she had been speaking, Mr. Justice Drew had been showing vigorous signs of disapproval, and she turned to him.

"My lord, I am not asking you to try this case again—that would be wrong. I am reminding you of what the jury heard that was favourable to the appellant. No jewels but one. How had he disposed of them? When had he the time? Those questions were never answered. But now—months after the crime—another jewel appears, and we have it in this court. Suppose your reasonable jury had known that? Suppose they had known there is a man walking around today who handled those ear-rings, that 'pretty piece,' as Mr. Green so quaintly called them, and perhaps other jewels, the rubies about which my friend was pleased to be amused? Where did he get them? Here is a man going around, months later, with the proceeds of a crime for which another man is being condemned to death. Suppose the jury had known that?"

"Very well: let us suppose it," said Mr. Justice Drew in his faintly querulous voice. "You heard the cross-examination by Mr. Kenyon."

"I did, my lord."

The judge looked at his notes and read aloud our old enemy's last three questions. " 'He could have come by the jewels in a dozen ways. . . . He could have come by them last week, or the week before—or on the night Miss Maudsley died.' " He glanced at her over the top of his rimless glasses. "Doesn't that take the point, Miss Kerrison? Isn't it exactly that? What is inconsistent between this mysterious visitor's possession of the jewels and the guilt of the appellant as attested on the plentiful evidence the jury had?"

"My lord, with respect, that is not an inconsistency that I must prove."

I saw Manning nod his head—from the beginning he had appeaerd to be the most favourably disposed towards us of the three. But Drew replied at once: "It is something that *we* may take account of when projecting ourselves, as you so picturesquely put it, into a jury's mind. What, after all, do juries expect? The duty of a prosecution is to prove its case to them. It is a matter of common sense. In this case the prosecution proved a series of lying statements by the accused; the possession of one of the stolen jewels; threatening words; presence in the neighbourhood of the crime; presence *inside* the house."

"By one witness, my lord. From photographs. In the dusk on an unlit staircase."

"Definite and repeated identification, all the same," the judge insisted. "And none of this is in any way contradicted by your new evidence. The Crown brought a great weight of testimony. Is it your suggestion that, on top of all this, it is also a prosecution's duty to go on and account for every receiver and every missing jewel?" He looked at her, inviting her to allow the absurdity. "Would not that appear to be an unreasonable burden, bearing in mind the fact that accused persons are not always helpful with the police?"

Kenyon was leaning back in his seat again and he made some whispered comment to Loader over his shoulder. But Marion showed no awareness of unfavourable weather signs and replied at once:

"My lords, in this case I suggest that the duty *was* owed by the prosecution in the court below. If the possession of one jewel was part of the accusation my client had to bear, the possession of these other jewels is just as much an accusation against some third person still unknown. Admittedly this third person *could* have received the ear-rings and rubies from the appellant. But there you encounter doubt: the *question mark* that must have been raised in any reasonable jury's mind if they had heard the witness Green give evidence. There is doubt at every turning of this case. Why should not the mysterious visitor have taken these jewels himself? It is surely a possibility. Indeed the identity of that man . . ."

"He has *no* identity that we can recognize," said Drew. "He was 'anyone in the wide world,' in a phrase to which your own witness agreed. I hope, Miss Kerrison," the judge continued, a most forbidding note coming into his voice, "that it was not your intention—on your own testimony, as it were—to provide a name for him?"

I put my hand out and touched her gown but she didn't notice. I don't think she was aware of anything except her own passionate vision of the truth.

"Not that. I am well aware of my duty to your lordships—and of my duty to my client too. But . . ."

"Miss Kerrison," the Lord Chief Justice said.

She stopped and turned to him. She was still capable of recognizing the kindness and goodwill that had sounded in every word he had addressed to her.

"Miss Kerrison, I do not think it is in your mind to press the matter further. But I think I should tell you now—in order to prevent any possible clouding in anyone's mind of the value of the skilled and devoted address you are making—that we could not possibly order the calling of any other witnesses. This

. . . this individual referred to is linked to the case by no positive threads at all."

She made him a dutiful bow and I am sure there was affection in it, the same almost filial feeling she had for Hesketh, but it was a measure of her quality that she didn't allow the rebuff, or the merciful way it had been expressed, to divert or soften her in any way but was back at once into her stride, as combative as ever.

"Doubts, my lords. I have submitted there is doubt at every turn. The prosecution's case was full of it. Here is a criminal who carries out a daring crime and disposes of jewels to the tune of eight thousand pounds. So efficient is his system that he disposes of these jewels or caches them in the short space of hours left to him between his crime and the arrival of the police." A fine incredulity began to sound in her voice as she went on. "Yet this efficient criminal has concealed one jewel worth £200 in a cistern where the first serious search will find it. This criminal is so efficient that he travels to the scene of his crime by taxi and gets off at the end of the drive. He knows the house well, for he has lived there, yet he chooses to commit his crime while two persons are at home. Why didn't he bide his time and wait for his aunt's and Birman's weekly visit to town, or at least for the cook's day out? There is the contrast: there is part of the doubt. Was ever efficiency and crass stupidity so mixed?"

She paused in the silent court. A faint smile appeared on her face and she added: "I can see that I *am* making a jury speech to your lordships. Yet those are the doubts—or some of them—that the jury must have had. On the evidence, they decided as we know.

But not on *all* the evidence—for that evidence was not available to them, and is not yet available even to us."

She swung round to the dock where Maudsley sat impassively.

"What does remain to us is the opportunity of righting what in my submission was a great wrong—a verdict delivered in ignorance of vital facts. If they had known! My lords, what reasonable jury could have ignored the stranger in the shop and the jewels, the whole suggestion of something unexplained?"

She paused. It may have been in her mind to speak of the greater uncertainties of life and death. But—"Perhaps one day we shall know," was all she said.

As she sat down I looked at Maudsley. There was a puzzled expression on his face, as though he had found the proceedings hard to fathom—so informal and polite that you might have wondered what the issue was.

I saw him glance at Kenyon, who had half-risen. I am sure he saw no significance in the way the advocate sat down again in response to an almost imperceptible gesture of the Lord Chief Justice's hand. The first words from the bench were formal, almost reassuring to those ignorant of courts, and there was praise of Marion and a statement of principles by which the judges would be bound. But for all that, it will not have taken him long to know, as I had known from the moment of Mr. Green's apostasy, that the Appeal had failed.

Chapter Thirteen

WE CAUGHT THE EVENING TRAIN north with ten minutes to spare, meeting Mr. Clive on the platform. By that time, MAUDSLEY APPEAL RESULT was appearing on the placards. I bought a paper, and it was all there: the judgement in the Stop Press, the jeweller's photograph on page 3, and the words MYSTERIOUS STRANGER fitting into the headlines as snugly as any sub-editor could wish.

How inevitable it looked as you glanced down the columns. In the Tube we had been surrounded by people reading of things which that morning had been known only to ourselves: the new initiates, the judges of the accomplished fact. The execution, one read, was fixed for Monday week (which left twelve days), and there, over-page, were the cricket scores and the results of the racing at Hurst Park.

Cynicism is often jejune and foolish and I did not give way to it for long, perhaps because I had not hoped greatly and could see that it was logical and right that Maudsley should be news for the day—a cautionary tale. "It's nobody's fault but his own, poor devil!" was how Mr. Clive expressed it as he showed us to the corner seats he had managed to keep for us. "If only he'd told us his story right from he first, eh, Miss Kerrison?" You could see that he was determined that this time she should not blame herself. "You could have used it then."

We couldn't say more, for the carriage was filling up. It was a melancholy journey through one of those grey evenings when summer seems the frumpiest of the seasons, without subtlety of shape and colour. Already there was a dullness of leaf that told you that autumn was not so very far away, in that march of nature which keeps pace with us on our short road. I wondered if Maudsley would have such thoughts, and whether he would see from the barred window of his car the countryside passing—dark, weed-strewn rivers; and trees, bottle-green and shapeless like Victorian matrons in crinolines. Six hours would see him back in his cell under the lamp with the porcelain shade, and then there were twelve days left, unless by some chance the Home Secretary decided to reprieve. I supposed we should go to see him, which was an ordeal I dreaded, for always in the past we had been able to hold out hope for him, and now the chances were that we shouldn't be able to any more.

The train drew into Peterborough, where you caught a glimpse of the cathedral behind the sprawling steel and brick of our age. Some people got out. By Newark, darkness had fallen; at Doncaster, where we were fairly back in our own country, the last of our fellow travellers descended.

Immediately Mr. Clive, who had been lying back for some time with his eyes shut, but awake and unrelaxed, got up and took down his brief case from the rack. I feared a post-mortem, but nothing could have been further from the mind of that persistent man: it was "the next stage" that he was concerned about.

While the train rattled on through the night, more slowly now, we held another of those conferences that had become a feature of our lives. I think it was the least realistic we ever took part in. No one wanted to admit that the fight was over and that there was nothing more we could do, for there is something very repugnant about facing realities of this sort and we were filled, like all those who preside over lost causes, with a sense of personal failure, no matter what we might say about it among ourselves or what justifications we might find.

"I don't like giving up," Mr. Clive kept saying, returning again and again to the barren ground. I noticed that Marion kept silent and showed no inclination to lead us as she usually did. "What do you think, Miss Kerrison?"

She shrugged her shoulders. "The same as you."

"That we've no case? There's no special point of law that could go to the House of Lords in this?"

"None," she said.

"And no chance of the Attorney-General's fiat?"

"Absolutely none."

He nodded. "I'm afraid you're right. It's up to the Home Secretary now and there's really nothing we can do. But one doesn't like to just sit by."

There was an air of the Prodigal, in deep contrast with this, about our return to chambers next morning.

Jaggers was there on the doorstep to greet us and

you could see that all was forgiven, for the papers had printed the Lord Chief Justice's encomiums, and there was a brief for me, marked ten guineas, and two for Marion, thus putting the worst of Jaggers's fears at rest. It would be a change for me, he remarked as he handed me mine, which was a Harfield "Black List" case of a peculiarly repulsive kind. He was all benevolence. Indeed, in chambers generally there was none of the tension that had followed the jury trial, when Marion's follies had appeared to be in spate, and even Fenney had become happy about us and was heard to remark that things had really worked out well, without any *trouble*, which was the important thing.

For the remainder of the week I was busy with my brief, relieved of care, in the knowledge of a short grace before the news came through. After working with Marion for so long it seemed odd to have something that was entirely my own to do, and I kept finding myself on the verge of consulting her on this and that point, though each time I checked myself, seeing that she too was busy with the new briefs, one of which was a big Conspiracy to Defraud, in which the prosecution was held by Hesketh with Serpell as junior. It was what she needed, I thought to myself, watching the energy with which she threw herself into these tasks, but I was surprised none the less, for I knew how much she had given to the Maudsley case and I had tried to prepare myself to face a different reaction.

On the following Tuesday I went to Harfield, where I was engaged all that day and most of the next—against Gilroy of all people, who introduced his ghastly facts and witnesses with so bland and holy an air that he almost made them sound respectable. I told him this over lunch. "Wait till you hear the rest of them, dear boy," he replied, not without reason as it turned out.

That night we dined together, and eschewing his case (which I was in a fair way to winning) he embarked on Maudsley—almost as obsessive a subject with him as it was with us.

"Won't the police help you?" he wanted to know.

I explained that our credit with them was quite exhausted. We were not believed. They would continue to search conscientiously for the jewels, and some form of watch might be kept on Berg, but it would be perfunctory at best, for Kenyon's cross-examination had disposed of any doubt in the official mind.

Not in Gilroy's, however: he was still unsatisfied. The judgement of the court had failed to convince him, though the law in it, he allowed grandly, was right enough. Where the mistake had lain was in our too-trusting natures and in our failure to frighten Green before Kenyon stepped in and did the job for us.

"I wouldn't have thought it of Kerrison," he said, shaking his head sadly over this failure to live up to the high Machiavellian standards he had set for her. "Perhaps she'll think of something else now," he added, cheering up a little, being now on his second brandy, which made the romantic in him come uppermost. We parted that night on the best of terms and on the understanding that really we should have done well to consult him from the first—an agreement which I hope consoled him for his beating next day in court.

I returned to chambers on the Wednesday afternoon.

We had now four clear days left, and I realized with a sense of shock that the result of the Home Secretary's review might be expected at any time. I tried to cheer myself with the assurance that it would be a very full and fair review, unhampered by strict rules of evidence, in which all the defence arguments, old and new, would be given their chance again.

No news came that night. All next day, Thursday, I was alone in our room, for Marion was in court, and every time the telephone rang or I heard visitors with Jaggers in the office I found my heart beating faster. I told myself that I was doing no service to Maudsley in this, but I couldn't help it: I could think only of him.

On the Friday, Marion was back in her place and I remember how glad I was to see her. I tried to sound her. I felt it would be easier if I could visualize somehow the circumstances in which the Minister's decision would be made and the advice he would have. I knew I was being foolish and that it couldn't make any difference, and that nothing I thought or said mattered any longer. There were times when I hoped, and times when, remembering the weight of the prosecution's evidence, I despaired, though always in my thoughts was the possibility that there might happen some providential thing, as the appearance of Green had seemed providential once.

Lunchtime came, and with it a routine report from Fox, listing the moves the police had made in their checks on jewellers' shops. I passed it to Marion, who hardly so much as glanced at it. I was angry, resenting a concentration on other things of which I was no longer capable and which I began to feel was callous and wrong. I couldn't bear to think that after all her efforts for Maudsley she should accept this final injustice of his death, for so I saw it, forgetting Oldfield and Birman and all the lies and prevarications of the past. The impotence of another was all the more painful because I myself knew that there was nothing to be done. Never had I felt so cut off from her. I loved her and I suppose wanted her happiness above all things, and yet at the same time I wanted to see a reflection of my own fears. Surely she must feel them. Yet when I looked at her I saw only the same calmness that had surprised me in court and in the train, particularly in her answers to Clive. She worked steadily, the new briefs and their fresh pink ribbons prominent on the desk in front of her. It was only in the afternoon, going to the window and passing close to her, that I saw, behind the barrier hiding them, she had the Maudsley papers open, and knew that she had been reading them all that time.

That night, about six o'clock, the news came through that the Home Secretary had declined to reprieve.

It remained to visit Maudsley in prison, and next day Marion and I went together. I had grown accustomed to the place—the towering walls and bastions, the interminable corridors and sour barrack-smell which seemed to linger everywhere, even in the offices of the Governor and his officials. Once you were inside it seemed easy to accept this world; nor do I believe that this was only insensitivity in me, the reaction of one who watches a dark routine without being part of it and indeed in the assurance that within an hour he will be outside again in the sunlight, for I think it is true that the smaller the cell, the more completely it becomes our home. So it is with the child in the womb and the dying man.

And so it was with Maudsley.

When we reached the administrative block in the bailey of the castle, as I suppose the Victorian builder must have thought of it, we found ourselves in the presence of the chaplain. We had seen him before in the offing, one of those Welfare officials in whom an anxious benevolence is an occupational disease. He had waylaid us. It was a signal, and rather a macabre one, though nothing could have been more open or pleasant than his manner as he introduced himself and led us into his office, a functional room with only a leather-bound Bible on the desk to remind you where you were. He must have noticed that Marion was not pleased at this intrusion, for he appealed to her directly: "You see, I visit him too. I want to help." I felt certain that he did, since we were in his province now along with Maudsley and all the rest. He wanted to prepare us—he had a great deal of experience of preparing people and had got into the way of it.

"You may find him changed," he told us. "Oh, don't mistake me, I'm using the word in the widest sense. He gives you the impression of being ingrown, the way they so often get. Quieter. More accepting of things."

I saw Marion's fingers close tightly on the papers she carried.

"He's a brave man," the chaplain said, perhaps noticing this also.

We might have been spared such a Job's Comforter, I thought as we went out, not appreciating that these valedictory remarks had slipped in all innocence from the good man's mind. But it was a melancholy walk through the corridors that resounded to the slow tread of feet and the clanging, far off, of iron grilles. You found yourself wondering about the routine of death. Inconceivable to the prisoner that it *was* a routine, and that the immensely personal and tragic moment was part of a plan that had been operated again and again over the years, with refinements of mercy—a sedative, perhaps, the shortest of walks, and apparatus that worked quickly.

The door of the cell opened and from the gloom of the corridor we saw Maudsley lying on his bed. It was hard not to think of the moment now so close when others would come and he would sit up, with the same questioning look of a man who still in spite of everything expects good news. I saw that they had told him. But after the first revealing glance he showed no weakness, nor did he ask us what we had done or what we hoped to do. I know I felt embarrassment, as one does when a trust is given us that we can't redeem, but nothing in his manner betrayed reproach or the despairing dependence some men show. He was calm, as the chaplain had told us. I wouldn't have said he was resigned or "accepting," for there was always a liveliness about him, and you could believe it would be with him to the end.

We asked if there was anything he wanted. Had he books?

"They've got quite a library," he replied, but I saw those the chaplain must have brought still piled on a table in a corner of the cell. "I'm not much of a reader," he explained, following my glance. "I play draughts and a bit of chess. The boys like that. They're good cobbers."

He broke off and for a moment we couldn't find anything to say: the unease was all on our side, for I don't think he resented us, as some condemned men are supposed to do, or that he wanted to be finished with us and left alone.

"Well, this is it," he said at last. "I don't suppose you'll be coming any more. I mean there's nothing you can do, now that it's decided."

"There's nothing more," she said.

He nodded, as though pleased at the way she had spoken out.

"Well, you did your best, and I always said that. I'd pick you again, you know. If I had it all over again I'd pick you, for you're my sort, d'you know that? You don't give up. And yet I made it hard for you."

"Yes."

"And I put you in wrong there with Lorne and the jury: telling you one story, and then another."

"Yes," she said, but in so low a voice you hardly heard her.

"Made it hard to trust me, didn't it?"

"At times."

"How does it feel now, when it's all over and all said? Don't tell me you still believe in me!"

"Yes, I do."

He came a step towards her, so strange an expression on his face that I thought he was going to confess.

"You're a queer one," he said. "Why did you come? To tell me that?"

She didn't answer.

"I think you did. By God, you're a queer one! Lady with the Lamp! Did you think it would cheer me up?"

"No."

He put out a hand towards her. There was rough humour in his voice, the bewilderment men feel for women's instincts, and gratitude and affection too. "Well, it does," he said. "And I'll tell you something. I never killed her. I was never in the house that night, and you can believe that, for there's no one left to hear it—only you. By God, you're the queerest one!"

I can still hear him saying that. He was a brave man.

And Marion went straight back, without a word, and sat down at her briefs. She had made her decision. It was to see Jane Birman.

Chapter Fourteen

THE HOUSE WAS ON THE ROAD TO "The Towers," about a mile nearer the centre of the town. No drive here, no gardens such as you would find in the intermediate territory where lilac trees rustle their leaves despondently in the wind. The house of Victorian red brick opened directly onto the street, a tall house of many windows, all curtained with net and roller blinds as though everlastingly ready for the undertaker's call. Yet those were flats: a board on the door proclaimed it: furnished flats.

We drove past slowly in the dusk of a stormy evening. "Springfields" the house was called, and there must have been fields around it in the early days when children played in its rooms and gardens among the aspidistras and pampas grass. The city had long since closed in on it: a wilderness of streets whose lintels and chimney pots continued the same falling curve, with breaks at ground level on the street corners where a few fly-blown shops displayed newspapers, cigarette cartons, and sweets in tall glass jars.

It was quiet there now that the children were in bed, and the sound of the traffic on the main road into the city, parallel to us a hundred yards away, could only be distinguished as a vague rumble, syncopated now and then by the whining of tramcars as they climbed the hill. A few lights showed in windows, for the evening was overcast, but in "Springfields" there was no sign of life. "Suppose she's not there?" Marion said, as I turned the car at the street end. We hadn't thought of this before. It had seemed natural in the moment of decision to assume she would be, but the doubt and question now were revealing.

I stopped the car some fifty yards off on the edge of some waste land and tried to reason with her. There had already been one heated scene between us, for it was an unheard-of thing that she was doing in going to a witness on the other side—something so unprofessional that it could mean the end of her career.

Yet no argument of mine could move her. "I could never practise again if I let this pass," was her answer to everything, and I could see that she was quite willing to let me think there was an element of self-seeking in actions which in fact were due only to the duty she felt she owed to Maudsley as long as he lived. The system had failed, but he didn't condemn it for one error it made, nor was she arrogant enough to be sure that she could right injustice, though she would try.

"No one's invulnerable," she said, when I pointed out the uselessness of appealing to so determined a woman. "Everyone has a weakness; something very small sometimes, as Clive used to say. I had one chance with her and I failed—perhaps because I was too certain of the kind of person she is. I have this second chance now."

"You always thought it would come, didn't you, Marri?" I said, remembering words whose meaning had escaped me at the time.

"Yes, I suppose so."

"What will you say to her?"

She didn't answer, but got out of the car. When I followed suit, however, she turned on me and told me flatly that she wanted to go alone.

"Don't be stupid," I said.

"But I do. This is my business."

I think she was remembering Berg and the glance he had given her in court, the sense of personal challenge that helped to support her now in the dangerous course she had chosen, but there were things I could not concede.

"And mine," I said.

It was very absurd of us standing there quarrelling like children over the choice of a game, but the truth was that we were both wrought up by the events of the day and the prospect awaiting us in that house. Darkness was falling and more lights were appearing in the street. Near by, a window was open, and above the sound of voices and laughter you could hear a radio playing some brassy tune.

"Don't let's fight each other, Marri," I said. "I can't let you go in there alone, and you know it."

"But it's my decision, and if it's unprofessional, as you say it is, and if they disbar you . . ."

"They won't. The case is over. We've rights as private people to see anyone we please."

She began to laugh—rather an uncertain sound.

"That wasn't what you said at first, Michael."

"Perhaps not."

"First one argument and then its opposite. Make up your mind."

"I have."

We started off towards the house, whose taller outline could be distinguished above the level of the street. The hour was striking from St. Andrew's near my home, for the wind was from that way and freshening—it was a familiar and comforting sound. When we got nearer to "Springfields" we could see that there were lights on now: one in an attic, presumably out of range of curiosity, for the curtains remained undrawn; one on the first floor, only a chink showing through the blinds—Jane's room, according to Fox.

At the door we hesitated, painfully aware that we had no plan. There was a bell ratchet and knocker, both of the antique shape that dares you to use them, but it occurred to me that it might be imprudent to announce ourselves in this way and I tried the door. It was on the latch. Inside was another door with panels of blue- and port-coloured glass, and then the hall, lit by a low-powered electric bulb and furnished with a grandfather clock and pictures of embattled stags on a moor.

All was quiet as we climbed the staircase, down whose banisters generations of children must have slid. It was almost dark there: much the same conditions in which Birman had seen her lover on the night of the murder, I thought, as we reached the landing, seeing at its far end, beyond the amorphous lumps of furniture, a thin ribbon of light.

We went softly forward till we were outside the door, behind which someone could be heard moving with the mysterious furtiveness which the ear, the gossip of the senses, is always reading into the most prosaic things. For an instant it occurred to me to wonder what Jaggers's high and hopeful imagination would have made of it. I was in a queer mood: wrought up, as I have said, in the grip of the obsession that Jane had always exercised over me. I can't imagine what I hoped for. There are times when only the dramatic and marvellous seem possible, and I know the rationalist in me had died the death the moment I had set foot on that stairway so strangely reminiscent of "The Towers," with the window through which the greying light came and the three doors in line.

I glanced at Marion, who was standing close beside me, so close that I could feel the slight tremor of her body. It was very unpleasant to feel that anxiety and fear in her. I remember that my sensations were not of the pleasantly protective kind that men are supposed to indulge in at such times, but more of anger with myself and a kind of impatience, so that I rapped quite loudly at the door.

Immediately the sounds behind it ceased. I don't know whether in some way the atmosphere of tension surrounding us can have projected itself to Jane, or whether she was by nature suspicious of visitors or was expecting someone. Certainly her actions gave an oddly secretive impression. We heard no movement, no sound of steps, she didn't call out any inquiry; but suddenly the door was opened and we saw her standing there in a brocade house-coat and mules of a pink, tartish shade.

"What do you want?" she demanded. She sounded truculent but I could see that she was really puzzled and frightened by our coming. There wasn't the same fire about her we had noticed in court, but she looked older and more careworn and there were streaks of grey in her hair—the fine lustrous hair she had been brushing in front of the mirror.

"What is it?" she said. It had seemed for a moment as though she was going to slam the door on us, but she must have thought better of it, for she made no protest as we went past her into the room—a modern room by "Springfields" standards, with a bed-settee already made up for the night, a boxed-in wash-stand, a wardrobe, and dressing-table, bulbous and gleaming with yellow veneers. She closed the door and followed us, obviously uncertain what to do. "Well, what is it?" she said again, addressing herself to me and ignoring Marion. "Why have you come?"

"To remind you of Maudsley, perhaps."

She gave a disagreeable laugh. "Do you think I need reminding? It's all in the papers, isn't it? I even had the Sunday reporters down here wanting a story."

"You should have told them one," I said.

She frowned, and I saw that my small sarcasm had gone deep. "I didn't want them and I told them so, and I don't want you. Why should you think I can be bothered? You had your turn in court when you asked questions and I had to answer them."

"Perhaps they were the wrong questions," Marion said.

Jane rounded on her with that "measuring" look women give one another. "What do you mean? You had your turn, whatever you made of it. So why think that by coming here now . . . ?" She broke off, and you could guess that what perplexed her was not our simplicity but her own. She had been alone for a long time and her thoughts could not have been pleasant ones. She knew the danger of speaking, yet she wanted to speak, and the questions she knew she should not answer fulfilled some need. "What a queer one you are!" she said to Marion in almost the same tones that Maudsley had used. "Why should you think I'll listen?"

"For the only reason one listens: because you want to. You want to be reassured somehow."

"By you! That's fanciful."

"No more so than thinking you can do an act and escape its consequences," Marion said. "Knowledge, for one. The knowledge, for instance, that it was *your* evidence that condemned him."

She didn't like that and replied at once: "No, it was the others."

"Oldfield, do you mean?"

"His own lying alibi too—and the ring he took."

Her voice had risen. I understood that these were things she needed to believe. She was not as hard as we had thought her or forgetful of Maudsley in his cell and the day that was now so close.

"Why did you give that evidence?" I said.

She didn't answer.

"Why? He never harmed you. He was quite innocent: rather a stupid, helpless man."

"Is that my fault?" she burst out. "Am I his keeper?"

I think we were both struck by the appositeness of that. Then Marion said: "What better word?"

Jane looked at us, uncertain what we meant. At that moment it was hard to think of her as the scheming, disloyal companion or even the false witness of the trial, for she seemed only pathetic, a woman lost and alone.

We began to make our last appeal to her. I had never allowed myself to hope anything from this, but now as we spoke it really seemed that she was listening. I couldn't believe it at first, but kept expecting her to break in with some protest or denial. She was not without conscience or compassion of a kind. She hadn't even hatred to sustain her, for I think her actions in identifying Maudsley had been no more than some dark inspiration of the moment.

But she didn't speak. She didn't look at us, but stood quite still in the middle of the room—an aging, rather ravaged woman in an old brocade coat, perhaps the gift of her father long ago. I couldn't know then what she felt, or how she saw herself or the future that Marion drew for her in words whose simplicity and tenderness must have touched her heart.

Suddenly she looked up. I was reminded of Marion's face after the trial: there was the same suggestion of weariness and strain almost beyond bearing. One never suspects it of the enemy "on the other side of the hill," for our own weakness is too near to us and pervasive. I had seen only our own problem, beset as it was by a thousand difficulties and disappointments, but I had not seen the central problem this woman had had to face in the house after the crime, in court, and in the loneliness of her room.

For an instant I think the balance wavered. There must have been the strongest temptation to confess, to speak and to have done with it. Reason has nothing to do with such feelings, which are as instinctive as the cry of pain, the old barber of the legend whispering his secret to the reeds. She wanted to confess, but something still forbade her.

"Won't you answer?" Marion said.

She turned away from us.

"Surely you must see it? Things like this can't be forgotten. You have the imagination to understand suffering, and if you let him die you will never rest, no matter where you go or what you do."

"It's no good," was all she said.

I knew that for all the lack of emotion behind them these were really decisive words. It was a frightening thing to come at last against this power of inertia that lies at the very heart of the citadel of human will. I knew the strength of it. Perhaps Marion did not, for with her generous instincts she must have found it hard to imagine that anyone could concede so much and still be adamant.

"You mean you'll let it happen?" I saw her face darken as she realized that it could be so—that the woman in front of us was capable of this cruel and monstrous action. Her passion for the truth and devotion to Maudsley, her own combative pride and hatred of wrongdoing, all seemed to unite in a surge of emotion that took possession of her being.

She took a step forward. I thought she was going to strike Jane—strike out blindly against the blind force resisting us.

"You can't let it happen. You know what they'll do to him. Only it will be *your* doing, do you understand that? *Answer!*" She raised her hand and I saw the knuckles clenched and white. "Why don't you tell the truth? Are you afraid for yourself if you do?"

"For myself indeed!"

It was a very small interruption—so small that it

was astonishing that Marion, in the flood of anger, caught it at all. Yet she did and recognized its meaning. Her arm fell to her side. "Doesn't that matter?" she said. "Is it only *Berg* who matters—or yourself in another way?" I heard the surprise in her voice, the sense of chance discovery and an intense excitement too. "Why! You're in love with him!" she cried.

She was interrupted by a denial so passionate that we knew at once that Marion's words were true. Jane's whole personality had altered. We had doubted too much the depth and devotion of her nature, but we had proof of it now in this disavowal of feelings that engaged all the ardour of her heart.

"And yet you *do* love him," Marion said.

"No, you're wrong, wrong. I hardly know him. You're quite wrong."

Marion pounced on that. "Why do you say that? Are you ashamed?"

"Ashamed—never. Ashamed of what?"

"You know that, surely?" They were face to face, and it occurred to me how much they resembled one another at that moment in the fierce single-mindedness of their natures.

"I know nothing," Jane replied.

"He's a murderer, isn't he?"

"No, no, he's not."

"How can you be sure? A stranger to you!"

"I'm sure of that."

"A murderer," Marion said, "and you love him. Yet you saw what he did."

"Nothing, I tell you."

"Did you think that on the stairs—that it was nothing? You were afraid for yourself then, weren't you?"

"I was never afraid."

"Perhaps some day you will be. Think about it. You have this knowledge and perhaps some day . . . yourself . . . your own life . . ."

"Do you think that means so much to me?" Jane said, and she was quite calm again. She had meant every word: her own danger from Berg went for nothing.

Marion had seen this, but she had seen also where it could lead. "What does count with you?" she said. "That you'll see him again? Do you think you will?"

"Perhaps."

"Where is he now?"

There was no answer.

"You don't know. Do you wonder if he loves you? Is that the great problem?" Yet she said this with so much gentleness that I felt certain that in some way divorced from her loyalties she understood and pitied Birman. "Why don't you tell the truth?" she said. "For the last time."

"I have done."

"In a sense, yes, and more than you know. And yet I never thought of it. I had a picture of you in my mind—it was wrong of me and foolish. I misjudged you. It's so strange to find love here—like a jewel." She paused, and I could see the veiled, reflective expression on her face. "You were more foolish than I was," she said. "You were more greatly deceived. Do you know that?"

There was no answer. A deep silence had fallen on the room.

"Think about it. You were deceived from the beginning. It was all planned—*even the killing*, I think. Oh, yes, there were two plans, yours and his, one upon the other, and the same scapegoat would do for both. But you found your error, didn't you, when you heard him still in the house and you came out onto the stairs? What did he say to you then?"

She waited, as though really expecting an answer.

"Did he say that he'd come back and that when it was all over you'd be together? Have you thought what use or danger you'll be to him when Maudsley dies? No one will believe you." She was close to Jane now, leaning forward as I had seen her so often in court, but her voice was very gentle. "He has everything he planned for, and you accept it . . . because you love him. And what have you?"

Birman had not moved: she had been so still that you might have doubted that she heard. But at these last words she made a small convulsive gesture of her hands—protectively, it seemed, though I think there was another and more poignant meaning and that this was the last denial. We saw then that, almost hidden by the housecoat, she was wearing something on a gold chain.

It was the little heart-shaped locket from Miss Maudsley's box.

Chapter Fifteen

SMALL FAILURES, SMALL WEAKNESSES! as Mr. Clive is never tired of saying.

Birman had this one token, value about ten pounds, and that was all. I suppose she had grown careless after the refusal of the reprieve, but I have never found anything surprising in the fact that she should have been wearing it that day—it was a pledge and a symbol, more valuable to her than all those other jewels her lover had.

It is over now, and nearly three years have gone by and Berg is dead. We had little share in what followed our visit to the flat: we were not even in court to hear them tried together in the same dock in which Maudsley had once stood. I hear they never spoke, never looked at one another until the end. Yet, for all that Marion said, I can't be sure in my mind to this day what they would have done if the plan had succeeded and Maudsley had died: they might be living contentedly together somewhere, model citizens, for murder is the strangest of crimes and has the most diverse clientele.

Shall I record the other more personal things?

Jaggers's problems and doubts continue. Is Marion after our marriage next month to practise in her maiden name? It is a nice point and there are no precedents that he can find; but practise she shall—this is Jaggers's diktat—for she has a future, and who can say to what heights he has aspired for her? Meanwhile, life goes on. Hesketh has the plums, Fenney has acquired the "manner," Serpell is still "the coming man," and Ross and Vivienne will wed—next spring is talked about.

The other day while I was sorting through some papers I came across my brief in R. v. *Maudsley*, and for the last time I opened it. "Leading you: Miss M. Kerrison," I read on the outer page, yellowing a little now, and I remembered Jaggers coming with the brief, and that earlier night when Marion had told me that the case was hers. Yet all the rest of it seemed very far away, like an old letter one reads, all its words remembered but no longer familiar, absorbed into the void we call experience.

I set most of it down in note form at the time, together with my reflections; and here is the record of it with much of its old shape retained; but as I write these last words, and glance back, it is not the old obsession that comes clearly to my mind but oddments by the way: the smell of the courtroom, the way the light strikes down on a jury-box, a street in the rain.

It is over, and Maudsley too, with his inheritance, has disappeared. We saw him once; and very grateful he was and pleased at our happiness. He was going back to Australia: a more predictable sort of country, he said.

Perhaps he is right; though I think they order Justice much the same there, and it is just as fallible, and just as certainly the best and fairest system that man, that poor fallible creature, has devised.

THE PERENNIAL LIBRARY MYSTERY SERIES

E. C. Bentley

TRENT'S LAST CASE

"One of the three best detective stories ever written."

—Agatha Christie

TRENT'S OWN CASE

"I won't waste time saying that the plot is sound and the detection satisfying. Trent has not altered a scrap and reappears with all his old humor and charm." —Dorothy L. Sayers

Gavin Black

A DRAGON FOR CHRISTMAS

"Potent excitement!" —*New York Herald Tribune*

THE EYES AROUND ME

"I stayed up until all hours last night reading *The Eyes Around Me,* which is something I do not do very often, but I was so intrigued by the ingeniousness of Mr. Black's plotting and the witty way in which he spins his mystery. I can only say that I enjoyed the book enormously."

—F. van Wyck Mason

YOU WANT TO DIE, JOHNNY?

"Gavin Black doesn't just develop a pressure plot in suspense, he adds uninfected wit, character, charm, and sharp knowledge of the Far East to make rereading as keen as the first race-through." —*Book Week*

Nicholas Blake

THE BEAST MUST DIE

"It remains one more proof that in the hands of a really first-class writer the detective novel can safely challenge comparison with any other variety of fiction." —*The Manchester Guardian*

THE CORPSE IN THE SNOWMAN

"If there is a distinction between the novel and the detective story (which we do not admit), then this book deserves a high place in both categories." —*The New York Times*

THE DREADFUL HOLLOW

"Pace unhurried, characters excellent, reasoning solid."

—*San Francisco Chronicle*

(Nicholas Blake continued)

END OF CHAPTER
". . . admirably solid . . . an adroit formal detective puzzle backed up by firm characterization and a knowing picture of London publishing."
—*The New York Times*

HEAD OF A TRAVELER
"Another grade A detective story of the right old jigsaw persuasion."
—*New York Herald Tribune Book Review*

MINUTE FOR MURDER
"An outstanding mystery novel. Mr. Blake's writing is a delight in itself."
—*The New York Times*

THE MORNING AFTER DEATH
"One of Blake's best."
—Rex Warner

A PENKNIFE IN MY HEART
"Style brilliant . . . and suspenseful."
—*San Francisco Chronicle*

A QUESTION OF PROOF
"The characters in this story are unusually well drawn, and the suspense is well sustained."
—*The New York Times*

THE SAD VARIETY
"It is a stunner. I read it instead of eating, instead of sleeping."
—Dorothy Salisbury Davis

THE SMILER WITH THE KNIFE
"An extraordinarily well written and entertaining thriller."
—*Saturday Review of Literature*

THOU SHELL OF DEATH
"It has all the virtues of culture, intelligence and sensibility that the most exacting connoisseur could ask of detective fiction."
—*The Times* [London] *Literary Supplement*

THE WHISPER IN THE GLOOM
"One of the most entertaining suspense-pursuit novels in many seasons."
—*The New York Times*

THE WIDOW'S CRUISE
"A stirring suspense. . . . The thrilling tale leaves nothing to be desired."
—*Springfield Republican*

THE WORM OF DEATH
"It [The Worm of Death] is one of Blake's very best—and his best is better than almost anyone's."
—Louis Untermeyer

George Harmon Coxe

MURDER WITH PICTURES
"[Coxe] has hit the bull's-eye with his first shot."
—*The New York Times*

Edmund Crispin

BURIED FOR PLEASURE
"Absolute and unalloyed delight."—Anthony Boucher, *The New York Times*

Kenneth Fearing

THE BIG CLOCK
"It will be some time before chill-hungry clients meet again so rare a compound of irony, satire, and icy-fingered narrative. *The Big Clock* is . . . a psychothriller you won't put down." —*Weekly Book Review*

Andrew Garve

A HERO FOR LEANDA
"One can trust Mr. Garve to put a fresh twist to any situation, and the ending is really a lovely surprise." —*The Manchester Guardian*

THE ASHES OF LODA
"Garve . . . embellishes a fine fast adventure story with a more credible picture of the U.S.S.R. than is offered in most thrillers."
—*The New York Times Book Review*

THE CUCKOO LINE AFFAIR
". . . an agreeable and ingenious piece of work." —*The New Yorker*

MURDER THROUGH THE LOOKING GLASS
". . . refreshingly out-of-the-way and enjoyable . . . highly recommended to all comers." —*Saturday Review*

NO TEARS FOR HILDA
"It starts fine and finishes finer. I got behind on breathing watching Max get not only his man but his woman, too." —Rex Stout

THE RIDDLE OF SAMSON
"The story is an excellent one, the people are quite likable, and the writing is superior." —*Springfield Republican*

Michael Gilbert

BLOOD AND JUDGMENT
"Gilbert readers need scarcely be told that the characters all come alive at first sight, and that his surpassing talent for narration enhances any plot. . . . Don't miss." —*San Francisco Chronicle*

THE BODY OF A GIRL
"Does what a good mystery should do: open up into all kinds of ramifications, with untold menace behind the action. At the end, there is a bang-up climax, and it is a pleasure to see how skilfully Gilbert wraps everything up." —*The New York Times Book Review*

THE DANGER WITHIN
"Michael Gilbert has nicely combined some elements of the straight detective story with plenty of action, suspense, and adventure, to produce a superior thriller." —*Saturday Review*

DEATH HAS DEEP ROOTS
"Trial scenes superb; prowl along Loire vivid chase stuff; funny in right places; a fine performance throughout." —*Saturday Review*

FEAR TO TREAD
"Merits serious consideration as a work of art."
—*The New York Times*

C. W. Grafton

BEYOND A REASONABLE DOUBT
"A very ingenious tale of murder . . . a brilliant and gripping narrative."
—Jacques Barzun and Wendell Hertig Taylor

Edward Grierson

THE SECOND MAN
"One of the best trial-testimony books to have come along in quite a while." —*The New Yorker*

Cyril Hare

AN ENGLISH MURDER
"By a long shot, the best crime story I have read for a long time. Everything is traditional, but originality does not suffer. The setting is perfect. Full marks to Mr. Hare." —*Irish Press*

(Cyril Hare continued)

TRAGEDY AT LAW

"An extremely urbane and well-written detective story."

—*The New York Times*

UNTIMELY DEATH

"The English detective story at its quiet best, meticulously underplayed, rich in perceivings of the droll human animal and ready at the last with a neat surprise which has been there all the while had we but wits to see it." —*New York Herald Tribune Book Review*

WHEN THE WIND BLOWS

"The best, unquestionably, of all the Hare stories, and a masterpiece by any standards."

—Jacques Barzun and Wendell Hertig Taylor, *A Catalogue of Crime*

WITH A BARE BODKIN

"One of the best detective stories published for a long time."

—*The Spectator*

James Hilton

WAS IT MURDER?

"The story is well planned and well written."

—*The New York Times*

Francis Iles

BEFORE THE FACT

"Not many 'serious' novelists have produced character studies to compare with Iles's internally terrifying portrait of the murderer in *Before the Fact,* his masterpiece and a work truly deserving the appellation of unique and beyond price." —Howard Haycraft

MALICE AFORETHOUGHT

"It is a long time since I have read anything so good as *Malice Aforethought,* with its cynical humour, acute criminology, plausible detail and rapid movement. It makes you hug yourself with pleasure."

—H. C. Harwood, *Saturday Review*

Lange Lewis

THE BIRTHDAY MURDER

"Almost perfect in its playlike purity and delightful prose."

—Jacques Barzun and Wendell Hertig Taylor

Arthur Maling

LUCKY DEVIL
"The plot unravels at a fast clip, the writing is breezy and Maling's approach is as fresh as today's stockmarket quotes."
—*Louisville Courier Journal*

RIPOFF
"A swiftly paced story of today's big business is larded with intrigue as a Ralph Nader-type investigates an insurance scandal and is soon on the run from a hired gun and his brother. . . . Engrossing and credible."
—*Booklist*

SCHROEDER'S GAME
"As the title indicates, this Schroeder is up to something, and the unravelling of his game is a diverting and sufficiently blood-soaked entertainment."
—*The New Yorker*

Julian Symons

THE BELTING INHERITANCE
"A superb whodunit in the best tradition of the detective story."
—August Derleth, *Madison Capital Times*

BLAND BEGINNING
"Mr. Symons displays a deft storytelling skill, a quiet and literate wit, a nice feeling for character, and detectival ingenuity of a high order."
—Anthony Boucher, *The New York Times*

BOGUE'S FORTUNE
"There's a touch of the old sardonic humour, and more than a touch of style."
—*The Spectator*

THE BROKEN PENNY
"The most exciting, astonishing and believable spy story to appear in years.
—Anthony Boucher, *The New York Times Book Review*

THE COLOR OF MURDER
"A singularly unostentatious and memorably brilliant detective story."
—*New York Herald Tribune Book Review*

THE 31ST OF FEBRUARY
"Nobody has painted a more gruesome picture of the advertising business since Dorothy Sayers wrote 'Murder Must Advertise', and very few people have written a more entertaining or dramatic mystery story."
—*The New Yorker*